Laurels for William Zink's Previous Works

The Hole

"This first work is a surprising and unlikely treasure from an author using a surprising and unlikely pseudonym. . . Highly recommended."
— Eric Robbins, Booklist

"*The Hole* is a strange and magical love story that is a joy to read."
— Larry Lawrence, Abilene Reporter-News

Ballad of the Confessor

"This is a muscular and gripping tale from inside the world of work. *The Confessor* brings home the real shape of a reality nearly erased by television and statistics. Is this the start of that much-needed social realist fiction? Perhaps. Zink is one hell of a writer."
— Andrei Codrescu

"A genuine southern masterpiece."
— The Charleston City Paper

"A lyrical and stark examination of working-class lifestyles. . . a compelling read."
— The Youngstown Vindicator

"It is tight and beautiful and glazed with the good kind of sweat."
— David Giffels, Akron Beacon Journal

Ohio River Dialogues

"Zink's characters are self-contradictory, arbitrary, generous, prejudiced, sensitive, self-pitying—complicated, in other words. You end up liking them in spite of it, or more probably because of it."
— The Pittsburgh City Paper

"William Zink's *Ohio River Dialogues* is. . . not quite a novel. Not exactly a play. Not a stream of seemingly disconnected stories that somehow magically intertwine perfectly at the end. Instead, he presents us with a hybrid of these, and what emerges is revolutionary. Indeed, Zink might soon be credited with creating a new form of literature."
— The Main Street Rag

Pieta

"*Pieta* is a true and generous wonder of a novel. In sharp, beautifully written prose, William Zink takes on big themes—love and devotion and family and death—and makes us all the better for it."
— Donald Ray Pollock

"This is a book every author will wish he or she had written: universal themes; innovatively descriptive language; likable characters true to their generation that are handled with resounding compassion; and, an authentically complex story."
— Curled Up with a Good Book

Eddy and Julia

William Zink

Sugar Loaf Press

Sugar Loaf Press
343 North Pearl Street
Granville, Oh. 43023

Cover photograph by Octavian A. Tudose
Back cover photograph by Marco P.

This is a work of fiction. People and events have been manufactured in the author's mind, and any resemblance to those in the real world is entirely coincidental.

Printed in the USA

.

This book is warmly dedicated to the people of Belgium.

Her Name was Julia

I was to meet Nico, a friend of Philippe's and the most esteemed photographer in Leuven, a half hour ago. I'd finished a three-hour training ride through some spectacular countryside, then stopped at Het Moorinneken in the Grote Markt for a couple quick beers. I would have stayed for a third but Emma, my Portuguese friend and waitress there, urged me along.

"Philippe sets up a meeting with Nico and you're late?" She shook her head, looking down at me as I finished my second Witkap, my preferred beer in this beer-crazy country. "How could you?"

"I'm not going to be late, Emma," I said.

"Don't you know who he is?"

"Yes," I said as if answering a nagging mother, "I know who he is." I stood up, wobbling, and reached for my helmet.

"You're drunk!"

"I'm not drunk. Two beers," I said, holding up two fingers.

"Yes, in less than ten minutes." She handed me my water bottle and shoved me playfully. "Get going now before Nico thinks you're a fool. Don't forget your camera!" She lifted it from the table—an old Hasselblad medium-format model—and I slung it over my shoulder. I straddled my bike, clipped in my left foot, and gazed up at the Town Hall's rococo exterior, the sun just dipping behind its spiky towers.

"You know, in all the times I've sat here, I've never once taken a picture of it," I said. "What does that say about me?"

"It says you're going to be late—now get going. Go!"

I pushed off and wound my way through the Markt, then turned onto the Bondgenotenlaan heading east, and before long I was on the edge of town. The road opened into spotty farms and villas, and I was able to make good time going close to twenty-five miles an hour. I dropped my head and shifted up a gear and I smiled to myself at my new-found freedom. I don't mean merely the freedom of the open road, but the freedom I'd given myself, the release from the cycle of pain I'd known since the day I was born. Even now I felt the uncomfortable ache in my chest that came with exertion. I lifted my hand and ran a finger vertically on my jersey, absently, habitually, along the scar beneath. I say *scar* as if singular. I've had exactly seven heart surgeries in my life, each new scar layered over the previous, hiding all but the most recent foray into my chest—the last one being two years ago.

I took comfort tracing the tip of my finger along the scar, knowing no scalpel would ever slice me open again. I'd come to Belgium to live out my final days, to enjoy them as I never had before, unencumbered by grief, in morbid anticipation of the unknown.

The house was a low, pale building with a long, slanted roof. Stout bushes ran along the perimeter, their tapered branches reaching pleadingly for sunlight. A warped fence encompassed the yard on three sides, all but the one facing the road. The most distinctive feature of the property, which was large, was the canopy of massive trees whose branches spread horizontally like roots in the sky. The trees let only speckled puzzle pieces of light through to shine on the dirt-and-grass ground. Two dogs stood back along the fence tied with rope to a tree. There was only dirt and no grass where they trod incessantly in an arc of hunger and hope.

Philippe was around back sitting at a picnic table watching Nico, who sat with splayed legs on a stool before an easel, painting. In front of Nico were three young women. They all had dark hair falling to their backs, and each wore a white formal blouse and a blue skirt, like something you'd wear at church. They sat in a slight curve facing Nico.

I was a bit confused. Nico was supposed to be a photographer. I was meeting him so he could teach me a few things and I could improve my own technique. I sat down beside Philippe, who moved his cane to make room for me, and whispered in his ear to which he replied, "Don't make a ruckus, but you certainly don't have to whisper."

"Yes, don't whisper," said Nico, "it makes me nervous. I would rather you just talked like a normal person."

"Sorry I'm late," I said to Philippe. "Traffic, you know."

"Ah," Philippe waved it off. "If that is your biggest crime, you are doing well."

Nico, who was shirtless, wore khaki pants and sandals. Modest layers of fat lay one atop the other over his belt like slim, stacked sandbags. His skin was dark, and though he was balding with greasy white hair slicked back on his bean-shaped head, the tan gave him a healthful appearance.

"Why is he painting?" I whispered.

"Again with the whispering!" said Nico. The girls, each of them, gave me a stern, frightened look.

"He has exceptionally good hearing, James," said Philippe. I fell silent, my eyebrows raised as I looked around guiltily. "He wants to know why you're painting," Philippe said to Nico.

"Why am I painting?"

"Yes, that's what he asked."

"Why doesn't he ask me?"

"I don't know." Then, to me, "Why don't you ask him?"

"I didn't want to bother you," I said to Nico.

"I already told you, your talking doesn't bother me. Are you the sort who needs to be told more than once to believe things?" Nico for the first time, brush aloft, turned to look at me. He seemed to be waiting, almost challenging me to say something. I felt like a fool sitting there with his dark eyes and that big sweaty stomach snickering at me.

"I didn't know you were a painter, too," I finally said, trying to be affable. The girl in the middle laughed into her hand.

"A painter, *too*?" said Nico, who was back at his canvas. He winced as if pained.

"I told him you were a photographer," said Philippe.

"Why would you tell him a thing like that?"

"In all fairness, the last time I saw you, you *were* a photographer."

"That was months ago," said Nico.

"Yes," said Philippe, "I should not have assumed so much."

"You don't do photography anymore?" I asked.

"Not if I can help it," said Nico.

"You don't enjoy it?"

"Detest it. Abhor it."

"Really, now," said Philippe, who seemed amused. The girl on the right, who was more slender and angular than the other two, kept looking at me with narrowed eyes and her chin slightly turned, as if I were being examined.

"I don't know what I was thinking. I wasted ten years peering through a square hole. Girls, your chins are dropping. As beautiful as you are, if you drop your chins you'll look suspicious instead of innocent. Do you understand?" Nico approached them and placed his fat, black-nailed thumb under their chins and brought them up.

"Are any of your pieces for sale?" Philippe asked.

"Which would those be?"

"The photographs."

"I think they've all been sold or thrown out," said Nico.

"You must be kidding," said Philippe, his mouth open.

"I'm sure there are some somewhere. I don't know. I suppose a few weren't all that bad."

Philippe turned his head away and shook it with real regret. "Nico. . ." he said. "You were the talk of the underground."

"I still am, so I hear," he winked.

"Yes, you are. You always have been. How many artists can move effortlessly from painting, to photography, and then back to painting again?"

"That's pretty God damn funny, Philippe, you thinking that I was still taking photographs. That was two lifetimes ago."

"Two?"

4

"Two, maybe three. You're not still living the life you did six months ago, are you?" He asked this with mild concern.

"I'm no artist like you, Nico," Philippe said.

"What the hell does that matter?" He had his brush in his teeth and sat admiring the three young women. They all had wide faces, high cheekbones, and dimpled chins. Their hair was terrifyingly dark, nearly black, and their lips were wide to complement their faces.

"He came to see your photographs," sighed Philippe, "and now there's nothing for him to see."

"Have a drink," Nico said to me. "Inside. In the kitchen."

I figured, why not? The meeting was pretty much a bust, though it was enjoyable enough listening to Philippe and Nico talk, and the three models weren't torture to look at. I went in and found beer in the refrigerator. I checked drawers until I found an opener, and then opened two bottles and came back out. One of the cats followed me, meowing.

"Here," I said, and offered a beer to Philippe. I knew he was drinking wine and he'd decline it, and then I'd have two beers instead of one.

"Nico?" I said, raising a bottle his way.

"It's all yours, kid," he said. "Drink, and watch me paint, and admire these beautiful creatures."

Nico decided to have one model, the one on the left, turn away so that her face was in profile. The other two remained looking at him. I stood up and walked behind him to see the women from his perspective, and to see what the painting looked like. The composition was from the waist up. The trunks of the trees behind the three ascended to the sky like pythons; this was not something Nico necessarily intended, but was a thought I had. Nico was painting over the first girl's face, the one in profile, replacing her features with clouds and a blue sky. The contrast of her realistic form and profile of clouds stunned me. I watched as Nico filled in the creases of the clouds and made them pop out of the canvas. Whether painting the clouds was something premeditated or an idea just occurring to him as he had her turn her face, it was clear he had caught an idea and knew there was importance in it. I waved at Philippe to take a look.

"Oh, that's marvelous," said Philippe.

"You think so?" Nico asked sincerely.

"I do."

"How about you?"

"He means you." Philippe gave me a nudge.

"I'm no expert on—"

"You've got two eyes, don't you? A brain?"

My eyebrows lifted with embarrassment. "Uh, yeah," I said. The girl on the right flashed her eyes at me, giving me a quick nod.

"There. You're qualified to have an opinion."

I moved my eyes from the painting, to the models, then down to the painting again. "It's good," I said. "It's really good. It makes my eyes want to move around."

"Best compliment you could hope for," said Philippe. "Anybody who says *good* isn't a bull shitter. A bull shitter would have used more syllables."

Nico laughed, then rubbed the now smooth protuberance of his arched stomach. "Girls," he said. "Come take a look."

They came around to look at the painting. The two with their faces still intact seemed pleased; the other one had some concerns.

"You painted clouds on my face," she said in broken English. "You have not yet finished mine, yes?"

Nico, sheepishly, raised his palms in surrender. "Well. . ." he said.

"But I have a real face—like them—look at it. Why did you paint clouds over my face and not theirs?"

I felt breathing on the back of my neck. The angular girl had moved behind me, her chin nearly on my shoulder. "Hands, eh?" she whispered.

"Because," said Nico, "the painting looks better that way."

This didn't go over well with the girl.

"But you did not paint over their faces—you hid only mine. Are you tired of my face, is that it?"

"Look," Nico tried explaining. "If I'd have painted your face just like theirs, you would be satisfied, right?"

She nodded, still with eyes glaring.

"Since I only painted *yours* with clouds, you noticed it right off. You ask me, *Nico, why do you only paint my lovely face with those puffy white clouds?*"

"I did not say that," she said with restrained bitterness.

"Instead of making you pleased, *merely* pleased, it made you think. A question popped into that pretty little head of yours—a question for which I have no answer."

"But no one has a face like that," said the girl, pointing viciously. "How can you have clouds where your eyes and nose are supposed to be? You make me look like a fool."

"On the contrary," said Nico. "I've turned you into a riddle."

"But I don't want to be a riddle. I want to be beautiful like my sisters. They look beautiful and I—I look foolish!"

She fled into the house. Nico sighed big, ruffled his wispy greasy hair, and shrugged.

"Am I that much of a pig," he muttered.

"She's always been sensitive," the youngest sister said. "Even as a girl."

The other one, who was now moving away from my shoulder, said, "It looks beautiful. Like all your paintings, it's beautiful." She kissed Nico on his dark cheek.

He had no choice but to go inside.

The other two stood for a moment, then hurried in as well. They returned with four bottles of beer and a bottle of wine and sat down with Philippe and me. When they were sitting for Nico, silent and still, they'd been like statues that you could appreciate, but not interact with. Soon the four of us were drinking quite fast and enjoying ourselves.

"He pays us very well," said the younger one, whose name was Gia. "More than we could make serving drinks to drunks." She burst out in laughter after the comment.

"And he *is* a great artist," added Julia, the eldest of the three, who was more thoughtful and spoke nearly perfect English. "I'd pose for Nico even if he didn't pay us," she said. She leaned forward looking directly into my eyes. "So, you photograph hands."

"Who told you that?"

"Nico," she said, then lay her own hand for a moment on mine. It was small and warm. "Don't worry—I think they're simply divine."

"You've seen them?"

"You don't think Nico would waste his time on some talentless hack, do you?"

"You don't look like a photographer," said Gia, teasing a fingernail between her teeth, her chin propped up on her palm.

"No?" I said still looking at Julia, but then turned my head. "What do I look like to you?"

"I'm not sure." She reached across the table to move my face left and right. "I think you look like a goat."

"Gia," scolded Julia. I laughed and so did Philippe.

"Well, he does. Did I say goats were ugly? It's obvious he doesn't look like a photographer. He looks like a goat. I like goats." She shoved her head forward for emphasis.

"Nico likes your work," said Julia. "He says you've got what it takes."

"He's a wonderful photographer," said Philippe.

"So, you're the one?" I said to him.

"As Julia said, Nico doesn't see just anyone. I had to show him a few samples of your work before he'd agree to meet with you. I hope you don't mind."

"I don't see what the big deal is," said Gia. "You like hands, so what? I like eyelashes, but you don't see me taking pictures of hundreds of eyelashes, do you?"

Julia took a swipe at her across the table. "You don't know which end of the camera is up," she said, narrowing her eyes derisively. "And if you did, you probably would take pictures of eyelashes since you spend all day in front of a mirror, anyway."

I flashed Philippe a grin, which Julia noticed. She gave me a swift shove. "I saw that."

Nico and the other sister, Valentina, returned.

"Valentina," called Gia, "don't you think this young man looks like a goat? He says he's a photographer, but I think he looks exactly like a goat—a young, handsome goat."

Valentina didn't seem to understand.

"That's enough," said Julia.

"But he *does*. He looks just like a goat."

"Enough." Julia raised her curled fist. "Beat it."

Gia stormed off in a huff.

"I'm glad to see you two smiling," said Philippe, meaning Nico and Valentina.

"Nothing that a good cry and a glass of milk won't cure," said Nico. "She's a bright girl. High-strung, but then all young intellectuals who are also beautiful are high-strung." He shrugged. "Take the good with the bad."

The sun shifted and the puzzle piece dabs of light moved from the ground to the wooden fence. Nico and Valentina were back at the painting. She took her seat on the stool, dropping her chin again until Nico reminded her and she raised it. Philippe got up and meandered around looking at the yard. You could hear his cane breaking small twigs as he went.

"You're a photographer, eh?"

"I try to be."

"And you came all the way out here because you thought Nico was a photographer."

"Sure," I said. "Philippe's been talking about him for weeks. I'd heard about his infrared photographs. I was hoping to see some."

Julia poured herself more wine and leaned forward and her eyes roamed over my face. It felt as if I were being sized up and judged. I grinned wide and took another drink. I'd given up women long ago. Well, long in a young man's life, anyway. I couldn't remember the last time I was with someone. Certainly, before I came to Belgium. I didn't see any point in pursuing sex, let alone a relationship, when there wasn't any possibility of a future. I suppose others would do just the opposite and try to grab as much as they could while they had time. I just didn't see the point. So as Julia stared into my eyes appraising me, I merely waited with the patience of indifference.

"And you like old things," she suddenly said. "Tell me about it, Eddy Merckx man. I want to know how it's done. How does a budding young Bresson like you capture the hands of time?"

I told her about my ride yesterday.

"I went out about twenty miles from Leuven," I said. "I can't remember the name of the town. Sometimes I ride until I get lost and then find my way back by way of the sun. It's a challenge, I suppose. Anyway, I stopped at this village and sat under some trees, and then along came this guy and his small dog, which seemed to be leading him. He must have lived through the war. I didn't know if he was old enough to have fought in it, or if he was a boy then, but he lived through it one way or another. He saw friends and relatives die. He wept as the Nazis moved in, then cheered when they were forced out. Yet, here he was, alone, walking his dog, invisible to everyone who passed by. I'd asked him to stop, which he was glad to do. I took pictures, not just of his hands, but of him and his little dog standing there."

She took another sip of wine, then lifted her chin to examine my face more closely.

"What's the obsession with old age, Eddy?" she said. "Somebody like you. Seems kind of weird. It doesn't add up."

Her staring had made me want to laugh but now, looking back into her eyes, I felt the quick rush of expectancy.

"I relate to old men," I told her. "It might be hard for you to understand that, but I just do. I feel comforted when I'm around them."

"Old men?"

I nodded.

"Most guys I know use the old SLR as chick bait."

I laughed. "Maybe I would if I were on the prowl," I said.

"Yeah, sure, maybe you would. I mean, why not? But then a guy like you—I doubt if he'd have to resort to such obvious carrots to snare the rabbit." She took a sip of her wine, sticking out her pinkie, never losing contact with my eyes. "What brings you to Belgium?"

I looked down to my cycling jersey and flashed my eyes to my helmet on the table.

"Only the cycling? Come on, there must be something besides the obvious." She leaned in, her knees pressing me. "Is it a girl? Is it, Eddy? Did you fly all the way over here for the romance and intrigue?"

"No," I said, "no girl. Should there be?"

"Should there be?" She leaned back in surprise, then came forward again. "Why, of course. Why do you think I'm here?"

"For a girl?"

She shoved me on the arm. "For the *romance*," she said. "To immerse myself in the pot, so to speak. To swim in the soup—drink it up and swallow it down and see how it feels in my stomach. What else is being young all about?"

"That's one way of looking at it."

"There's another way?" She looked at me, tilting her head.

"I'm not really worried about that," I said.

"Too busy with the hands?"

"Seems so." I took a drink from my beer.

She continued staring at me. Her eyes, except when she itched her upper thigh beneath her skirt suddenly, never left my face. I felt my cheeks burning from the alcohol and the heat and her scrutiny.

She suddenly stood, her legs like slender flying buttresses on either side of the bench. "Come on," she said and held out her hand.

She took me to the far side of the house where there was a covered porch. She made sure the door was closed and brought a finger to her lips, indicating that I should make no noise. Poised on her toes, though there seemed no reason for it, she pulled away a tarp to reveal stacks of boxes. In the boxes were photographs. Some were matted, but most weren't. They were neatly piled with large books in between the layers to keep them flat. I began looking through them, astonished as much with the care she had given them as with the prints themselves.

"Nico would kill me if he knew," she said.

"He doesn't know these are here?"

"Every time he dumped them into the trash, I pulled them out. He burned an awful lot, and that couldn't be helped. But he never comes back here. He thinks there's nothing but old tires and junk, and before I started hiding his photographs that *was* all that was back here. He's only been in this room once that I remember, and that was because he was drunk and he was looking for the toilet."

The photographs were all in black and white—I knew Nico never worked in color. I found some infrared and these I examined more closely. The infrared were mostly landscapes where the white foliage contrasted with the darkness of everything else. There were many nudes, mostly of the three sisters. I found one of Julia sitting on a fence, clothed, with cows and the setting sun behind her. I don't know why, but I looked at this one longer than the others until I was aware of her gazing over my shoulder. She perched her chin there, breathing into my neck.

"I was scared to death," she said. "That's a bull, not a cow. Nico wanted me to get in with it. I told him he was nuts."

I set the picture down and continued on, casually, but kept the corner tip exposed as I lay others over it in the vague hope of finding it later. "Are you going to keep them?"

She moved to my side and shook her head almost fearfully. "These are Nico's, not mine. Heck, what would I do with them?"

"They're probably worth a lot of money," I said. I said it to see how she'd respond.

"Aw, I wouldn't sell them," she said. "I just can't see these things going to the dumpster, is all. Today he says he's a painter, and tomorrow he might pick up his camera again—who knows? But when the day comes and he changes his mind, I'm going to pull back this tarp and give him the biggest surprise of his life. Can you imagine? I mean, can you *imagine*?"

I nodded, but I was only half listening. I came across another picture of her sitting in a wicker chair holding a cat. Sunlight washed the right side of her face casting the other side in deep shadow. Her eyes appeared heavy, as if caught at the beginning of a blink or, perhaps, because she was fatigued. Her chin was thrust upward, further turning her eyes into slices of mystery. She had the quality of seeming sad and happy at the same time.

I liked this one better than the one with the bull. "Can I take this?"

She seemed surprised. "You want that one? There are loads more better than that one."

"But I like this one," I said, smiling.

She snatched the photograph from my hand and looked it over. "I remember the day he took it. I was hungry—famished—but there wasn't a thing to eat in the house and so I rode into town right after and had the biggest bowl of rice you ever saw." She rubbed her finger over the print as if trying to wipe away a smudge. She passed it back. "Take it, Eddy, but don't let Nico see you with it. Not unless you want to see him blow his top."

The photograph wasn't matted, so I rolled it neatly and slipped it in the back pouch of my riding jersey. We left the house and returned to the others. The sun was falling. Nico had started a fire and I thought about staying—Philippe could have put my bike in his trunk and given me a ride—but I wanted to get home before dark.

"I'm heading out to the botanical gardens tomorrow," I said. "You should come along." We were sitting together on the bench of the picnic table, legs extended, watching the fire.

"What for? I mean, do you like flowers?"

I lifted the camera from my side. "I do this, remember?"

"Sure, you do." She smiled, suddenly and comically, as if I were taking her picture. "All right—that sounds rather whimsically unusual—but I can't in the morning. Classes. How about the afternoon?"

"Okay," I said. "I'll come over and we can ride there together. Do you have a bike?"

"Nothing like yours, but I have a bike."

"You don't need a bike like mine," I said. "It's going to be a joy ride."

"Is that a promise or a hope, Eddy?"

I grinned. "Oh, let's just wait and see."

I stood up and gathered my helmet from the table.

"You don't have to leave just yet, do you?" She touched me on the arm.

"I'm afraid so."

"But why? We've only just started the fire. Nico hasn't done his impressions yet. You just *have* to see him do his impressions."

"I'd like to," I said, "but I'm beat. I rode fifty miles before coming out. You wouldn't want me falling asleep at the wheel, would you?"

"Heck no." Her hand hadn't left my arm. She squeezed it. "Be very, very careful," she said.

I put on my helmet and glasses and straddled my bike, then clipped in my left foot. "I'll see you tomorrow, then."

"Yeah, sure. See you tomorrow." She leaned in and gave me a sincere, hopeful look. "It's going to be epic."

I coasted over to Nico and Philippe and thanked them. Nico told me to come again any time I wanted and he'd tell me everything he could remember about his former life when he was a photographer. I pushed off and passed beneath the big dark trees, then turned onto the road. My legs felt heavy now. I was dizzy from all the alcohol and from talking to Julia. It was a good kind of dizziness and I wanted it to linger. I felt the rolled-up photograph on my back, and I thought about her all the way home. I rode steadily, not fast, so I could remember all the things we said to each other.

Cosmic Compatibility Test

I woke but didn't hear the birds, which is what usually wakes me. Instead, there was this vague presence jabbing at me. It confused me and, to be honest, frightened me until I opened my eyes and saw Rick standing in the middle of the room. As soon as I opened my eyes he sat down in a chair opposite the couch. He was agitated as hell.

"Rick," I said, trying to gather myself, sitting upright.

"I don't know what to do," he said.

I forced my eyes to open wider. I felt hot and sticky. I'd come home from Nico's, laid down on the couch, and fell dead asleep.

"About what?" I said.

"You know."

"Well, maybe I do."

"Sure, you do."

"Okay, yeah, I guess I do."

"So, she left, you know."

"Who?"

"Elle—who do you think? She left for Ireland."

I looked at him. He was a mess. His hair was stiff and his clothes were wrinkled and his eyes bugged out at me red and desperate.

"I thought that was just talk."

"When Elle talks about something like that, it's not just talk."

"Gee, Rick," I said. "Maybe you can meet her there?"

"Don't be ridiculous; I don't want to go to Ireland—and sure as hell not with her and some Irish band."

"I'm sorry."

"I don't know what to do." Rick blinked manically. "I just don't know what to do."

"I'm not sure if there's anything you can do," I said. "I don't know the ins and outs of your relationship, but I don't think in situations like these there's a whole lot that can be done." I wasn't trying to be philosophical, I just wanted to make the poor guy feel better.

"Of course, I can't *stop* her," he said, "but she's out of control—completely out of control." He leaned forward. "She's going to get hurt."

"Yeah, but you said it yourself, she's used to doing this kind of thing. She'll be all right."

"Are you kidding? She's a child. A middle-aged child."

Rick's eyes seemed as if they'd pop out any second.

"Look," I said, standing up. "How about if I get a shower and then we'll talk about it. What time is it, anyway?" I scratched my head, looking around for my watch.

"Almost eleven."

"*Eleven?*" My hand stopped, grabbing my hair. "Jesus. Well, there's beer in the fridge, help yourself. I'll get a shower and then we can talk about it. There's some ham in there, too. Have whatever you want. I have to spray all this salt off me before I can do anything else. I'll just be a few minutes."

I showered, lathering twice to get the grime from yesterday's ride off. I dried and wrapped a towel around my waist. I'd left the door ajar. I peeked through the crack to see where Rick was, but didn't see him. I eased the door all the way shut and locked it.

I opened the medicine cabinet and brought down the pill case. I always felt ashamed, even when I was alone, whenever I took the pills. They were keeping me alive and, though I'd accepted my fate in general terms, I wasn't suicidal. There were seven pills in all, some large and hard to swallow, some easy. I started from largest to smallest, and by the

16

time I was finished taking them the nausea had already started. I needed to get something in my stomach before it overtook me.

When I stepped out of the bathroom Rick was gone. There was a half-drunk bottle of beer on the counter. I took two slices of bread and ate them plain, quickly, washing them down with Rick's beer. I went to the balcony and looked down to the canal. I followed some ducks swimming in the water and waited and soon the nausea stabilized, but it didn't go away completely and so I ate a banana. I went back into the living room to the long table crowded with photographs. Some had been there a while, and some I'd just printed the day before and left them there to dry. I examined the new ones. Most were of the old man and his dog. The contrast between the old man and the cheerful dog was interesting. It was interesting visually and symbolically. The nausea from the pills was beginning to wane, but now there was the different nausea of hunger. I hadn't eaten, other than the two slices of bread and the banana, since yesterday afternoon before the training ride. I felt like I should eat, but I resisted. Sometimes I allowed myself to grow terribly hungry. It wasn't a form of masochism, I don't think, but a test. Of what, I couldn't say.

I dropped the towel from my waist and stood on the scale, which wasn't in the bathroom, but just outside it in the hall; I'd converted the bathroom into a darkroom. The scale read 172 pounds. I hadn't lost weight in over a week. I stepped off the scale and stood sideways before the full-length mirror, looking at my ribs, then turned to face myself straight on. The lines of my ribs continued down into the lines of my stomach muscles. All excess fat had vanished from my frame. I was still well-muscled, but showed hints of the gauntness that comes with being ill. I picked my camera up from the table and took two pictures of myself. I'd begun doing this recently, though not with total regularity. I had some vague notion of documenting my decline. Earlier images of my body were on other rolls I'd developed, but I hadn't made any prints yet. I didn't know if I ever would.

I decided to have lunch at Het Moorinneken before meeting Julia. The hunger was too intense and I knew I wouldn't be able to enjoy myself if I didn't eat. I had a salmon salad with a baguette, but ate very little of either. Harry and Marta came by and we had a drink, then a second. The conversation was light and superficial, just the way I liked it with those two. After they left I ordered one more beer. It wasn't long before I spotted Philippe swaying beside St. Peter's Church, slowly making his way toward me.

"Ah, James," came his quiet call as he wedged himself between the compact tables.

"How's it going, Philippe?" I rose to my feet.

"Sit—no, no—sit down."

I sat back down but upright, not slouched as I'd been before. Philippe pulled out his chair, made a quick pivot on his good leg, and sat down sideways on it. He seldom faced you straight on. Whether for comfort or effect, this was his preferred posture for dialogue. He put his hands, one on the other, on top of his cane. His scruffy, pointed chin below that wry grin and blue eyes gave off an optimism that I found irresistible.

"The dynamic duo's not here?"

"Them? They left a while ago."

He eyed the empty glasses. "You mean these are not all yours?"

"Come on, what do you take me for?"

"I take you for a man of leisure, fully capable of holding down more than his share of the barley." Philippe, always dressed smartly in pastel khakis and fitted, long-sleeved shirt, tilted his head. "Have you been out taking pictures?"

"I just got up."

"You just got *up*?"

"Crazy. I came home last night, laid down on the couch and next thing I knew it was mid-morning. If it hadn't been for Rick stopping by, I'd probably still be asleep."

"Goodness," he said leaning toward me with concern. "Are you ill?"

"No," I said. "Just a little tired is all."

"Well, when you get that much sleep it means your body needs it."

Philippe got the attention of a waitress and ordered a cava. He was well-known at the café and commanded respect. This was different from me, who they viewed as just another patron, albeit a wealthy one.

"Did you enjoy yourself last night?" he said.

"Very much," I said. "Wow. What a character."

"Oh, you haven't seen anything."

"Can't believe he gave up photography."

"He didn't give it up. Don't let Nico's showmanship fool you."

"No?"

"He might *think* he's given it up, but he's too good. He's just bored. He'll come back around."

I rubbed the back of my neck, grinning, looking up at him sheepishly. "We looked at some of his pictures."

"You and the girl?"

"Julia."

"Yes, Julia," he said all bright and excited. "And what did you think of her? She's quite a beauty. All three of them."

"She's nice," I said. "Yeah, she's really nice."

Philippe's cava arrived. He felt the slim stem with his fingertips, twirling the tall glass slowly.

"Santé," he said, and lifted it toward me.

"Santé," I said, raising my glass of Witkap.

We each took a sip and smiled warmly at one another.

"Nice, eh?"

"I think so."

"Are you smitten with her?"

"*Smitten?* No, I'm not *smitten*."

"It sure seemed like you were last night."

I shrugged. "We're riding out to the botanical gardens."

"Today?"

"After her classes."

Philippe reached across the table and lifted away my beer.

"Hey!"

"You've had enough. You don't show up on a young woman's doorstep half-drunk. Shame on you." I tried to reach for it but he lifted his cane in warning. "Not another sip."

I chuckled to myself looking away. I knew he was right, and I probably did drink too much.

"What's their story?" I said.

"The three sisters? I don't know very much about them, other than they're from Italy and live with Nico."

"And he's Italian?"

"Greek."

"That's a little strange, don't you think?"

"That he's Greek?"

"That he's got three young women living with him."

"I believe he's a friend of the family, though I'm not certain of that. I really don't know, I never asked."

I rubbed my chin, eyeing my estranged beer, then Philippe. I'd been wanting to tell him. I knew he was going to get a kick out of it, and so I was waiting for the right moment. "Harry thinks he can take me on a bike," I said. "He challenged me to a race."

Philippe, whose lips were just to his cava, nearly sputtered in his glass.

"Does he know you're one of the best cyclists in Leuven?"

I paused and then slowly shook my head. "He seemed pretty arrogant; you know how he gets. I figure why tell him. He'll find out soon enough."

"He wants to race you? Oh, James, shame on you. How utterly wicked of you."

"He was showing off in front of Marta. I mentioned something about riding to the Ardennes and back, and he said that was nothing, that he could do it no problem. Before you know it, he's bragging about how much better he is than me and then Marta said we ought to race. You know Harry—he couldn't resist."

"And you accepted?"

"I've got a thousand euros riding on it," I said.

"A thousand euros? That's no small change. Poor Harry," he said. "He never knows when to shut that big mouth of his."

Philippe took a swift drink, then gave me his look. He was the only one who could make me laugh without saying a word.

"You and Julia, then?" he said, still with the look.

"Yup." I couldn't look him in the eyes.

"Out for a spring joy ride."

"You got it." I stared into the cobblestone, wincing.

"Does *she* think you look like a goat?"

I finally gazed back at him without any expression, challenging him with drooping eyes, then looked away before I laughed.

"A goat—you look just like a goat. A cute little goat."

I had to stand up and look away. I stood for a moment and then, shoving my mouth into my shoulder, headed inside.

"A g-g-g-g-goat!" I heard him call. *"A cute little g-g-g-g-goat!"*

I remembered passing a florist on the way to Nico's. I stopped and went in the rickety old greenhouse. The guy working behind the big table laid out with cut flowers asked me what kind I wanted. I told him daisies. He stared back at me behind his black glasses and suggested roses. I told him I didn't want roses, I wanted daisies. This obviously disappointed him. He took the first cluster in the bucket, but the flowers were already turning brown. I made him show me all the clusters before picking out the very best one. He wrapped the flowers carefully, his stone expression unchanged, and rang me up on some ancient ten-ton register. I rode with the daisies against my body to protect them from the wind.

When I arrived, I knocked on the door and Julia answered. She took the flowers and gave me a kiss on the cheek. She led me in and skipped to the old porcelain sink and filled a vase with water and placed the daisies in, one stem at a time.

"Follow me, Eddy," she said, and she took me through a set of French doors to where she and her sisters lived, on the west side of the house. They had a long open room with three single beds against the wall, some bookshelves, an easel, a few bargain chairs, and a couch that was made from a mammoth old bumper, upturned, adorned with green and yellow cushions. It was a comfortable, casual room and smelled of incense, though I saw none burning.

We sat on the bumper couch. I wasn't nervous really, but it had been a long time since I'd been alone with a girl. I jiggled my glass, now just ice after I'd finished all the water. She sat forward, her slim arms on her knees, and was unusually quiet.

"What year is it?" I said, glancing around me at the couch. "It looks like a '55 Chevy, but I'm not an expert on cars."

"I think so," she said. "A '55 Chevy sounds right."

"Could be a '56, though."

She looked down and to the right and left. "Sure, could be."

"Might even be a Ford or a Porsche."

"Could be a Volvo."

"Hard to tell from a bumper alone," I said.

"Well, it's like taking a dinosaur tooth and saying whether it was a T. rex or a stegosaurus, isn't it."

"Do you think they really died out because of some big asteroid?"

"What, the dinosaurs?" she said. "I don't see why not."

"Who's to say? I mean, the dinosaurs aren't around to vouch for one theory or another. It's complete conjecture."

Jesus, I thought to myself, what am I doing? I went to drink more water but got a nose full of ice. I felt her leg brushing against mine. It was just a leg. I'd brushed tons of legs in cafés and none of them had registered even the slightest blip. She had on perfume, and as I breathed it in it combined with her bare thigh to make me light-headed.

"They really are beautiful flowers," she said, lifting her eyes to the table.

"I didn't know what kind you liked. Everybody likes roses, but I don't. I always liked daisies better. I didn't know what kind you liked, so I gambled on daisies."

"I love them, Eddy, I really love them. Daisies are my favorite."

There was dead silence. I jiggled the ice in my glass and looked around the room and nodded appreciatively.

"Where are your sisters?"

"Oh, they made themselves scarce," she said. "I *made* them make themselves scarce. What about you—you have any brothers or sisters to terrorize?"

"I'm an only child," I said.

"Gee," she said, "that's sad."

We decided to get going. I handed her the glass of ice and she set it on the coffee table next to hers.

It was hot. We were both in shorts and short-sleeved shirts, but still it was oppressive. I'd ridden my touring bike, which more closely matched hers, and we went along easily and leisurely into town. We went side-by-side until we hit heavier traffic and then I let her go ahead of me. Finally, when we reached the center of town, we dismounted and walked our bikes through the crowd.

"These damn tourists!" I called ahead.

"I know—especially the Americans!"

"Ha!"

We wound through the Grote Markt and then the Oude Markt. Just before turning onto the Minderbroedersstraat, she pulled to the side and leaned her bicycle against a stone wall.

"Do you mind?" she said. "Since we're so close, I wanted to stop in the bookstore."

The bookstore was a small inconspicuous shop whose name, painted above the front window, was so faded it could barely be read: *In Our Time*.

It was tidy and compact, comprising no more than six tightly aligned aisles and a small area near the counter where a single customer might stand while paying. African music, low and mellow, thumped from a CD player behind the old woman who sat reclined in a chair, an afghan over her legs, rocking as she talked to the cat on her lap. The woman's name was Lily Lolimper, an English expat and, as it turned out, a dear friend of Julia's.

The women, one young and one old, hugged, not across the counter crowded with fliers for poetry readings, lost dogs, and yoga classes, but in the bookstore space proper, what little there was of it, Lily herself waddling around to wrap her arms around Julia, whose chin lit gently and snugly on top of her head.

"My lovely girl," said Lily. She squeezed and squeezed and didn't appear as if she would ever let go. When she finally did release her grip she went to the door, pulled down the shade, and locked it. "Goodbye and come back tomorrow."

Julia made introductions and I shook Lily's hand, making sure not to squeeze too tight.

"I haven't seen you in ages," said Lily. She motioned for Julia to follow her as she waddled back to her chair. She sat down and pulled Julia onto her lap. It was a sensible move, considering there was nowhere near enough space for the three of us to carry on a conversation where we were.

"How have you been?" said Julia, who kissed the top of Lily's head.

"Lonesome as hell and as loony as a tune," she said. "Nothing's changed here, sister."

"Have you collected anymore canes?" Julia gave me a wink.

"The last thing I need is another cane," said Lily. She gazed up and over the counter to me. "I have thirteen canes. Hey—you—are you listening? Thirteen is not an unlucky number. Only fools and druids think that. Each one of my canes has a distinct personality and a name. There's the Southern Belle, Miss Genevieve Whitehead, regal spinster that she is. And there's Alice Mudslinger, a fearless dame who climbs trees saving lost baby squirrels. Oh, then there's my slut cane."

"Ha!" Julia clapped a hand over her mouth.

"I'm sorry, sis, I know she offends your Catholic sensibilities. But she is what she is, as they say, and nobody's going to tell *that* woman what choo-choo train to hop on or off. There's—"

"Lily," said Julia, giving her a warm-hearted shake. "We're here for the test."

Lily, as if waking from a dream, cocked her head at Julia and gasped. She shook her one free hand with excitement.

"What test?" I said, my eyes darting around the room anxiously.

"Our future cosmic compatibility test," said Julia. "I bring in every guy I think I might eventually someday fall in love with, which is why I haven't seen Lily for quite some time, quite some time, I'll have to say. I mean, why spend months and months dating only to find out you're going to end up miserable as two bulls in a bull ring together when you can avoid the headache, broken family, and stretch marks, and zero in on the one and only yin to your yang? Lily has powers."

I felt as if I'd just been slapped in the face. My throat was dry. My eyes burned.

"Powers?" I could only utter.

"What you might call psychic powers. *We* don't call them that, but close enough for lay people such as yourself. So, what do you think?" She hopped off Lily's lap. "You ready?"

"Cos-cosmic com—"

"Cosmic compatibility test," Lily said. "You hard of hearing or something?"

"It's all right, Lil'—don't hold the stuttering against him. Some of the world's best crooners are former stutterers; not that this specimen's got the pipes of anything more than a plumber. Trying my best not to get my hopes up this time. The point is, he brought me flowers and put on his finest pressed polo and that's a start. Let's not jump to conclusions and invalidate the results. I'd hate to have to drag him back in here tomorrow."

I couldn't possibly process all that I'd heard in the time given. I nodded my head weakly as Julia faced me, staring into my eyes.

Her gaze grew intense and I thought she might burst into tears. Then, still staring, she reached down and removed her shoes and socks and dropped them to the side. Well, this wasn't such a bad thing, I thought. I reached for the button of my shorts. Her eyes did a dance and her hands fell to mine.

"No, silly. Footwear. Only the footwear."

I swiftly buttoned up and did as I was told. I waited for Lily to give a signal that things were getting started, but I soon realized Julia had performed this ritual so many times she needed no guidance. Lily eased into her chair, closing her eyes.

Julia took my hands in hers, lifting them to the level of our faces. Her toes, inching forward like caterpillars, sought a similar entanglement, though this took more time due to the less dexterous capabilities of the lower phalanges. She leaned forward so that our waists and chests touched, but not our faces. Our lips and noses remained inches apart. I glanced over to Lily, who sat nearly comatose, arms and legs splayed dead to the world, head thrown back, lips twitching and, occasionally, mumbling incoherent babble. The incense combined with her perfume and sweat and the must of the old books made my head swirl. Julia's eyes hopped between mine, growing immense, and seemed to ask questions for which I had no answers. I felt a growing desire to kiss her, which she must have been able to see. She tilted her head, closed her eyes, and leaned up toward me. Then, Lily began to moan. Not a low, muffled moan you could ignore, but a full-bore dying-water-buffalo plea for mercy. I gazed past Julia, whose eyes were now wide open, to see Lily, mouth agape, head thrashing side-to-side. I thought she was having a heart attack and went to break our communion, but Julia shook her head to let me know she was all right. She leaned into me farther, prompting a reaction from me that, well, let's just say hasn't occurred in the company of a woman in quite some time. She raised an eyebrow and cocked her head. Her toes flitted across mine. Her palms—or maybe mine—were sweaty. Lily's moans grew louder and more agonizing. Julia closed her eyes and then I did the same, leaning in to finally kiss her—when there came a sudden and moment-ruining clap.

We both lurched and shrieked.

Julia ran to the old woman, now in moderate convulsions. I was about to jump outside to call for help when she came out of it. The two women hugged, cried, and laughed. Lily whispered into Julia's ear, not some brief message, but a full diatribe taking five minutes. A while later we left Lily, bidding her goodbye and giving thanks. We mounted our bikes and continued toward the gardens along the Minderbroedersstraat.

"Well?" I said, riding behind her.

"I know you want to know, Eddy," she answered, "but I can't tell."

"You can't?"

"Sorry," she called back. "You wouldn't want to fiddle with fate, would you?"

"But—but wait a minute; you're fiddling—I want to do some fiddling, too."

"I'm *not* fiddling. I'm the female. I know and accept. You're the male—the one who'll try and change the course of pre-determined events if he can. But you can't. Our course is already set—whether together or apart—there's nothing to do about it. To mess with that, well, you'd be fucking with some pretty high rollers, mister."

"I won't—promise!"

"Not a chance, my dearest. Accept—that's all there is."

We rolled across the Dijle, passed St. Mary's Anglican Church, then dismounted just before the tall, stone archway. We walked through it, and then the gardens were around us in all their vibrant splendor. We set our bikes in a bike rack and began wandering around. On either side of the crushed stone walkway were flowers of every color, texture, and scent. Manicured shrubs rose from the palette like waiting spacecrafts, while others were trimmed so tightly they looked as though they were firm green mattresses that could be laid upon.

I took out my camera and moved ahead of her, snapping pictures as I walked backwards. She ignored me, then made faces, then exaggerated her walk as if she were a model strutting down a catwalk. We came to a small pond completely overtaken with lily pads, and I had her stand on a deck overlooking it. It was frightening how quickly and smoothly she changed expressions, switching yet again to a mood of serenity and intro-spection. She lowered her head, demure, the outline of her form popping out against the layers of foliage and the pond behind her. I paused, lower-ing the camera. She seemed to be putting on a show, yet nothing about her felt forced, as if giving a performance was as easy and natural as any-thing. I was stunned and mesmerized.

She slipped away from the deck along the trail, tossing pebbles into the pond as she went. It was all I could do to keep up. We went through a carpet of bluebells and onto an open field of grass where she twirled in place like a dancer, head thrown back until she lost control and tumbled to the ground. I followed her, firing the camera, until I went to advance the frame and it didn't move. I tossed myself to the ground beside her and began advancing the film in the magazine.

"Oh, Eddy," she sighed, her eyes cast to the sky, heaving delightfully, "this truly is a wonderful place, isn't it. I'm so glad you brought me here. Is this where you bring all your pretty dates?"

"Every single one," I said.

"I knew it. A brilliant young photographer such as yourself is bound to have all sorts of girls clamoring for attention." Her smile remained. "It doesn't matter. It's a wonderful place and a wonderful day. Don't you think clouds are heaven's way of saying everything's going to be all right? That even when it seems like there's no hope, no hope in the least, things move along and something truly new and exciting is bound to come your way?" She turned on her side to face me. "Don't you think so?"

"That's what all my pretty dates say," I said.

"Oh, stop." She pushed me. "Now you're making fun of me."

"I wouldn't make fun of you," I told her. "Never."

"But you are, of course you are. I'm not jealous, am I? I'm merely making a statement, an observation based on your qualifications as a desirable young man with good looks, a sensitive nature, and quiet charm."

"And money—don't forget the money."

Her eyes got big. "Money? Really, Eddy? Are you really loaded?"

"Beyond your wildest imagination," I said.

"Not that *I* care, mind you. Oh, but that does make you even more of a catch for our hoard of female fanatics. What's your preference— blonde, redhead, dark hair?"

I lifted my head giving her a quick once-over. "Definitely brunette. Something like yours, actually."

"How serendipitous! You have good taste, Eddy. Most young men of your qualifications make a bee line straight for the platinum—heaven knows why, but they do. I'm glad to hear you're a naturalist and don't go in for any of those phony-baloney bleach-blonde shenanigans. . . Say, what kind of device is that, anyway?"

I held up the camera, then popped off the back magazine so I could retrieve the wound-up roll of film. "Just something from the olden days," I said.

"Does it still work?"

"Better than anything made in the last forty years."

"How consistent of you, to cling to that old pile of gears and rust, just like all the old people you seem so obsessed with. It *is* an obsession, you know. Anything requiring more than 20.5% of your waking hours, per day, over a period of six months, can categorically and reasonably be described as an obsession. I read that somewhere."

I pulled a new roll of film from my pocket, loaded the magazine, and clipped it back onto the body of the camera. She watched me the whole time.

"Here," I said, handing it to her and then placing the strap over her neck.

"What are you trying to do, Eddy, turn me into your own personal sherpa?"

"Have you ever been behind the camera before?" She sat up, the camera swinging until she took it in her hands and began looking it over. "Did you ever think about becoming a photographer?"

"Now how would I ever have time to do that when I'm in school half the day and posing for Nico the other half?"

"You should," I said and stood up, wiping my hands of grass. I started walking away from her. She hurried after me, camera bobbing.

"Hold on a minute," she said. "Why would *I* want to do something as crazy and fiscally damaging as *that*? You trying to send me to the poor house?"

"I'm just saying, someone with your curiosity and *talent*. I know it when I see it."

She trotted just ahead of me, stopping me with her hand, clutching my shirt.

"*Talent?* That's a loaded cannonball of unsubstantiated compliment you've tossed out there, Eddy. Just where do you get off telling me I've got talent? Why, I might be dumber than a dodo and as thick as mud. I've got no natural acumen for the arts."

"I could take pictures of you all day, Julia," I said. "And I'd love every minute of it. But I don't think Lily, in all the things she saw in your future, had you sitting on a stool posing for somebody else for the rest of your life."

That comment must have struck something in her, for she stood there in a daze, still pinching my shirt. She snapped out of it, looked at me, then gave me a mild shove.

We went along a colonnade of conical bushes set in a bed of irises and ivy. She lifted the camera casually, almost insolently to her eye without stopping, then dropped it. She took exaggerated, loping strides as if she were being dragged along. A squirrel danced across the path. It was tame and took its time, and once we'd passed it she turned and stared at it. The squirrel stared back so, for spite, she took a picture of it. We stepped into the greenhouse, which was not nearly as hot as I thought it would be. Still, she waved her hands dramatically and felt her forehead with the back of her hand, then dropped her head against my shoulder, limply, as if she couldn't possibly take another step. I thought she'd remain only a moment, but she didn't leave, rolling her head back and forth. I lifted my hands and went to comfort her, but refrained. I reconsidered and, just as my hands touched her shoulders, she lifted her head. Tears streaked down either cheek pitifully.

"Nobody's ever bought me flowers before, Eddy, you sweet son-of-a-bitch. And now you tell me I'm more than just a pretty face. What are you trying to do to me? It's too much."

She fell against me again and this time I did embrace her. She reached her arms around my waist, turning her head to the side. I'd nearly laughed, but I now took seriously her overdramatic outbursts as signs of real struggle. I held her for a good long while.

We reversed roles and she made me stand in front of a woody old tropical plant with vines spiraling up its trunk. She had trouble finding the focus, so I showed her. I showed her where the aperture setting was, and the shutter speed. She seemed pleased and told me to take my position again. She fired off several shots as I stood there, not nearly so enthusiastically or aesthetically pleasing to look at, but I smiled warmly at her. We left the greenhouse and found a mass of wisteria hanging heavy and plump over a trellis. We took turns being the model and then the photographer. When she modeled she did so in a more reserved manner than earlier, and at first I was disappointed; I so enjoyed her theatrics. But as I zoomed in, I saw her defiance and courage against whatever it was she was fighting, as bold and bright as the flowers around her. She gazed back looking right through my camera lens, and I was sure she was reading my thoughts.

We walked without saying much. I felt her hand bump mine a few times and took it as a signal. I held her hand. She ground her thumb into my palm gently, barely, so it tickled. I made plans to kiss her. I hadn't wanted anything so much in years—right then I felt I couldn't let her go without feeling her in my arms and kissing her.

"Let's go over there," I said, and steered her off the path.

"Where?"

"There," I said, nodding to a cluster of giant old yews.

The yews formed a tall, ragtag hedge providing good cover. We stopped beside them. I turned to face her, taking her other hand.

"Gosh, Eddy," she said, "what's this all about?"

I leaned in and kissed her. I let go of her hands and took her in my arms. Her lips were hot and receptive and she kissed me back. I felt her lose tenseness as she fell against me. There was the scent of her perfume and her skin and the yew—all swirling in my head together. We kissed for a long time. We kissed until we heard people talking on the other side of the yews. We didn't stop immediately, but kissed a few more times and then returned to the path.

We rode back to the Oude Markt where we stopped, straddling our bicycles. She went to give me back the camera but I told her to keep it. There was half a roll left; I told her she should take pictures of whatever she wanted and then we'd get together again and I'd show her how to develop the film and make prints. She slung the camera over her shoulder and I told her she looked like a real pro. She leaned over our bikes and kissed me, nearly knocking us both down. She abruptly turned and marched her bike through the crowd. I watched her until she disappeared into the sea of heads bobbing beneath the blinding sun.

My Idyllic Day

Harry and I had been out for over two hours, winding our way through the small towns east of Leuven on an unusually brutal day. During the first hour we talked casually about the heat and joked about the competition. We sat upright much of the time, peddling with one or sometimes neither hand on the handlebars, sipping water idly, pointing out some unique building or a beautiful horse. It was our first ride together, and I knew that Harry wanted to prove something. As for me, I wanted to enjoy the scenery. I didn't often have time to notice it when I was training. I watched him from the corner of my eye. He was pretending to be taking it easy when I knew he was plotting his attack. I felt really bad for him, and more than a little guilty.

When we came to the first hill he made a surge. He gathered speed leading up to it, then geared down and increased his cadence. The hill wasn't steep, but it was long and required endurance to keep up a good pace. The hill for me was of little challenge, but I purposely lagged behind. I watched Harry, his legs peddling away like mad. He approached the crest and, when he saw that I was still behind him, lifted his arms from the handlebars in victory.

The next hill was half a mile away, steeper and longer than the first. Harry gathered speed leading up to it while I shadowed him, waiting. He attacked just as he had on the first hill and I decided to have some fun. I swerved out wide and blew on past him. Half a minute later, I turned to look back. He was fifty meters behind and struggling to keep up. I backed off, pretending to be struggling myself, and allowed him to gain some but I didn't allow him to catch me. I reached the summit, wincing, as if it'd been a real effort. We reached for our water bottles and coasted down the steep backside. The wind pushed the sweat from my face and I lifted my arms to catch as much of it as I could.

The hills went on for some time and we took turns leading the way up, that is until we were about two miles from our destination. Harry suddenly accelerated, bearing down on his bike to get more power. I knew what he was doing. He wanted to show me up in front of the others, who were waiting for us. I sat upright watching him struggle, and smiled. He arrived at the cemetery fifty meters ahead. He didn't let up until he'd crossed the parking lot entrance, which I guess he considered to be the finish line. I pitied him. I pitied him for much more than this bit of grandstanding. He pulled over, waiting for me, then slapped me on the back in a show of disingenuous sportsmanship.

Philippe, Marta, and Emma were waiting just outside the woods near the cemetery. They'd arrived some time earlier, along with the catering truck I'd arranged. I gave specific instructions for a long, multiple-leaved table to be carried to the spot, and on it was spread a feast of pastries, breads, meats, cheeses, smoked fish, vegetables, wine, and a tub of ice filled with an assortment of Belgian beer. All this was laid on a white antique tablecloth adorned with fresh-cut flowers. I'd purchased the chairs recently at an estate sale—the backs were carved in various medieval scenes and the seats had been re-upholstered in beige linen just two days ago. Philippe was seated at the far end, his back to two bartenders dressed in white short-sleeved shirts, identically mustached as it were. Marta and Emma were on either side of him, each with a drink and a small plate of food. Harry and I leaned our bikes against a tree and approached them.

"There they are," Philippe said, "our two riders." He had his hands on his cane and gazed at us admiringly. "Tell us, how did it go? A bit hot for cycling, eh?"

"Warm enough," I said. Though the ride hadn't been strenuous, I was sweating profusely. I stood with my hands on my hips looking down at the table, trying to decide what I wanted. Harry had already made his way to the beer and was being helped by not one, but both bartenders.

"I'm sure it was," said Philippe. "It's hot enough sitting here in the shade not doing a thing."

"Who won?" said Emma. I was glad she'd come. She never got a break from waitressing and it was good seeing her on the receiving end of a table for a change.

"It wasn't a race," said Philippe.

"It's always a race," she said, sucking on an olive. "Come on, don't tell me it didn't turn into a race."

"As a matter of fact, it did," I said. "Harry took off with two miles to go and never looked back."

"Didn't you see us come in?" Harry said, his hopeful eyes moving around the table.

"The girls were preoccupied, I think," said Philippe. "We have very attentive servers." He grinned at them all. He so enjoyed scandal, however small, in whatever guise.

Harry sat down next to Marta. She draped her arm around his sweaty neck and kissed him. One of the bartenders brought me a Witkap, along with a plate filled with salmon, cheese, and grapes. I sat down next to Philippe, slumping back in the high-backed chair in my normal posture, but then I remembered how sweaty I was and I sat up.

"So," I said, "are we drunk yet?"

"We thought we'd be good guests and wait until you two arrived," said Emma.

"Liar," I said, "but it's a nice thought."

"I never get drunk anymore," said Philippe. "I find that I miss too much once everyone else gets drunk."

"He's writing a memoir," said Marta, having just pulled her arm from around Harry's neck. "He needs to stay sober."

"Is that right, Philippe?" asked Harry.

"And what if I were?"

"Better watch what you say," said Emma. "I think the cane is a ruse."

"You mean he's got a recorder in there?" I inched slowly toward Philippe, eyeing the cane suspiciously.

"How on earth would I fit a recorder in this thing?" He lifted it up, grasping it midway like a spear, and shook it near my head.

"Must be somewhere else. Perhaps those two?" I nodded to the mustached bartenders. "You two aren't spies for our good friend, are you?" The two looked at one another and shook their heads uneasily.

"I may just write a memoir someday," said Philippe, "but it won't include this sorry lot."

"I'm hurt," I said. "I'm really hurt. Are you suggesting we're uninteresting drunks—that is, when we get drunk?"

"You're extremely interesting drunks, which is what draws me like a happy honey bee to your bouquet of insights and pithy remarks."

"Santé," I said and lifted my glass.

"Santé," said Philippe, but the others all said, "Cheers."

"Emma," I said, "where is Derek? I thought he was coming."

"He paints all day."

"I figured he might take a break, you know, get out of the studio for a while."

"That's impossible," she said. "You know that."

"Sure, it's just that I thought he'd have a good time with everyone, that's all."

"He lives for his painting. I did not expect him to take the afternoon off to sit beneath trees chit-chatting."

"He doesn't drink, you know," said Harry.

I thought he was joking, but then realized he was serious. "Yeah, I know he doesn't drink."

"That's probably why he didn't want to come," continued Harry, sitting with one leg over the other. "I'm sure it's nothing more than that."

"We should all be so dedicated," said Philippe. "Instead, here we are eating and drinking to our hearts' content."

"I don't know," I said. "What else is there but to live and drink and live more from the insights of drinking?"

"Making art," said Emma.

"Yes," said Philippe. "On top of living and drinking, there is art."

"Are you saying that this is a waste of time?" I said.

"No, I didn't say that," said Emma. "You asked what more there is to life than drinking, and I said *art*."

"I didn't say *just* drinking," I corrected. "I said living and drinking, and more living."

"You're an artist yourself," she pointed out. "Surely, you would understand."

"But my art, the photographs I take, are nothing but images of people living—"

"And drinking," added Harry, wagging a finger.

"A man can't create truthful art unless he lives," I said.

"Now *there's* insight," said Emma facetiously, slapping the table. "Where did you read that?"

"I didn't read it. It becomes obvious to anyone after a very short time." I raised my empty glass, prompting Harry to raise his. Our glasses were promptly filled and returned by the two bartenders. "Derek gets out plenty. I know he prefers a strict routine where he works during the day and then kicks back in the evenings. I do the opposite. Besides, taking photographs is different from painting. I have to go into my subject matter. If somebody sees me with my camera, they either shut down or ham it up and either way it makes the picture unusable. The more time I spend at the cafés and on the streets, the more I become invisible. My strategy every morning is to become invisible so I can capture reality."

"But," said Emma, "why are drunks more interesting than, say, a businessman on his way to work, or a mother on her way to the bakery with her two children? What makes a drunk so appealing? Don't you think that's a tired cliché of what good art is?"

"I don't think drunks are more interesting," I said. "I shoot plenty of people besides café rats. But I've given up my suit and tie, and I have no idea what it is to be a parent. I could photograph them and I'm sure my images would have some aesthetic value, but I'd be an outsider, a voyeur, which is an entirely different thing."

"Being an outsider has its advantages," said Emma. "Sometimes when you get too close to something you can't see it properly. Your focus can become a hindrance."

I thought about it. "I guess so. But now you're getting into the realm of self-analysis, and there's nothing deadlier to an artist than *that*."

"James *has* found a new subject matter recently," said Philippe. "He is moving away from drunks to the elderly men and women of our area, those who lived through the last war."

"Are you, James?" said Harry raising his glass. "Bravo for you."

"I agree with you, Emma," I said. "There's only so much you can squeeze from café life. It's something I've known, but now it's time to move on."

"There you go," she said, "an outside observer—a *foreign* observer, in fact. What prompted the shift in subject matter?"

"I don't know," I said. "I guess I just want to get down whatever I can in the time I have left, to document as much as I can about the people who lived here during the war before they're all gone."

Emma, holding an olive in midair, seemed surprised. "In the time you have left? Are you leaving us, James?"

The table suddenly grew quiet as they waited for an answer. I'd been debating about whether to tell them. Part of the reason for the picnic had been some vague scheme of gathering them together and explaining my situation. I wanted to tell them; I wanted to tell *someone*. But I couldn't. I didn't want them to look at me any differently. I wanted to remain as I was, without their pity.

"You didn't think I was going to stay here forever?" I said to Emma, but meant it for the whole group. "My father. . ." And here I drifted away in thought—for, the very mention of my father brought up unresolved, uncomfortable emotions. I looked at them all looking at me, waiting. "My father wants a return on his investment," I said, smiling. "I'll need to go back some time."

"Well," said Emma, "I think that's quite admirable. Not that your café pictures weren't interesting. But now you've taken on something of real importance, James. Instead of stealing away life from your subjects, you are giving something in return. There is no greater tool for the artist than empathy."

There was an awkward silence. Philippe, whose head was lowered as he stared into the table, looked up.

"So," he said, "when is your beautiful young friend arriving?"

"Friend?" said Marta. "Oh, please do tell."

I shook my head in embarrassment. "They should be here soon. Maybe they got lost."

"They?" said Harry.

"She doesn't drive. I believe Nico, her. . ."

"Another friend," said Philippe.

"Yeah, another friend, that's right. He's supposed to be driving her out. I thought they'd be here by now."

"James," said Marta, "you have the look of a young man in love. Are you?"

Philippe, without saying anything, nodded excitedly.

"You mean it's true? James, you are really, finally in love?"

"I think we ought to let actions speak for themselves," said Philippe. "She will be here soon enough. If everyone could refrain from interrogating the poor girl the minute she arrives, James would be eternally grateful."

I raised my glass to Philippe. "That's right—I want everybody to behave. She's no mouse, but how about if you all count to ten before you start firing away?"

"Why, James," said Emma, leaning forward with the widest grin. "How very nice."

Julia arrived a short while later, striding through the waving field. I saw her and jumped to my feet and ran out to her. She leaped into my arms, wrapping her legs around my waist, and I carried her like this until she finally slid down and we walked together, hand-in-hand. She leaned against me, squeezing my hand as I made introductions. Philippe stood up and gave her a hug.

"No Nico?" he said.

"Not today," said Julia.

"He could have stayed for something to eat," Philippe said mildly offended. "I told him we were having a feast."

She said nothing, then flashed her eyes from behind her hair. "Drama," she said. "Valentina threw a knife at him."

"Oh, dear me. Is everyone unscathed?"

"It was just a bread knife. Got him on the forearm pretty good, but he's all right. They have spats sometimes."

Everyone chuckled uneasily.

I asked her what she wanted to eat, and I made up a plate for her. The bartenders offered her something to drink, but she said she just wanted a bottle of water. We sat down beside Philippe, who had cleared a spot on the table, flicking an ant with his finger as a final act of hospitality.

All eyes were on her. She glanced around, and then pushed a finger toward her opened mouth as if she were about to vomit. Everybody laughed.

"Holy everything," she said. "Who's the one putting on this banquet?"

"That would be Philippe," I said, giving him a nod. I lifted my chin and my eyes went around to each of them in firm warning.

"Gee, my idea of a picnic is a dirty old blanket and a couple sandwiches. This—this is something else. *Nice*—don't get me wrong. But crazy over-the-top."

"Philippe's an over-the-top kind of man," I said. "Aren't you, Philippe?"

Philippe lifted himself in surprise. "I guess I am!"

"So," said Harry with hands clasped, elbows on the table, "are you a student?"

"Does Putin like mirrors?"

Marta choked on a laugh.

"Sorry, I'm being obtuse. Sure, I'm a student. And before you ask—it's philosophy, that dying field of naval gazing and star pondering."

"How interesting," said Harry. "Someone under the age of twenty-five who's not majoring in international business."

"*I'm* not majoring in international business," said Emma, leaning

40

forward to look down at Harry.

"Yeah? What's your major?"

"Undecided," she said, folding her arms in self-satisfaction.

"All my friends are undecided," said Julia. "Or else philosophy majors. Not much difference between the two when you get down to the short and fat of it."

"Julia is from Italy," said Philippe. "She's visiting with her two sisters. They all model for Nico, one of the most esteemed photographers in Belgium."

"Not half as esteemed as *this* boy's going to be," she said. "You wait and see."

"What part of Italy are you from?" said Harry. "Your English is remarkable."

"Some little place you never heard of. Pretty, though. Quaint. Olive oil dripping from the clouds."

"Are your sisters studying here as well?"

"Nope." She broke off a hunk of baguette and chewed it, over-emphasizing the difficulty of the act. "They just do the statue routine for Nico. Ambition, at least the gray matter kind, never was their strong suit. Oh, not that they're dumbos or anything. Lots of geniuses decide to do nothing with their lives. And I'm not saying posing for Nico is doing nothing, either. He's somebody you can really learn from. Why do you think he and Valentina have it out every day? He challenges her in ways she's not comfortable with. It ruffles her feathers. Breaks those icicles. Not always a pleasant ride, if you know what I mean, but once you've done all the loop-de-loops and walked over the coals of humility, there's something waiting at the finish line. Something you can really chew on for the rest of your life."

"Do you get a chance to return to Italy often?" said Emma.

Julia paused, a piece of baguette in one hand and a knife tipped with butter in the other. She stared into the table. "I haven't been home in two years." Then, as quickly as she'd shut down, she lighted up again and began buttering the baguette. "Can't afford to. Plus, with school, when is there time except for summer? Nico likes the heat, so we're busy as beavers in summer." She stopped herself again, a bit put off. "Why does somebody's bad health have to sink a torpedo in the family cruise ship? We send every spare euro we make back home and it doesn't make the tiniest little dent in the mountain of debt we've accumulated. Why, you stick out your tongue and say *Aaaaaah* and there goes six months of sitting on a stool breaking your back in front of Nico's drooling mug. Willy Boy had it all wrong—don't kill all the lawyers, kill all the doctors and insurance agents."

"Willy Boy?" Harry said, lifting his chin away from his curled hand in confusion.

"Oh, goodness," said Philippe. "Go on, dear. This is marvelous."

"I don't know," she sighed. "I guess my cross isn't any bigger than anybody else's. It just feels like a hippo, is all. Sometimes it's just so hopeless. I mean, it's so hopeless I just don't know what to do. I wish I could see my dear old mother, that's for sure. When I think of her wasting away in that dark room, all alone except for my aunt, who's not in the greatest shape herself. . . It just tears me to pieces, it does. The hopelessness of everything. I don't know how people don't fall apart all over the world. I really don't."

She ate her plate of food and then had another half-plate, and then she asked in a whisper if I wanted to check out the woods. I told the others we were taking a walk and we'd be back in a while. Philippe said he was going to look at the horses near the cemetery, and Emma said she'd like to go with him.

I held Julia's hand as we walked, helping her across small tree trunks and stones. We came to a nearly dry creek and I lifted her by the waist over it. There was a clearing with wildflowers blowing in the slight breeze.

"Here," she said, and from the waistband of her skirt she took out a roll of film. "Nico showed me how to rewind it. You didn't tell me this was infrared, Eddy. Nico says it's hot stuff, though I did want to see the wisteria all bright and cheery purple. I finished the roll as soon as I got home. Couldn't wait to get at it. He wanted to develop the roll himself but I told him to get his big fat mitts off—this is very personal stuff—

only to be shared with humanity if we both give the thumbs up. I'm afraid I can't do the lab work beside you, though. Barely had two ticks of the clock to come out here today—you'll have to do it yourself and show me some other time."

She allowed herself to fall against a tree.

"Well, now," she said. "Aren't you going to kiss me? I shaved my legs and put on my favorite earrings and everything. I'm about as plump with hormones as it gets."

She reached out her hand and I took it, letting my body press hers.

"Oh, Eddy, you're such a beast. Lily said you were a beast and she was right. She's always right."

We kissed against the tree. I took her hands in mine and lifted them above her head and pinned them to the bark. I kept them there with one hand and with the other slowly unbuttoned her blouse. I kissed her neck and then on down. I grazed the curves of her bosoms with the back of my hand, still held by her bra, then kissed her nipple through the gauzy material. My hand slid under her skirt passing over her glass thighs. I let go of her hands, but she kept them above her head as I slid down her body. Her skirt was not tight and so I lifted it and tucked a portion of it into the waistband to hold it up. I kissed the fronts of her thighs and her waist and the gentle rise beneath her scant panties. I pulled the panties down to her knees. My lips moved over her, everywhere, my eyes closed, hands sunk like talons into the flesh of her cheeks, and I lost myself in her scent and taste.

The Scar Revealed

I lay in bed listening to the birds. Morning was a pleasant time, and I always had difficulty getting out of bed. But this particular morning I lingered longer than usual as I thought of Julia and our brief time in the woods. It had been a while since I'd held a girl in my arms. I'd forgotten what it felt like to kiss and be kissed, to have someone move beneath me, to desire me as much as I desired her. My pillow, though she had not been here, held her smell. I rolled to my side and breathed deep and it hurt inside to think of her not being beside me. My mind obsessed over the little details of our time together at the botanical gardens, and prior to that when we were sitting on the bumper couch, and then recently in the woods. I kept thinking of her hair in my face, how her neck opened for me to be kissed, the soft points of her breasts as we embraced, and the low, aching moans she made as I pulled her closer. I was sure she was in a similar state in her own bed thinking of me, longing for my hands on her body, reliving our kisses, imagining more. I'd had girlfriends before, but had never been in love. I didn't know if I loved Julia. It felt like love, but I had nothing to compare it against. It felt different than anything before, and better, and it was more intoxicating.

I rolled onto my other side and drifted back to sleep, then woke when Derek came into the flat. I heard an unusual sound and realized he was eating an apple. I got up and trudged out of the bedroom.

Derek sat sideways in a chair eating the apple, looking at the recent images I'd put on the wall, turning his head at different angles to change his perspective. I stood to the side, barely awake, waiting for him to say something.

"Well?" I yawned.

"I'm not done," he said, lifting a pinkie from his apple. "Hold on."

He chewed the apple as his eyes darted between the images. Suddenly, he leaned forward like he was ready to charge ahead, then relaxed and sat back again.

"Jesus, Derek, come on."

"Your message said you wanted my opinion," he said. "An opinion requires an informed mind."

"I just wanted to know what you thought about her," I said, folding my arms.

"Are you looking for an opinion on the girl herself, or her ability as a photographer? Or, do you mean you want an opinion on the images, as art, that you've taken, irrespective of her aesthetic qualifications?"

I breathed deep, allowing myself to digest the question.

"I guess all of that."

Derek took a final bite of the apple and let it drop to the floor. He wiped his hands together and then, not satisfied, wiped them on the front of his shirt.

"She's a stunner, all right," he said. Again, he leaned forward. "Yeah... *Yeah*... Not in the classical, drop-dead gorgeous predictable way, but in the much more interesting, intelligent way. She's got class. She's got mystery. What's her name?"

"Julia."

"Julia?" He pushed out his lip. "She doesn't look like a Julia. But if you say so, okay."

I walked in front of the photographs. "How about these," I said, "the ones of her hands?"

"Oh, those are really nice. I haven't seen a pair of hands like that since this commercial for dishwashing soap on TV."

"She took them. Do you know why?"

"To show off her recent manicure?" He waved his hand. "You're in the way."

I moved aside. "I told her how I'd been taking pictures of old men, you know, especially their hands. She went home after our day together and immediately took these."

"Well, she probably thinks you have a hand fetish. You might be on to something with this one."

"She doesn't think I have a *hand fetish*," I said. I picked up the dropped apple core by the stem and walked it like a dead mouse to the kitchen trash can. "It's like. . . she's three steps ahead intellectually, yet something's holding her back. Like she's afraid."

"Of what?"

"Beats me. I get the feeling she can't process everything racing through her head. It's really strange. It's not a lack of confidence, I don't think. I don't know what it is."

Derek stood up and approached the images. We looked at them together.

"I'll have to say, they're certainly well-composed," he said.

He gave me a pat on the back and said he needed to get back to his studio and start painting—said he should have been at it an hour ago. I got dressed and worked in the darkroom for several hours. I wanted to go out on a ride, but I was tired. I lay down on the couch and woke up some time in the afternoon. When I woke I was sweating. It was the second time I'd had the sweats in two weeks. When I stood on the scale I saw that I'd lost three pounds.

I didn't see Julia for nearly a week. I wondered what she was doing throughout the day, whether she was in class, or posing for Nico, or studying, or maybe she was seeing someone else. She said she'd never been given flowers before, but of course that wasn't true, it couldn't be. Maybe she was just being grateful, but it bothered me that she couldn't accept the gesture without making such a hyperbolic comment like that. Yet, that very exaggeration of everything she said was part of what made her so attractive. Nico said he'd turned Valentina into a riddle, yet Julia's entire background was a riddle, in particular her speech. She had very little accent and used phrases and slang only an American would use. If Valentina and Gia were her sisters, why were they so different from her?

I decided the best thing to do would be to go about my normal routine without obsessing over her. It was hard at first. I missed her buoyant presence, her voice, the way she put things. But after a couple days I was able to push thoughts of her to the side and resume my activities.

I went out each morning when it was cool and the canals were still. I'd never seen anything alive in them. It didn't mean they held no life, only that I was too impatient to wait for signs to present themselves. Cats walked the ledges. These came in a variety of pedigrees, colors, and amiability toward people. They strode forward as cats the world over do, heads and tails erect, as if the walls had been built specifically for their use. I took pictures of them, not as subjects, but as points of departure for other images or as juxtapositions within an image itself. They led me from the still canals to other places. They guided me with their haughty confidence. I caressed them when they allowed it, and cautioned them about the long fall down and how the saying about nine lives was nothing to put your faith in.

I found a small café where I sat beneath dense trees and sipped a cappuccino. My trick was to pretend to be examining my camera, to feign confusion as if I had some mechanical problem with it, when really I was waiting for the right moment when someone interesting walked by and then I'd take the picture.

After the café, I wandered through the middle of the city beneath the old trees which dropped small almond-shaped leaves and lay like yellow Corn Flakes on the cobblestones. Along the canal I found Rick, sitting on a bench. He wore a corduroy jacket and a scarf because he believed it gave him a more European look. I initially thought he was an old man and was anxious to begin framing him against the dark stone of the wall behind him, then realized who he was. Rick taught at a small liberal arts college back home and had come over for a series of lectures at the university. The lectures finished several weeks ago. Rick, I presumed, was still waiting for the arrival of Elle, who was not yet back from Ireland.

We walked along the canal to the Grote Markt and went inside The Carousal and sat at the bar with all its goose neck taps and glassware dripping from the ceiling like stalactites. Rick gave a sigh and winced. He sat with his hands curled around the wide-mouthed glass of beer. When he talked it was from the side. His eyes were on his beer, a raspberry sour, but his ears were listening.

"How do you like it?" Rick winced. He winced after each sip. It was a habit that went well with his corduroy and scarf.

"It's okay," I said. I'd ordered the same beer as Rick instead of my usual Witkap.

"Elle—all she'll drink are sours. At least in Belgium."

"Bring her here, then. She'll be in heaven."

"Oh, she's been here, don't you worry about that. She knows every bar there is to know in Leuven for a semi-affluent middle-aged redhead from America."

"It's not that I dislike it," I said. "I don't think there's a beer in this country I dislike, and I like sours. It's the raspberries. I'm not a big fan of sticking things into beers that shouldn't be there." I took another small sip. "My ambivalence about it is slowing me down, which is probably a good thing."

"A brewer like you, you must be in heaven over here," he said.

"You don't have to be a brewer to be in heaven in this country."

"Still," Rick flitted his fingers along the side of his glass, "it has to be an inspiration. Something to take back home, I mean."

"I don't want to think about going back home. I thought we agreed about that. I won't bring up Elle and you don't bring up my brewery."

"I don't mind talking about Elle. She's fine to talk about."

"That's not what you said the other night," I said.

"You recording our conversations or something?" Rick laughed into his glass of beer. The glass of beer meant more to him than just about anything. "I don't remember."

"I still have the bruise on my arm when you grabbed me," I said. "You were pretty adamant."

"I apologize profusely. I'm not a man of violence under normal circumstances."

"You had a pretty strong grip."

"I'm really sorry, James," he said. "I don't remember any of it."

I extended my arm and showed him. "Around back there. I don't bruise easily, but you got me good."

Rick kept his eyes on his glass. He winced, but it was the wince of being embarrassed and not an affectation to go with his corduroy and scarf.

"What is it about her?" I said.

"What do you mean?"

"Seems like there's a lot of animosity between the two of you."

Rick seemed surprised. His brown eyes got big so you could see the veins in them. "What makes you think that?"

"The bruise, I suppose," I said.

"The bruise. You keep bringing that up. I told you I was sorry."

"The other night when you grabbed me, you mentioned something about a cigarette. You kept going on and on about the cigarette. I thought you were going to break down and cry."

"Me cry?" Rick said making a grumbling sound. "Never."

"Well, almost."

"I'm a college professor, James. I don't cry. I drink, but I don't cry."

"I could be wrong on the crying part. And I said almost—*almost*. So, when is she coming back?"

"She's coming when she gets here," said Rick. "Exactly when she gets here."

"I see."

"Do you?"

"Not everything, but enough." I took a sip of my beer. "That's a lot to live with, Rick."

Rick's face turned sour. He stared into his beer and the rims of his eyes shook with hatred. "That Irish *band*." He'd begun telling this story the other night, but didn't get too far into it before his anger took over:

"It was a lovely evening, just the two of us walking the river, when we stopped in a café on the Île Saint-Louis. It was on a corner, an open-air place, perfect for drinking and watching. It was lovely, just lovely. A man came around to all the cafés playing his saxophone looking for money. A drunk, you see. A man who once possessed real talent, now groveling whimsically from café to café. Harmless in every sense of the word, memorable even, for tourists like us. The managers tolerated him and the patrons found him amusing, but he was finally sent on his way after striking up a conversation with a woman wearing very gaudy jewelry and red high heels. Her date didn't mind, but the manager of that particular establishment had had enough. There we were casually drinking our beers—that's something I love about Elle, she's a beer drinker, has no use for wine whatsoever—when we met the band. Not a traditional Irish band, a rock band. They'd stopped in for a quick pint, you see, in their black T-shirts and leather jackets smelling like Dublin, which is to say smoke. Nice enough guys. They sat down with us. We had ourselves a good chat. Snarled on about the sax player getting the boot—took it quite personally."

"Have to love the Irish," I said. "Punch right through snobbery, they do."

"They were in Paris for a few gigs. Three, four, maybe five—I can't remember. They weren't talking to *me*, you understand. You do understand, don't you?"

"I think I have the gist of it."

"I wasn't listening so much as *observing*."

"Got it."

"Before you know it she's—*we've*—been invited to see them play that night at wherever it was they were playing. Which we did, of course."

"How did they sound?" I took another sip of beer.

"They sounded very loud. Very Irish. She loved the whole thing. You see, I've omitted to tell you that my wife has in the past year or so morphed into a sort of middle-aged groupie. She leaves on Friday and returns Sunday evening, hoarse, sick, and scant on details. She's in Chicago one weekend, Atlanta the next, San Francisco the following. She has several bands she follows religiously now, and a whole new set of—I guess you'd call them friends—she tramps around with. Between concerts she's on her phone or computer planning the next adventure, or reliving the last one. A remarkable thing to watch, really. The utter and complete abandonment of one kind of life—ours—for a new one based on sixteen-year-old idol-worshipping. I'd go with her, other than the fact that standing in line for eight hours to get a spot on the rail isn't my idea of a good time, not to mention she'd rather I not go with her anyway." Rick waved his hands. "This is all beside the point. The point *is*, after the gig, the gig with the Irish lads, Elle and—surprise, surprise—the lead singer formed a bond, a friendship, if you will."

"Isn't that convenient."

"You see where this thing is headed," Rick lifted his eyebrows, which were bushy and wide, frayed at the tips like two used paint brushes. "And here I thought I was going to spring it on you. So yeah, they start buddying around in between the gigs while I'm hitting the Bouquinistes looking for something good to read. A couple days later I come trudging up to the flat—five stories up, mind you. Dirtiest carpet you ever saw. Never seen a college apartment that had dirtier stairs than that place. But the inside, nice as can be. Great view—even a peek at the Eiffel Tower herself. So up I go, but nobody's home. I figure I'll lie down on the bed and take a quick nap before she gets back. That's when I notice something on the floor. I look down and sure enough I'm not seeing things. It's a cigarette. Not a cigarette butt, but a new one, though bent, nearly broken in half. I'm not sure if I told you but I don't smoke, and neither does my wife."

"Of course."

"I'll let you connect the dots."

"Done," I said taking a quick sip of beer.

"Naturally, I was stunned. Well, not completely. It's not like I haven't been down *that* road before. Still, it's always a shock."

"I imagine so. Christ."

"The band was in Paris a few more days, during which time I spent roughly four waking hours with her. They invited *us* back to Ireland for the continuation of their worldwide tour. My wife, I knew, was going whether I went or not. There was no question about that. To save what little dignity I had left, I made her return to Leuven first in the wild hope she'd change her mind. Not the first time I've had such foolish hopes." He closed his eyes, dropped back his head, and finished his beer. "And that, my friend, is that."

"How long has she been gone now?"

"I believe it's been two weeks. Haven't heard hide nor hair from the redheaded ballbuster. No email. No text. Not a thing."

"Are you worried?"

Rick lifted his winged eyebrows and made a face. "I think she's got things pretty well under control."

"Jesus." I took another drink. "What's she doing for money?"

Rick laughed. It was the very first time I'd heard him truly laugh. "And I thought you were the professional dot-connector."

"I see."

"Do you?"

"Not everything, but enough. That's a lot to live with."

"Don't," Rick said giving me a look. It was a hard look to give a friend. "I told you, I don't want your pity."

"All right," I said.

"The last thing I need is for you or anybody else to look at me like I'm some beat dog. I'm *not*." He clenched his fist on the bar top.

"I didn't mean anything by it," I said. "And I understand, about not wanting pity."

"You?" Rick looked at me like I'd said some kind of joke. "You have no idea."

I said nothing. Rick's story *was* pitiful, but I tried not to think about it. I'd heard many such stories sitting in the cafés. I knew that the single most common element weaving individuals together was stories just like Rick's. There was nothing to be done about it, but listen and allow the tragedies of others to lessen your own.

· · ·

A few days later I returned home from an afternoon ride to find Julia sitting cross-legged outside my building facing the canal. She seemed to be meditating, though I couldn't be sure.

"I'm trying to call life-forms from the depths of your waterway," she said in a low, serious voice. I waited. A few moments later she pushed herself up, wiped off her hands, and turned to face me. "I think it's deader than disco."

I carried my bike up to the flat as she followed close behind. When we stepped inside she waited for me to set the bike on the hook in the ceiling, then pulled me close and we kissed. She kissed as if she'd been thinking about me all this time. I held her cheeks in my hands and then pushed aside her hair and began kissing her ear. She giggled. A moment later, she pulled back making a dramatic sweep of her hand across her forehead.

"Whew! Electricity's not a problem in *this* pair bond." She turned her gaze to the ceiling. "Thanks, Lily. So far, so good."

She saw the photographs on the wall and gave them a cursory glance, then traipsed around surveying the place.

"Not bad, not bad for a *presumed* bachelor. I think this will do very nicely, very nicely indeed."

She pushed open the bathroom door. "Some nooks are still a work in progress, I see. No problem, we can work with that. A darkroom—how resourceful of you, Eddy. Doesn't allow for the Spanish moss of bras and like unmentionables drying from the shower curtain, but art does have its sovereignty. I approve and will abide."

She strode out to the living room again and went back to the photographs on the table, flipping through them. "These are pretty darn good," she said. "You are a budding genius. I've been around enough of them and you, my friend, have the gift."

Then, as if as an afterthought, she gazed at the photographs on the wall. "Well, well, what do we have here? Not too shabby. Not too shabby at all. You make me look like a real dancer, Eddy. You really know how to capture the spirit of a person, don't you. And hey—mine aren't so bad either. God, I botched *that* one, but some aren't so bad. I do have nice hands—everybody says so. The longest fingers in the family, and we come from a long line of giraffe-fingered femmes. Had a devil of a time holding the camera with one hand, framing it up just so, then clicking the pic. But somehow I managed. A bit of perseverance, a little luck, and you can do just about anything." She stopped for a breath and reached inside her purse. "Here," and she handed me three rolls of film. "Nico has tons—he said I can have as many as I want. No infrared, but I figure that's okay—we don't want to be in competition, now, do we? Would you mind doing the chemical magic and turning these pods into something the eye can look at? If you don't have time, I understand, we're all short on the fourth dimension. We can make some popcorn and do it together some time—let's make a date. Who knows what might happen when the lights go out and two strangers set foot in the fixer?"

I poured us each a glass of ice water. I drank mine down without pause, set the glass on the corner of the table beside all the photographs, placed my hands on her waist, and brought her close. I kissed her.

We made our way to the couch, where I began unbuttoning her silk blouse. Apparently, I was performing the task too slowly, so she yanked up what was tucked into her skirt and helped me, unbuttoning from the bottom until our hands met. She wriggled out of the blouse and reached back and unsnapped her bra. She pushed me down and started kissing the side of my neck.

"Mm. . ." she said, smacking her lips. "Salty."

She wanted to go farther down my chest, but my jersey and bibs were in the way. She lifted me up, helped extricate me from the tight sweaty jersey, and pushed down the straps of my bibs. When I leaned back down she saw my scar and gasped.

"My, Eddy," she said. "Dear me!"

She leaned forward pressing our chests together, then held the sides of my face and kissed me. I felt the heat from her chest and from her cheeks and it made my head swim. She lay her head on my chest and traced a finger along my scar.

"Do you want to tell me about it?" Her voice was low and sincere and I felt I was talking to the real Julia without any façade between us.

"I'd rather not," I said.

"I didn't mean to be nosy."

"No, it's all right. I'd be curious, too."

Her touch was light. She moved her finger like an inch worm repeatedly over the scar. "Does it hurt?"

"Not anymore," I said. "Not for a long time."

"It's all right, Eddy," she said. "It must be something monumental. I don't blame you one atom for keeping it to yourself."

I stroked her hair, then pulled it back so I could see her cheek from above, and her finger moving slowly along the numbed scar.

"I have this condition," I said. "I've had it since birth. I had my first operation that day, the day I was born, and since then I've had several more. The last one was a couple years ago."

She placed her ear on my chest and listened. "Gee, Eddy, it sure sounds like a winner to me. Is everything all fixed now?"

I breathed deep, my fingers pushing into her silky hair. "Oh, not exactly."

"Not exactly? That's not what you're supposed to say."

"I came to Belgium because they say, the doctors I mean, that I need another overhaul."

She waited for me to go on, but I was having difficulty. "So that's why you're here? To have the operation?"

"No," I said to her in a low voice.

My breathing lifted her head several times as she thought about what I'd said. Her finger stopped moving along the scar.

"Oh," she said, barely audible.

"The thing is, I can't."

"Oh."

"I wish I had the courage, but it's all used up. I'm sorry."

"Gosh, Eddy, why are you telling me you're sorry? I'm the one who's sorry. I'm just as sorry as can be." She lifted her head to look up at me. Tears fell from her eyes. I touched her cheek. "I don't understand. You're about the biggest, strongest brute I know. Why, you go miles and miles on that bike of yours. How could you—" But she stopped herself. "How

55

long do you have? Tell me, Eddy—how long?"

"It's hard to say. Maybe a few months. Maybe a little more."

Her eyes bulged and then she buried her face in my chest. I stroked the back of her head and tried to soothe her. She lay there softly crying, and then eventually fell asleep. I didn't sleep at first, but watched her until I, too, drifted off. When I woke, she was no longer on top of me. I heard a sound in the bathroom, and then she emerged, picking up the camera from the table. I looked at her curiously.

"What are you doing?"

"Stay there," she whispered. "Don't move."

She pushed a potted plant to the far side of the coffee table so it wouldn't be in the way, and began taking pictures. I was uncomfortable at first, but then grew used to it. Then, she lowered the camera from her eyes and held it to her side, standing plainly and openly on the other side of the coffee table. "Pull them down," she said.

After only a brief pause, I slid out of the bibs to lie nude before her for the first time. She didn't direct me to pose in any certain way. I remained as I was, shifting my position slightly. She came closer, focusing on whatever seemed of interest. She moved swiftly, as if she were in a hurry, or maybe she thought I'd become embarrassed or tired with it. But I remained as I was, determined to allow her the freedom I had when I was the photographer. Even as she changed rolls, her fingers fumbling, cheeks flushed, I waited where I was and then took whatever direction she gave me.

When she finished the roll, as she was changing film again, I approached her. I gathered the camera and the film and motioned for her to trade places with me on the couch. She still wore her skirt, but nothing more. I took a few shots and then told her to remove it. She became shy and lay on her stomach, her hair spilling into her eyes. I was glad she was timid. Her demureness said many things about her, all of them good.

Cinder Roads

For several days we rode into the countryside. We found barns and fences, flocks of sheep and cows and goats, villages older than anything back home in America, but not older than those in Italy. I sought, as usual, men who looked as though they might have survived the war. In the beginning she did the same, following me where I went, photographing whatever I did. It wasn't long, however, before she drifted off on her own. She found a group of teens, then a small bakery just open for business with its breads and pastries in the window, then the sun rising brightly behind the old village skyline. It was obvious she gravitated toward optimism and hope, not melancholy. We stepped inside a village church and I photographed the patina of the pews and the grotesque paintings of the decapitation of some saint, while she tilted her camera to the light of the stained glass glowing in a colonnade above us.

We sat on a bench beneath a tree kicking our legs. I felt a compulsion to tell her things I hadn't told anyone before. The contrast of the images she was taking from the ones I took was stark and undeniable. It made me want to tell her about a part of my youth.

"When I was a boy," I said, "we'd have people come over—relatives for the holidays or business associates of my father's and their families. I seldom played with the other children my age. I always sat with the adults, sometimes right with them and sometimes off to the side listening to their complaints about their aches. It's where I felt most at home. I could relate to that. Every time I had a surgery I was in rehab for months, and then it took another good half a year or more before I'd be back to normal—whatever that was. Pain was something I lived with all the time. I had no idea what a carefree childhood felt like. The old folks, they enjoyed having me around. None of the other kids wanted to listen to them, but I found what they had to say fascinating." I paused and took her hand, rolling it in my own, then kissed it. "I don't know why I'm telling you this. I take photographs of the old because I feel old, because in terms of the span of my life, I *am* old. But you're not. You're a beautiful young woman, and seeing you react to the other beautiful things around you, it's nice. I find it really refreshing."

We took a cinder road out farther away from the towns, where the houses were sparse and the trees grew wild and the pastures weren't so manicured. We played follow-the-leader, winding in sweeping arcs along the deserted road. When she was in front, she'd suddenly hit her brakes and I'd have to slam on my own breaks to keep from ramming into her. She thought it was a riot, though I told her I was seriously going to rear-end her and we'd both go crashing to the ground. Julia didn't care. She didn't give a thought to the next minute. She didn't think of consequences; she only cared about enjoying herself in the moment. I led and she followed for a while. I stopped my bike and balanced on the two wheels and told her she needed to do the same. She tried and tried, but fell each time, laughing, clutching herself like she was having some kind of fit. Finally, I went to pull her up and she yanked on my arm and I fell on top of her. We rolled on the cinders laughing, not caring what might be coming at us.

Her hand swept over my hair, her fingers digging into the now filthy mass.

"Tell me about your parents, Eddy," she said. "What are they like?"

"They're just parents," I said.

"Are you close? So, no brothers or sisters?"

I shook my head. "Nope and no."

"Is that another subject you don't like talking about?"

"I don't mind talking about them. I'd rather talk about you, though."

"Oh, please," she said. "I'm as pedestrian as they come."

"You're anything but. How about you; what's the situation with your mom?"

She propped herself up on an elbow. "She's not well, Eddy, not well at all."

"Is your dad still around?"

"Oh, sure, he's around. Drinks the vino like acqua, so he's not much help. He hasn't worked in ages."

"What's wrong with her?"

"She and the Marlboro Man had quite the romance," she said. "She quit smoking five years ago, but only after half a lung was hacked out. She has circulation issues and dementia's setting in. She knows who we are, mostly, but can't remember what day it is or which drawer her socks are in. Funny how that works. Besides that, they think she's got cancer."

"What do you mean, they *think*; don't they know?"

"She hasn't been in to see the doc in almost a year. She hates them— thinks they're all in some conspiracy to rob her jewelry."

"So, you and your sisters are here for work?"

"Italy's a dumpster fire," she said. "What good would it do to go back? We can make three times the money in Belgium. We send home everything we can, Eddy, but it's still not very much."

"And Nico, does he charge you much to stay there?"

"Well, nothing's free in this world, Eddy."

"Meaning?"

"Meaning I'm just glad Valentina's taking the baton for a while. That fat old man's nothing to write home about behind closed doors, if you know what I mean."

"You and Nico?" I said, trying not to show my surprise.

"Sure, me and Nico. Why not?"

I didn't know what to say.

"I didn't know—"

"Look, Eddy—you think it's anything but transactional? Quid pro quo, quid pro quo is what it is. He's not so bad, or *wasn't*. Like I said,

Valentina's taken the reins for a while." She could see my shock. She took my hands and shook them. "It doesn't mean a thing," she said. "You think I'd do such a thing if I didn't absolutely have to? You think I didn't have to think of my dear old mom every time he laid his fat fingers on me? What's a girl to do? Grin and bear it and remind myself that every hour staring at the ceiling was another day closer to when Mom might finally head back to the hospital and get well again. Oh, I know she'll never get completely well. But, she could be a lot better off than she is now. She's too young to be wasting away in that dark room." She gave my hands a firm tug. "You do understand, don't you?"

My heart sank, I can't deny it. I tried to convince myself that what she'd told me was all right. It made me mad that she had to prostitute herself while her mother wasted away in Italy.

"I've got no claims on you," I said.

"It doesn't mean a thing, Eddy," she said. "Not a God damn thing."

We stood up, brushed ourselves off, and started riding again. The mood had dimmed and our pace was sluggish, almost painful. I tried to reconcile everything she told me. The reality was, I didn't have the right to make judgements about what she did or how she lived her life. Intellectually I knew this, but what I felt viscerally was something completely different. The longer we rode the more it sank in and the sullener I grew. I was angry at myself for falling for her so quickly. I felt a fool.

We passed through another village, barely a crossroads, where there was a fountain in the center of town. We stopped and filled our water bottles. She took several pictures of the fountain, and then the few shops behind it standing silent and stoic. She seemed to know I was having difficulty, and she left me alone to my thoughts. I remained straddling my bike waiting for her.

"No rush," I said to her.

I wished I was back in my flat alone. I began thinking of ways to avoid her in the coming days. I considered moving to another city, or out of Belgium altogether, but I had no idea where I could go. I'd heard northern Scotland was remote. It would be warm enough this time of year. I could rent a small cottage near some loch, and sit in the mornings and watch the birds fly over the water the way I watched them now skim the surface of the canal. There'd be miles and miles of isolated roads I could cycle on where no one would bother me. I kept going back to what a fool I'd been for thinking I could have a relationship at this stage. My expression remained neutral, or so I hoped, as I tried not to come apart.

I told her we ought to think about turning back. She said she didn't want to go back the same way we came, and so we turned onto a gravel road where the territory became wilder and the farms gave way to woods, the ancient limbs arching above us like the tines of giant pitchforks. We rolled over a small bridge and beyond it, not far, was a chapel. We stopped and set our bikes in the long, untended grass.

The chapel was very small, stone, its tile roof shot through with several large holes. Ruddy moss covered the entire structure giving it the appearance of being brushed with rust. We took out our cameras and photographed it from a distance, then moved closer. The stone steps were worn and crumbled. Beer bottles and other debris were strewn obscenely behind the bushes and in the stringy grass.

The inside was little more than a shrine where two rows of pews led to a statue of the Virgin Mary. The statue was in poor condition, having been severely vandalized. Its nose was missing, along with one arm and the tips of both bosoms. Weeds grew behind it in the cracks of the walls.

She moved around the statue, looking at it from all angles.

"Holy Moses," she said. The comment struck me as being funny and I laughed. I needed to laugh.

She touched the statue curiously and though I didn't think she was overly religious, she appeared quite sad seeing the icon treated with such disrespect. I sat in one of the pews gazing at the dereliction and wondered what the chapel looked like years ago.

"Do you think anybody ever got married here?" she whispered. "Do you, Eddy?"

"I suppose so. Sure, I bet lots of people did."

"If I ever get married, I want it to be in a place like this. I wouldn't even care if rain came pouring through the roof."

"I didn't think you liked old things," I said.

"Now, that's a horrible thing to say. I love Lily Lolimper to death, and she's about five hundred years old if she's a day. I like this better than most churches."

"Better? How so?"

"It's the ideal profaned by the obscene," she said. "It's unfortunate and totally unnecessary how it's been abused—by time and by punks—but isn't that closer to reality? I don't believe in fantasies, Eddy, not if I can help it. Do you? I sure hope not."

She wandered outside while I remained, sitting in the pew. Though my eyes moved slowly around the chapel, I kept coming back to the statue of the Virgin. It was so abused that if you hadn't seen it in the context of the chapel, you might think it was a secular piece.

I went out and found her beneath a pine tree where the grass wasn't so tall. She wasn't doing anything but waiting for me.

"How was it, Eddy?"

"It's peaceful in there," I said.

I sat down beside her. She took my hand and dropped her head against me.

"How come days with you seem like they could go on forever?" she said. "Or at least I wish they could."

I lifted her hand and kissed it.

Ten minutes earlier I was ready to discard all thoughts of her, and now I couldn't imagine being without her. I put the other thing out of my mind and concentrated only on now, how she was with me.

"How much does your mom need?" I said.

"You mean the medical bills?" She'd raised her head, then lowered it again. "Gosh, I don't really know. I'd say a cool hundred thousand, give or take."

"You say there are certain treatments that could improve things for her if she had the money."

"Oh, sure," she said.

"Would you return to Italy?"

"What—you mean if I somehow stumbled on that pot of gold? That's an awful good question. I really don't know. If I knew Mom was being looked after, if I knew she was happy and sort of back to her old self. . . I don't know. I'm halfway through school—I don't know if I could go back and marry the local turnip man and pop out five kids. That sounds bad, doesn't it. I guess, as much as I love her, I've been away so long. . . I think I'd about lose my mind back home. But I'd do it if I needed to."

"I can give you the money," I said.

"Aw, isn't that sweet of you. I bet you would."

"It might take a little time, hopefully not too long."

"You are just a pot of honey, aren't you," she said kissing me on the shoulder.

I knew that she wasn't taking me seriously. I took a piece of grass and wiggled it in front of her eyes.

"Hey, I mean it."

She stopped my hand and pulled away to look at me.

"Don't. Don't, Eddy, unless you really do mean it."

"But I do," I said.

"Where are you going to get a hundred thousand euros?"

"Don't worry about it."

"But how can't I worry about it when you promise something like that and I don't see how in the world you're going to come up with the goods? It's not like you to lie, Eddy."

I put a finger to her lips.

"Remember when I told you I was rich beyond your wildest imagination? You thought I was kidding. Well, I wasn't."

She fell silent trying to understand what I'd said.

"Gee, I don't know what to say. That puts a whole new spin on things and sort of raises the quid pro quo bar, doesn't it."

"There's no quid pro quo here, Julia," I said.

"Nobody gives something like that for nothing. You'd be the first."

"But I already have what I want."

"Oh, yeah? What's that?"

I placed my finger at the top of her chest and drew a line down her sternum, then tapped her gently.

"You."

Elle Returns

Julia had exams and I didn't see her for a week. I had my routine of taking pictures in the morning, cycling before the midday heat, then relaxing in the cafés in the afternoon. In the evenings, I developed film and made prints. This was the same schedule I'd kept before meeting her, but now there was an emptiness to it, as if it really were just a schedule of things to check off and be done with. When I went out taking pictures, I thought only of her. When I was on my bike, I found myself losing concentration and wondering where she was or what she was doing. In the cafés, whether alone or with friends, I'd gaze at other couples in envy and wish she were with me, sitting by my side, entertaining me with her unusual wit. The worst were evenings when I had to develop film I'd taken alone, not with her. My images no longer seemed vital. They looked uninspired in every way and it was a chore to make contact sheets and then prints. After dark I'd sit on the balcony and look down at the canal shimmering with the lights of the old buildings, and I felt utterly alone. This was a complete reversal. The balcony had been my refuge where I collected my thoughts from the day and forged the courage for the next. It's where I centered myself and, when I hit difficult patches, where I strategized on how to move forward. Now, because I could think of nothing but her, I sat with my beer in hand staring into the darkness, lonesome and lost.

She had a cell phone, but because I didn't, and since she wasn't one to talk on the phone, we didn't communicate much while we were apart. She did leave notes, however, when she could. These she left on the outside of my door. They said things like, *Missed you again, Eddy. I'm studying hard. I want you to be proud of your Italian girl.* Or, *Dear Eddy, I stopped by but you must be out on the two-wheeled rocket. You've got the heart of a lion and the legs of a god. Your Italian girl, Julia.* Another time she wrote, *God, how I miss you, Eddy! Do you know how much? Here's a kiss just for you. Put it wherever you want!* And below the writing was the imprint of her lips in red lipstick.

The strange thing was, I was always out when she stopped by. I tried staying home a couple mornings, and then waiting to ride until later in the afternoon, but I didn't see her. Invariably, I'd arrive home to find a note taped to my door. As much as I didn't want to think about it, it became obvious that she was avoiding me. But why, if she took the time to stop by and leave a note, didn't she want to actually see me, if only for a few minutes?

I began leaving notes of my own. *Hey, kiddo—I miss your beautiful smile. I miss your laugh. I miss the mole behind your ear. I miss everything about you. Eddy.* Or, *Julia, last night I sat on the balcony and saw your reflection in the lifeless waters. Lo and behold, something emerged from below. It was the hand of God touching your cheek with His purity and grace. Eddy.* Or, *Julia, I lay in bed last night with the kiss you gave me. I carried you to the tree by the chapel and made love to you. It was beautiful. Your Eddy.* The next note, the next day, was adorned with her red lips. *Dear Eddy. Why didn't you take me under that tree, you fool. Didn't you know I wanted you to! Hint-hint—when a girl leans her head against you under a shady tree far far from mankind, and she's rubbing the inside of your thigh, it means she wants you to lay her down on the soft pine needles and do sweet sweet things to her. God, I miss you. Julia Botticelli*

I wrote her back, but the note remained on my door the entire day, and the next morning I took it down. There was no new note from her. As much as I wanted to see her, I tried to think of her as little as I could. Not as retribution for her mysterious evasiveness, but for my own sanity.

.   .   .

I met Derek, Emma, Harry, Marta, and Philippe at St. Peter's. Only Philippe and I had been inside, though it dominated one side of the Grote Markt, just opposite the spectacular Town Hall. We were standing between two of the white columns whispering, huddled together in a circle. Philippe was apart from us near the altar. Not long after, Rick arrived and joined us.

"What are you doing?" he whispered.

"Hey, Rick," I said.

"What are you guys doing?" he repeated.

"We just got done praying."

"Are you Catholic?"

"Close enough."

"Close enough; what's that supposed to mean?"

"Yeah," I said. "I'm Catholic."

"Why were you praying?" said Rick.

"We're in a church, you know," I said, making a face.

"I know we're in a church."

"Then I don't understand the question."

"All right," said Rick. "It's just that I've never known you—any of you—to attend church, is all."

"I go to church," said Emma.

"Of course you do," said Rick. "You're Portuguese."

"Look," I said, "you sort of came at a, well, inopportune time."

"You want me to leave?"

"*Shhhh. . .*" I said. "Keep it down. No, not really. Unless you want to."

"Why does he have to leave?" said Derek, who was part of the circle but not part of the conspiracy.

"He doesn't have to leave," I said. "Rick, you don't have to leave."

"What's going on?" he said.

I felt embarrassed and didn't want to say. I made a strange face.

"He has a hamster in his pocket," said Emma.

Rick, who I'm sure was accustomed to unpredictable things coming from the mouths of university students, merely made his eyebrows jump. "Okay," he said.

"Don't you want to know why?" said Emma.

"Sure."

"It's always getting loose," I said.

"Tell him," said Emma.

"I didn't know what a mess it would make."

"Go on. Tell him."

"And, well, do you remember the part in the Bible where Jesus goes into the Temple and turns over the tables and shoos all the money changers out?"

"It rings a bell," said Rick.

"You guys are a bunch of idiots," said Derek, looking nervously behind us, chuckling.

"He was trying to cleanse the Temple of unsavory elements," I said. "The Temple wasn't a bank—it wasn't a place of commerce. It was a place of worship. A place to worship God."

"*God*, Rick," said Emma. *"God."*

"Just like this church. *This* is a place of worship," I said. "But you'd never know it by all the tourists scurrying around snapping their pictures. I mean, this place is nothing but a stream of guided tours bumping into statues and pillars because they've got their heads in brochures. It's not a church anymore, but a museum or worse, a mausoleum, as if God really were dead."

"Well, the jury's still out on that," said Rick noncommittally.

Emma lowered her already low voice. "He's going to let the hamster loose. You know, shake things up. Cleanse the Temple. What do you think," said Emma. "Isn't it brilliant?"

"Childish. Wicked. . . But brilliant?" Rick was amused, but unconvinced.

Philippe, who was admiring the altar, slowly wandered in our direction. He looked at us suspiciously.

"I sense something mischievous bubbling in the cauldron," he said.

"Something tasty, I hope?"

I gave a sheepish look. I'd hoped the deed would have been done before Philippe came back around. He enjoyed a good laugh as much as anybody, but he respected certain institutions and didn't go for making a mockery of them. The church, perhaps, was the institution he esteemed most. I saw the innocence and faith in his eyes—not religious faith, but faith in *us*. I felt ashamed.

"Come on," I said. "We're finished here."

We shuffled outside and then, allowing the others to walk ahead, I bent down and released the hamster along the edge of the church. I gave the little creature an adieu and a goodbye salute.

We decided to have a drink at The Green Lantern. Derek declined, reminding us that his paintings didn't paint themselves. I knew his reluctance to go with us was because he didn't want to be around a bunch of people drinking, and I couldn't blame him. He'd mentioned recently that he'd begun to crave a drink more and more. He felt he had to dedicate himself to a strict routine while he could.

The Oude Markt was alive with students and tourists, who mistakenly believed it was an extension of the Grote Markt with its much more subdued cafés and restaurants. When we arrived at The Green Lantern Rick's wife, Elle, was already there, sitting with two university students. The students quickly sized up the situation and, after the obligatory introductions, said they had to be going, much to Elle's disappointment. We all sat down and Rick introduced her to everyone.

"I hear you were in Ireland," said Philippe. "I hope the climate was better there than it has been here. The heat we've had!"

Elle, who wore a tight shirt, was braless and obviously so. It seemed to make Rick uneasy.

"It was amazing," she gushed, sitting forward on her seat, arching her body.

"Were you visiting friends or family?"

"Oh, I wasn't *visiting* family," she said. "My sisters were over here with me. We were all in Paris together. They decided to stay in Paris but I've never been to Ireland—I figured why not? I'm a big girl—I can go on my own if I have to."

"That's the spirit," said Philippe, who I could tell was immediately taken with her. "How long did you stay?"

"Oh," she thought, "about two weeks, I think." Then, looking to Rick who was several seats over, "Wasn't it about two weeks, honey? I'm so bad with time." She burst into laughter and her body jumped like somebody poked her.

"How nice is that," said Emma. "I'd love to see Ireland."

"You should come," said Elle, her body again lurching with excitement.

"To Ireland?"

"Come on," Elle challenged her, "let's go. We can leave tomorrow."

Emma rolled her eyes. "Yeah, maybe someday."

"Why not? I know a few people we can stay with in Galway. Come on—it would be fun."

"If I only could," Emma sighed. "I couldn't leave Derek. And I have school. I couldn't."

Elle turned toward me. "How about it? Want to go to Ireland?"

"Ireland?"

"Why not?" When she spoke she showed her teeth big and wide, and her eyes squeezed down into slits of anticipation. "We should all go. I mean, I can't drag Rick away from that school, but it doesn't mean the rest of us have to stay here. It'll be an adventure."

"I'd love to go," said Marta. She turned to Harry. "Do you want to go to Ireland?"

Harry shrugged. "Sure, why not?"

"Have you ever been there?"

"Nope," he said. "You?"

"Once. I was in Dublin for a week."

Elle leaned into the table, lifting herself a few inches off her seat. "You have the most beautiful hair," she said. "You have the lips of a—" But she cut herself off, looking at Marta with big throbbing eyes. Everything she did, everything she said, was now before a rapt audience. "You should be a model."

Philippe broke in, "She is!"

"Was," said Marta.

"Was, is, makes no difference," said Philippe.

"You *are*?" said Elle, astonished.

"I *was*."

"Here in Leuven?"

"Oh, heavens no," said Philippe. "She modeled in Paris, Brussels, London. All over Europe."

"I didn't know that," said Emma. "You mean serious stuff, like real modeling?"

"Marta was one of the top young models in Europe," Philippe said. "The most beautiful woman to come out of Russia in a decade, and that's saying something. Her face was all over the place. I can show you."

"But you're not modeling anymore?" asked Elle.

"Oh, God no," Marta said, as if the idea was absurd. "Such a boring thing, this modeling. I know it sounds very glamorous, but that is the part you see. The face in a magazine. The images of models in exotic locations making millions of dollars. Models dating famous movie stars."

"Sounds good to me," said Elle, prompting the table to laugh.

"I know, I know," she said, waving at us. "I know you don't believe me. But, you would get bored, too. There is much sitting around. Much doing things you don't want to do. There are many kind people, and there are many not so kind people. And the pay, unless you are a super model, is not very good. You have to buy expensive clothes, you are constantly getting your hair done; the shoes alone can cause bankruptcy."

Everyone laughed.

"I am much happier now. Thanks to Philippe, I have found a new home. And Harry, of course!" she added, seizing him by the hands. "These two men are like two pillars of strength for me. They have shown me so much kindness. I like it very much here in Leuven. I will let little girls chase the glamour. I prefer real stars, the stars of my true destiny, the stars of happiness."

Philippe ordered another round of drinks. We wouldn't hear of it, but he insisted on paying. We had several more rounds, each of us buying.

70

Elle must have had a few before we arrived; she grew pretty sloppy and emotional and you could tell Rick was embarrassed and irritated with her. By the time we finished it was getting late. We said our goodbyes and then, as we were parting, Elle said she was too wound up from the trip and wanted to stay out a bit longer. Rick offered to walk Emma home. Philippe was too tired and scoffed at the idea of staying out any longer. He turned his back and began the slow trek back up to the Grote Markt, and then on to his flat. It was decided that Harry, Marta, and I would accompany Elle for one final drink.

We found a bar that served American IPAs and Guinness. I ordered a Guinness, while Harry and Elle ordered IPAs. Marta wanted only water. We sat around a table for four near the open entranceway.

"Cheers," I said, raising my glass.

"Cheers," Harry and Elle said, but Marta said, "Santé."

Elle, who had been perched on her chair at The Green Lantern, sat upright now with her elbows jutting back, holding onto the armrests. This accentuated her already prominent breasts so much that it was ridiculous not to openly look at them. After a while Marta decided to have a vodka. Elle had nearly finished her pint and went to order another IPA, but I insisted she try a Guinness as a tip of her hat to her recent Irish trip. When I told her I was a brewer she slammed her glass on the table in a spontaneous fit of disbelief, causing the entire bar to look over.

"Why didn't you tell me you were a brewer?" She laughed. "I think we're going to become fast friends."

She told us in more detail about her trip. She said that since Rick couldn't get away from his duties at the university, she decided to go alone. She stayed in Dublin for a while, checking out the music scene there, and then heard about a band in Galway worth seeing. She went there and sure enough, the band was excellent. They happened to start up a conversation with her during one of their breaks and invited her to their next gig the following night. She went and soon became friends with the band.

"They're so *smart*," she said in a slurred, sloppy declaration. "They're just a bunch of young guys, but they have it all figured out."

She tapped the side of her head, hitting a different spot each time. "They're just a bunch of really cool guys," she added wistfully.

She decided to follow them as they made their way around Ireland. They called her their good luck charm. Before each gig they'd rub the top of her head and they'd all down a Guinness in a single breath. She knew that she was spending a lot of money and because she didn't want Rick to get mad, she decided to sleep on the couch of whatever room the band was staying in. "A sheet always stayed between me and those horny lads," she laughed. She felt as if she were witnessing the birth of something very big and important. She said she had seen a fair number of bands in recent years, and these guys were by far the most talented and the most ambitious.

Marta cleared her throat hesitantly, as if she were in a theater. She moved in her seat, crossing her legs slowly. She took Harry's hand, squeezing it.

"Rick just doesn't *get it*," she went on. "All he wants to do is stay home and read books. Well, I'm sorry, but that's boring. I don't want to do that night after night. . . It was so exciting being around a group of just. . . creative, talented people. What's wrong with that? Is that a crime?"

"It is no crime to live," said Marta. "It is certainly no crime to live."

"That's right," agreed Elle, now sitting forward again as she had at The Green Lantern, and making as if to slap her thighs. She did this in slow motion, for effect. "Pretty soon we'll all be dead. *Dead*, you hear me? The last thing I want on *my* tombstone are the words, *Here lies a professional book reader. She spent her days in a chair eating carrot sticks and reading books!*" She wagged a finger at us. "I'm not going to let anybody put *me* in a cage. I'm not!"

There was a group of three Germans sitting a couple tables over who kept looking at her. Elle had on two occasions lifted her pint glass toward them, but said nothing. A while later she excused herself to use the toilet.

Marta shook her hand, which still held Harry's, and leaned against him. "I think we must be getting home before my eyelids fall to the floor."

"Will you carry me?" he said.

"We can always get an Uber."

"At this hour? Fat chance."

Elle didn't return from the toilet for half an hour. As she sat down the Germans filed past our table noisily and drunkenly, and they bid Elle goodnight. She lowered her head as if blushing, but she wasn't blushing, she was sniggering into the top of her shirt.

We left the bar. Marta and Harry went one way and Elle and I went the other. I was going the opposite direction of my flat, but I wanted to see her home. We went up through the Grote Markt, which was emptying out, and passed St. Peter's. A group of drunk students hollered at her from a distance. They kept it up even after I turned and gave them a look.

"Hold my hand," she said.

It didn't stop their heckling, but soon we were around the corner and then there were only their occasional fading hoots.

"Rick told me about you," she said. She hadn't let go of my hand, and now had her head dropped on my arm. "You're a really nice guy."

I said nothing. I figured that, under the circumstances, it was the best thing to do.

"He says you're *rich*." She didn't actually say *rich*, but slurred it into *ridge*.

"You must be awfully tired," I said. I was hoping Rick wasn't up and waiting for her. I thought about leaving her a block from their flat, but knew I couldn't in the state she was in.

"I like you, Jeems," she slurred. "Yeah. I like you a lot."

She had on heels higher than you'd want to wear walking the cobblestones of Leuven, and she kept tripping over herself. I really didn't want Rick to see us walking to the door.

When we arrived at their flat she asked me if I wanted to come in. The lights inside were out, as they were in all the other flats on the street. I said I better not, since Rick was probably asleep and it would be rude to wake him up. She stood and waited and I knew she was waiting for me to do something. I tried the door and thankfully it was unlocked. I pushed it open and told her goodnight and left. As I headed back toward my flat I kicked myself. I really should have said something. It wasn't any of my business, but Rick was my friend. I really should have told her that her shirt was inside-out after coming back from the toilet.

The Storms: Part One

For a week the city broiled beneath cloudless skies and a sun that glared down like an angry white eye. There was no breeze, no respite at night or in the mornings. It was as if some harsh lesson were being taught, and it forced you to reevaluate your belief in deities and the wrath of gods.

The cafés bulged with tourists seeking refuge beneath umbrellas, or air conditioning inside. Those outside drank beer exclusively, or water, but never other liquors that only made you warm in the face. Men and women shed inhibitions and wore as little as possible or, alternately, some donned baggy long-sleeved shirts and pants to the ankles, but never tight, always permitting air to circulate. Women carried umbrellas to block the sun. Bicyclists peddled with languid strokes reminiscent of old men. The areas of the city with trees along the canal and in the parks became havens for groups of kids and lovers who couldn't be kept inside. People sat on the stone walls of the canal. There was no real breeze, it was true, but the shade made it seem like there was, and the coolness of the canal water every so often swirled upward and gave hope to all along it that rain was coming, or that there would be some other change. After a week of scorching heat, change did come. The storm marched through like an invading army.

It hit Leuven at two o'clock in the afternoon. It wasn't as if it was a surprise. Windows were closed, some shops latched their storm shutters, and afternoon classes at the university were cancelled. Most cafés took down their umbrellas and refused service outside. Some made an event of it. Rick told me about The Carousal. He said it was packed, standing room only. When the rain started, everybody cheered. He said they cheered as if Leuven had won the league championship on a last second goal. Then came the wind gusts bringing waves of rain instead of the constant sheet. The gusts blew sideways and when they hit the front windows everybody *oooohed* and *aaaahed* the way you do when you see something truly dangerous from a distance. Umbrellas, those that were left standing, flip-flopped across the Grote Markt. Chairs blew past like tumbleweed. When the wind really got going there came a whistling sound from outside the door. When this began, the laughter died down and everybody listened. The whistling became a howl, and then a roar, and then the power went out.

It was the wind alone that pushed over trees, mostly on the outskirts of the city, bringing down electric wires. The city outage was massive: eighty percent of Leuven was without power for some period of time. The storm hit all of Belgium and much of Europe. There were no extra crews available to help, so priorities were set as to the order areas would have their power restored. It would be two weeks before all of Leuven had power again. Meanwhile, the heat that had been given a brief respite by the storm, returned. Generators were everywhere, spewing black smoke into the streets and, as all complained, increasing the heat further.

I was with Julia when it blew in. She'd brought some of her things for an extended stay. We sat on the balcony watching the gray skies become darker. The water on the canal whipped up with small whitecaps, and ducks huddled on shore in the nooks of the larger trees.

"Let's go out," she said to me.

"I think it's about ready to let loose," I said skeptically.

"Aw, come on, Eddy. It'll be a day to remember."

We slipped on our sandals and hurried down. It wasn't as noticeable on the balcony, but everything seemed to have a purplish tint to it. It was beautiful and strange and it felt like we'd walked into a different world. We went to the edge of the canal and looked down. The canal, always so serene, looked dangerous with the small whitecaps. I told her to step away from the ledge and I took her hand and led her on. We went beneath the trees that dropped the almond-shaped leaves. The leaves swirled in mini cyclones as the wind began picking up. She ran from one to the next, trying to stand in their midst, and she laughed whenever she got in the middle of one. I took several pictures of her and then we moved on to the Grote Markt. It was nearly deserted with only a few adventurous souls like us out. I didn't know Rick was in The Carousal or we'd have stopped in for a beer. We watched as one of the umbrellas was swept up and flopped across—it frightened her—and we ran down toward the Oude Markt. Before we got there she stopped suddenly and pulled me into a tight alleyway. She kissed me hard.

"Oh, Eddy," she said, "you don't know how much I've missed you."

We didn't stay long. The wind really picked up and it began to rain. I grabbed her hand and we headed toward my flat, ducking beneath awnings when we could, but it was hopeless. By the time we made it back it was pouring and we were soaked all the way through. I'd tried to protect the camera but it was wet—I took a towel to it right away. Julia, standing in the middle of the room, began to strip out of her wet clothes. I'd turned my back to her, out of respect, and then I felt her hands on my shoulders. She pressed her body against me. I turned and set the camera on the table and wrapped my arms around her. Her skin was covered in goose bumps and she shivered uncontrollably. I kissed her, moving my hands over her, trying to warm her. My hands traveled up and down her back, down the sides of her upper legs, around back to hold the two halves of her cheeks, then around front where I cupped my hand between her legs. She gasped and rose up on her toes, then began rising and falling to my movements. She lay her head against my shoulder and bit down with restraint. She gave a sudden shiver and then withdrew.

"Come on," she said and led me to the shower.

We moved the hanging strips of film and the trays of chemicals out and got the water going good and hot, and stepped in together. She laughed and jumped in place as the spray hit her body. She took the bar of soap and started lathering me, leaning up to kiss me every so often.

She took hold of me, stroking me, squeezing, then letting go. She did this several times and then, gazing down before giving me the soap said, "Holy cow, Eddy, today's my lucky day."

I soaped her back, which was red from the hot spray of the shower, and then I turned her to face me again and did her chest and legs. We kissed hard. She pulled away and kneeled down on floor and leaned over. "I want you to do me really hard, Eddy," she said. "I want you to do it like you don't have a few months, but like it's your last day on earth."

I made love to her the way she asked, then fell onto her back afterward, heaving. I lay there, my eyes closed, my heart racing. She raised herself on her knees and I held her, cupping her breasts, kissing her neck. I remained inside moving slowly, and then my hand moved down lightly and rubbed her. Not soon after she let out a shout that I'm sure the neighbors heard through the thin walls, but I didn't care—I didn't care at all.

We dried ourselves off, our bodies warmed. We peered out the balcony door at the fury of the storm. The downspouts from the buildings across the canal gushed like fire hoses, and trees thrashed around helplessly. I shook my head thinking I wouldn't want to be out there now.

I took her into my bedroom and laid her on the bed. Our lovemaking in the shower had been an urgent release, but now I wanted to see her, to slow down. Just as we faced each other the light in the hall, the only light on, flickered and went out. We wouldn't have power for many days. I smiled as I touched the outline of her body. She, in return, reached her hand to my scar, grazing it, and then flattened her hand and seemed to listen to my heartbeat with her palm. I moved closer, nuzzling my face into her neck, kissing her, caressing her.

I rolled her onto her back and made love to her as slowly as I had frantically in the shower. At times I barely moved at all, but allowed myself to throb, and then she'd squeeze back, as we remained locked in a slow, deep kiss. The window was open and gushes of air came through to blow over us. Lightning flashed, sending baritone moans of thunder against the walls that shook the flat and made an empty glass on the nightstand vibrate. We made love for several hours until dusk approached. We fell asleep and in the morning, when we woke up, we began again beneath the oppressive heat.

I sat with Philippe a few days after the storm at a café on the edge of the Grote Markt. The café didn't have electricity or a generator, but we were in shade and it wasn't too bad. Philippe had cold coffee while I had a bottled water.

"I ran into Rick," I said.

"How's he doing?" Philippe meant the question in the specific context of having had his wife run off to Ireland to follow a band of twenty-somethings.

"Not so great, I'm afraid. I think he's going to lose it. I really do. She's not home much these days."

Philippe shook his head and sipped his coffee. "I was afraid of that."

"He doesn't know where she goes, but. . ."

"But?"

"She's been staying at Harry's. Not all the time, but some of the time. God only knows where she goes other nights."

"And Marta?"

"I think she moved out," I said.

"I see," said Philippe.

"It was bound to happen. Those two were never going to make it."

"No, I would think not."

"Still, it has to be tough on Marta."

"Oh, I don't know," said Philippe philosophically. "I think their relationship was one of convenience. I had the impression she was waiting. Now, the wait is over."

I took a drink from my bottle, pressing it to the side of my cheek.

Philippe wiped his forehead with a paper napkin. "Lord, when is it ever going to stop."

"Julia's been staying over," I said.

"Oh, yes," he said anxiously. "How is that going?"

"Good," I said.

"Good? Just good?"

"All we do is sleep and. . . This is the first real break I've had in two days."

"You're going to kill the girl," he said. "She didn't know what she was getting herself into."

"She gives as good as she gets, you can believe that."

"Has she moved in?"

"Moved in?" I paused, thinking about it. "No, she hasn't moved in."

"I see," said Philippe. "Nico will be displeased if he loses one of his sirens. I'm happy for you. She seems like a nice girl."

"She is a nice girl," I said. "Like someone dropped from the heavens."

"Really?"

"I should think," I said, teasing him with one of his own phrases.

"That's exciting news. Good for you, James. You deserve a nice girl. I'm very happy for you."

"We'll see. So far, so good."

I hadn't eaten in over a day; it suddenly hit me how hungry I was. I went inside and bought a bagel and brought it back out. I'd been wanting to talk to Philippe for some time.

"Philippe," I said, "do you remember what I told you a while ago?"

"You mean a while ago as in a few minutes ago, in this conversation?"

I shook my head. "No, do you remember when I told you about my relationship with my parents?"

He thought for a minute. "You aren't close," he said. "I remember. I'm sorry."

I waved at him. "No, Philippe, it's all right." I paused to find the right words. "It has something to do with them. But, well, I didn't tell you everything about my youth."

"No?" he lifted his head, listening intently.

"There have been certain developments," I said. "With me." I sat back against the chair. Even those few words felt like I'd unburdened myself.

"Good developments?"

"As you might say, I wouldn't think so." I forced a smile, which he didn't return. "I told you about my mother's coldness, how she was emotionally unavailable and distant. Our relationship is in many ways worse than the relationship I have with my father. I haven't told you what pushed her away from me. You think I idle my days away, sitting in cafés getting drunk for nothing; but I've learned a lot sitting and thinking about things."

"No one thinks you're a drunk, James, I can assure you."

"Well, anyway. You see, I was born with a pretty bad heart." I glanced up at him. "Really bad. I've had more surgeries than I care to remember, the first being when I was born. The doctors said I wouldn't live past my teens. My teens came, and I lived, I graduated from high school. It was a surprise to everyone, including myself. It was a surprise to *her*." I looked away to the few sloth-like people trudging across the Markt, the sun pounding them unmercifully. "She wasn't the type of person to be burdened with a thing like that."

"Burdened?"

"My words, not hers," I said.

"I'm sure you weren't a burden in any way, James," said Philippe.

"She just didn't know how to handle the situation. She was there, of course, by my side at the hospital for each procedure, and when I came home she looked in on me. She and the nurses. My father used work as a way of keeping it away; this is something I've just recently understood. But my mother, with each surgery, drew further and further away as well. Listen," I said, "I don't want pity. This isn't about pity. I'm trying to tell you the facts as clearly as I know them. . . They drew back and I had nothing to fall back on. The nurses kept me alive as my heart healed each time. You'd think that I yearned for their affection, being so close to death, but I didn't. Their coldness became instilled in me. I didn't see the void in their souls, and never thought there was one in mine." I paused, staring deep in thought. I looked at Philippe.

"About two years ago, I had another surgery. It went well. A success, so the doctors said. Once I built my strength back up, I began working at the brewery again, riding my bike each morning to increase my stamina.

My father softened a little. He began treating me as his son. He'd always treated me as something less, but now he treated me more like a son, I think trying to make up for lost time. My mother. . . She remained as she was. She's never changed, other than her drinking has increased." I paused again, sighing big, and then continued. "Shortly before I came to Leuven, I saw the doctors. They said things weren't going so well. They told me I needed another surgery or I wouldn't see the end of the year. That's why I've come to Leuven. To live out the remainder of the time I have left. I can't do it anymore."

Philippe's face dropped. His usual energy was replaced by the worst kind of anguish.

"You mean you've come to Leuven. . . to die?"

I nodded. "Yes," I said.

His eyes wandered around, lost, and he fumbled for his cane. He wiped a hand over his face. I couldn't look at him. I stared into the table instead.

"How much time do you have?" he asked delicately.

"A few months. Give or take."

"A few months? Dear God."

"I wanted to tell you sooner," I said. "I really did. It's not like I wanted to hide anything from anyone, especially you. I've lived my whole life being sick and having people look at me differently. I wanted to be normal for the first time. Not some frail invalid, but just another guy. You can't imagine how good that feels."

"Julia," he said in near panic. "Please tell me you've told her."

I put my hand over his and finally looked into his eyes. "Yes," I said. "She knows. I didn't want to tell her, just like I didn't want to tell you, but when she saw the scar. . ."

"Ah, yes, I imagine that would have raised a question or two," he said.

I gave his hand a shake and let go, sitting back.

"The thing is. . ."

"Yes?" he said, as if alerted.

I wasn't sure exactly how I felt or what I wanted to say, but talking it through with him helped.

"I don't see how I can go through another surgery and the whole re-covery process, but I don't see how I can just willfully drift away from Julia. I can't imagine not being with her."

He leaned forward seizing me by the forearm.

"You really do love her, don't you!" He smiled like I'd never seen him smile.

"I think I do," I told him.

"What do you mean, you think you do? Of course, you do."

"I've never been in love," I said.

"You love her," he said. "You have a reason to live!"

"I think I do," I said. "But I'm still not sure."

"Be sure, James—be as sure as you can. What do you think love is for—but to give someone a reason to get up in the morning—a reason to carry on with some dreadfully boring job—a reason to have hope when there doesn't seem to be any. A reason to *live*," he said, his eyes throbbing wildly. "That's what love is, that's what love can do. You've never had it before—of course it's unfamiliar territory—but love like yours, the love I see in your eyes every time you talk about Julia—the way your voice changes, the way your eyes have brightened like polished dia-monds over the last few weeks—it's rare, James—rare and worth doing everything in your power to hold and to protect."

Philippe's enthusiasm was captivating, and I knew he spoke from a place of friendship and trust. Yet, I still wasn't sure. I'd come to Leuven accepting my fate, and now that the possibility of returning to the same desperate treadmill faced me, I just didn't know if I could do it.

"I haven't decided what I'm going to do," I said.

"No matter," he said undeterred. "You've grasped the branch. You're hanging on. Now, with every fiber of your being, you must find the strength to pull yourself up!"

The Storms: Part Two

She lay face-down on the bed, her head to the side. We'd brought the bed into the living room next to the window. Our electricity had returned, but the flat had no air conditioning. I had a fan I kept on us, which helped. Sometimes there were slight breezes drifting through the window, but we still sweated constantly under the unrelenting heat.

I stood in the kitchen at the sink. In it was a small bag of ice. I'd found a student who was dealing in ice. He'd sell you two bags, no more, for ten euros each. I'd bought two and now they were in the sink covered in a towel. We'd had the ice for several hours. We had iced tea, iced water, iced beer, and now she requested something else. I used a table knife to chisel off some wedges. The wedges had begun fusing together from melting and then refreezing. I put the broken off wedges in a bowl. They were slippery, like little fish. I sat on the edge of the bed and she reached out and took my hand and squeezed it.

"Do you want more to drink?" I asked her.

"I'm fine," she said. "It felt good going down."

I held up my glass. "I don't know why there's such an aversion to ice in beer. If beer is good, it's good with ice."

"It's a cultural thing," she said. When she talked her head rose and fell as her jaw moved against the mattress."

"Yes," I said. "I think you're right."

"You're not the kind of guy to care about cultural things."

"No, I'm certainly not."

I drank some of my beer and set the glass on a stack of books on the side table.

"Are you ready?" I asked her.

"Yes, Eddy, go ahead."

"It's going to shock you."

"I don't care. I want to be shocked."

She reached up and pulled her hair to the side, exposing her shoulders and back. I took a wedge and held it over her. Soon, cold water dripped from my fingertips. Her body twisted when the first drop hit her back, and then on the second, and the third, but by the fourth she was used to it. When the wedge had melted I took another and this time moved it to different locations so that she didn't know where a drop would hit next. The uncertainty made her jump each time. Water meandered down her spine laying like a great river from her neck to her tailbone, some of it evaporating along the way, but much of it pooling in her lower back just above the twin hills of her cheeks. I took a finger and made small splashes. The water was warm already. I moved my finger away from the pool, drawing lines like spokes from a wheel. The lines evaporated quickly. I did this again and this time made a final line below her spine to the top of her tailbone. I rubbed my finger there, which seemed to please her. The ice wedge melted and so I took another one and I pressed the flat side of it directly to her skin—she lurched off the mattress making a gasp—and I passed it across her back doing sleepy figure eights. I ran the ice in stripes up and down her back until it was gone, and then took another wedge and slid it over her upturned legs. Her legs were long, and I covered them in cold water from the melting ice.

She rolled over and kissed me. When my hand touched her side she gasped, but then sought my lips again and pulled down on the back of my neck. I was familiar now with her kissing, but it was still new enough to surprise me. She smelled of the sun, the air, the humidity of the room, and the musty canal.

I pulled away. There were still wedges of ice in the bowl. I took one and, as she watched, dribbled the cold water on her chest and stomach. I heard the girl from across the canal. Each day after school she came home and played music on her balcony. I gazed up to look at her, and when I returned my attention to Julia her nakedness struck me. I bent to her, rubbed ice over a nipple, then sucked on it hard. I did the same to her other nipple and she twitched when I bit gently on the tip. Her eyes, glazed and dark, waited for what was coming. I'd done it hours earlier without planning to do it—it just happened, it was completely spontaneous—but now she knew it was coming and her breathing heightened in anticipation. I took a wedge of ice and, after a brief pass along her thigh, slipped it inside. I held it there as she stiffened clutching my neck, her body writhing as the spasms leaped within her. I watched as her expressions changed the way a kaleidoscope changes color. I whispered to her as she held on, shaking, and I kissed her neck and stroked her hair with my free hand. I held her this way for several minutes until the ice had melted and the water returned to me hot in my palm.

We slept, the girl across the canal and her music vibrating in my ear. When we woke we got dressed and went down to a café for iced coffee. Afterwards, we strolled under the trees along with the others. I'd needed a haircut for some time. She knew a salon that wasn't too pricey, but good. I sat reclined in the chair with the white towel secured around my neck while she sat on a stool bobbing her leg telling the girl how she should cut my hair.

"Not too short," she said. "Short in the back and around the ears, but not too short on top. He has the most beautiful hair and it shouldn't be sheared down to the bone."

I thought that was a funny way of putting it.

"How long were you without power?" I asked the girl. It was the usual thing you said in Leuven since the storm.

"We never lost it," said the girl.

"Now, there's some luck."

"I sleep in the back. I still don't have power in my flat."

"I bet you're a popular salon."

"Kids come in just to get out of the heat. We let them stand near the windows as long as they don't bother the customers."

The girl did a pretty good job trimming my hair. It was subtle so there wasn't any white next to my tanned skin.

"You look like a real photographer now," said Julia. She lifted her camera and took a few pictures.

"You need a hat," said the girl.

"A hat?"

"She's right, Eddy—you need a hat."

"What do you mean—Nico doesn't wear a hat."

"And you're going to base your fashion sense on Nico?" She gave me a look of mild disappointment. "You need a beret."

"Then you're getting one, too," I said.

"Really, Eddy?" she said. "You really want me to get one?"

"Sure," I said. "You need a beret more than I do."

We walked the streets looking for berets. We stopped in a bakery after an hour and bought croissants, mine with meat, and we ate them as we went. We stopped in a bookstore, and several women's clothing boutiques. In one, she tried on some dresses with colorful floral prints.

"Sweet," I told her.

"Sweet, Eddy?" she said, turning to look at herself in front of the mirror. "Do you really think so?"

"Really sweet."

"I guess I don't look too bad all prettied up, do I? Amazing what the right dress will do for a girl."

She went to duck back into the dressing stall, but I told her she should have it—she was young and beautiful and now was the time of her life to enjoy it. I told her I'd buy the dress with the stipulation that she wear it.

"That's all you want me to do—wear this pretty thing and you'll buy it for me?"

"I'll be getting the better end of the deal," I said.

She wore the dress, a blue one fitted around her slender frame. She nearly skipped out of the boutique, taking my hand, and we wound our way through the university admiring the old buildings. The university regained power after only a few days and classes had resumed. Students lounged in the grass beneath trees or along the low walls reading or talking. They seemed oblivious to the stifling heat.

"You forgot your books," I said to her.

"I have the week off," she said.

"And they don't?"

"My main philosophy class was cancelled an extra two days because the prof, who lives twenty miles down the pike, still doesn't have power and won't leave his wife. I don't have classes on Fridays, which leaves only Tuesday and Wednesday. But those are my independent study days and so I've got the entire week off."

"And who says you don't live a charmed life." I swung our arms forward and backward like a kid. "Which buildings do you have classes in?"

"Which buildings? Oh, just about every building you can see. Close your eyes, point your finger, and you're bound to hit one."

"I hear the library's something else," I said. "A real architectural wonder. Let's go."

"Let's go?"

"Come on," I said. "I've always wanted to see it. Which way?"

I took her hand and started walking, but she yanked it, standing firm. She pulled me close, nuzzling her cheek into my shoulder.

"Aw, Eddy honey, I don't want to trudge all the way over to that old place. I'm there just about every day of my life. Can't you give a girl a break?" She leaned up and kissed me. "I feel about as pretty as a princess—I don't want to spoil the mood traipsing around rows and rows of musty old books."

I paused, waiting to see if she'd change her mind.

"Then what do you want to do?"

She gave it some thought. "Gee, I don't know. Maybe we could still find you one of those berets. You really do need one if you're going to be taken at all seriously by the established art community. Come on—I know a few more places where we can look."

We walked a few blocks and stopped in three shops before finding one with hats of any kind.

"Here you go—catch!" She tossed me a brown, woolen flat cap. I put it on, showing her with crossed arms.

"Not really you, Eddy. Too workingman. Not that you're not a work-ingman. But I think the look you want to go with is more urbane—more Paris and less Glasgow."

She searched through the bins until she found a beret. She held it up and made it spin on her finger.

"Nice," I said. "Toss it over."

"That's a woman's hat, Eddy."

"Could've fooled me."

"Ah-*ha*!" She pulled up a light blue one and stuck it on her head. "What do you think of this one?"

I went over to her. "It looks good. Yeah, I'd say so."

"It does look amazing, doesn't it? And it goes with my new dress." She looked at me, her hands at her sides as if making her case. "Please, Eddy? I'm not sure I could scrape two dimes together if I dumped every drawer in my room. But I'll pay you back—really, I will. Would you—oh, could you?"

"Give me a flash," I said.

"Come again, love?"

"I said, give me a flash." I motioned toward her dress. "You lift the hem of that dress and the beret is yours.'"

A quick, wicked smile spread across her face.

"Aw, Eddy, really?" And with that, she lifted it, once for every third or fourth word: "*That's* about the *easiest* beret this school girl is *ever* going to *earn*. You *need* to try *harder* next time and make me *do* something really *naughty*, like—"

The matronly proprietress was making her way over, having noticed Julia's flaunting of bare flesh. I grabbed her hand and we dashed between racks, dodging the old woman. I stopped—briefly—at the counter where I tossed down a hundred-euro bill and we raced out of there. We ran down the alley, turned a corner and banged against the building, falling on top of each other laughing.

We walked the alleys, always staying on the shady side, and bought some Italian ice cream, licking fast. I had my camera and took a few shots from behind as she trailed away from me down the zig-zags of the cobblestone lane. I paused, watching her as she gazed back. She seemed hopeful in the dress and beret, as if she'd gotten away with something and had atoned for it. I don't know why, but there was a certain sadness in her slow walk. I lowered the camera to my chest and watched as she faded away from me, then suddenly gripped it with both hands and ran after her.

We stopped and had iced coffee at a small café in the alley. She sat beside me, not across the table, sipping the cold drink through a straw.

"Sometimes, do you ever just wonder what makes people tick? Do you, Eddy?"

"In what way?"

"In every way possible," she said. "I mean, look at all these people. To think that every single one of them is like you or me, planning what they're going to have for dinner, heading to pick up their kid from preschool, or maybe they've just fallen in love and are on their way to meet whoever the lucky someone might be. It's like they're moving pictures right before our eyes, like they've been put here for our benefit, to watch and wonder about. We know they're people, but we don't consider that each and every one of them has hopes and dreams just like you and me. Gosh, Eddy, it's simply terrifying."

It was later afternoon when we arrived back at the flat. We were hot and sticky and so we took off our clothes to be as cool as we could. The ice in the sink had melted.

"I'll get some more," I said, but she said no, she didn't want me to leave.

We took a cool shower together. She kissed my soapy shoulder as she ran the bar over my back and down my legs. She wrapped her arms around my waist and squeezed tight. I turned around and she wouldn't let go—her eyes clenched shut. She said a prayer. The prayer started out as an Our Father, then became something of her own. She asked for more time, for me and for us, and she thanked God for allowing us to find one another in the sea of anonymous humanity. She mentioned Lily Lolimper, and asked her to use all her powers to make her visions come true. She said everything was going according to plan, but there was the one big gap in the train tracks and she needed her help mending it.

I washed her, kissing her body along the way, and stepped from the shower. She hesitated.

"I want you to do something for me, Eddy," she said with big, anxious eyes. "I'm going to stand under the shower and I want you to slowly turn it colder and colder until it's really ice cold, until I want to scream— and I just may. Will you do that?"

"Whatever you want," I told her. "Just don't expect me to get in there with you."

She braced herself cupping her hands over her face. I reached around the shower curtain and nudged the knob, turning it colder. I gave it another nudge, then another. She gave no reaction and so I moved it a bit more.

She suddenly flapped her hands. "You're going the wrong way— that's making it hotter! Oh, Eddy, turn it back!"

Quickly, I turned it back the other way and soon after she gave a shriek.

"Keep going! ... Do it, Eddy—make it ridiculously frigid! I'm so damn tired of this heat—I want to sock it right in the nose!"

I turned the knob until it wouldn't move any more. I stuck my hand into the spray and immediately pulled it back. I watched her, fascinated, as she stood clutching herself, shivering in near convulsions.

"Now, Eddy—turn it off!" she screamed.

She stood nearly paralyzed, shaking uncontrollably as I turned off the water and led her out. I wrapped a towel around her and began rubbing it briskly over her body.

"You're nuts," I said.

"Take me to the bed, Eddy," she said, but she didn't wait for me, shuffling past the hanging rolls of film and into the living room. She threw off the towel and lay down, curling herself into a fetal position. "Hold me," she said. "Put your arms around me. Just *hold me*, Eddy—

hold me until I stop shaking. I want you to do it before the heat takes over, before the evil descends. I want you to protect me—do you understand? Oh, do you!"

I lay behind her, wrapping my arms around her as she'd asked. She shook until my body warmed her. I felt her body twitch and knew she was weeping, but for joy or sadness, I didn't know.

When dusk came we lit candles. I had this large candelabra at the corner of the bed which provided ample light to see her form. The light from outside was nearly gone, except for the muted glow from the buildings across the canal. I'd never seen such beauty. The girls I'd been with before were superficial associations, and our time in bed together was always urgent and brief. Seldom had I been given an open and prolonged view of female nakedness. I didn't know whether to look at her, softly run my hand over her, or make love to her. I wanted to do all these things at once. We made love slowly, as if we were the gods of time. Instead of an explosion, it was like lava creeping through our bodies, burning us without a true beginning or end. She wouldn't let me leave, but kept her legs locked around my back, holding me close, and I would begin again having never stopped completely. The wind picked up, sending gusts through the flat, and then it began to rain. It was a gentle rain with low, ominous thunder and distant flashes of lightning. I pulled away, nudging her. She thought I meant for her to roll all the way over, but I stopped her when she was on her side and began again as she looked back at me. I rode on top of one leg while holding the other aloft at a wide angle. I gripped her flesh, giving it light pats that grew harder, eliciting short quips of shock from her lips. She alternated between glancing back at me, her eyes glazed, and closing her eyes as she hugged her angled leg to further split her body in two. I didn't know what I was doing. I was an amateur and did what came naturally in reaction to her—what I felt she wanted or needed. I'd had so little experience, I felt there was nothing impossible or unnatural that could occur between us.

It was the second storm that finally broke the heat wave. It continued to rain into the next morning. The temperature dropped and suddenly the Grote Markt was alive with black umbrellas and rain jackets. Power returned to all of Leuven. The city went on as it had before and people talked of the great heat wave and the storms, but not for very long. There was life to be lived.

A Day in Bruges

I waited in the Markt in Bruges where the old bell tower, standing erect like some medieval rocket ready to blast off, was in plain view, sitting on the circular lip surrounding the great statue where I could see and be seen. I was to meet Elle there at 1 p.m. I kept gazing up at the clock, its gold hands seemingly frozen in place against the Roman numerals. Every time I looked it was only a few minutes later. At 1:30 I bought some frites at a stand nearby and sat back down where I'd been and began spearing them with the little plastic fork, dipping each one in the pile of mayonnaise. I wasn't all that hungry, only bored. At 1:45 I ordered a beer at one of the cafés along the great arc of the Markt. The waiter was hesitant to seat me as a single, but I explained that my friend, a girl, was due any minute. The waiter only sat me when I handed him ten euros. From then on he was attentive and friendly, and introduced himself as Rafael.

"She is late?" Rafael said now in English. He'd spoken French during our short seating negotiation.

"Very late," I said.

"Is she beautiful?"

"Yes, she is that."

"Then it is okay," said Rafael. "A small price to pay for lunch in Bruges on a day such as this."

"Along with the ten euros for the seat," I nodded, raising my glass.

"I am sure she is well worth it," said Rafael.

"She's not *my* girl."

"If she is beautiful, a girl is a girl. You will be the envy of every man in the café."

Rafael went off and I worked on my beer. I was halfway through it when I spotted Elle. She was standing at the edge of the Markt talking to two young men. They were tall, blonde, perhaps Swedish. She wore sunglasses but still held a hand in the air as if shielding her eyes. Their conversation, at least on her end, was animated. She talked to the young men for a few minutes, then leaned up and kissed them goodbye. She stood where she was, turning a full 360 as she scanned the Markt.

I decided to have a little fun. I held the big liter glass to my lips, hiding behind it, as she looked my way. She didn't see me and gradually began wandering through the crowd and took a seat at a café just down from me. She was given one of the better seats with a full view of the Markt. She ordered a beer, a full liter, and struck up a conversation with an elderly man in a gray suit who was reading a newspaper.

The man didn't lower his paper immediately, but he eventually folded it and turned to face her, and they had what appeared to be an engrossing conversation at very close range. Every time she laughed she reared back, attracting a great deal of attention, and then placed her hand on the shoulder of his gray suit, prompting him to move incrementally closer. I looked up at the bell tower; it was 2:30. A bottle of wine arrived and she motioned that she didn't want it, but the man insisted and poured her a glass anyway. He draped his arm around her chair. I was really enjoying this and ordered a second liter. The man put a hand on her leg, which she didn't remove. He kissed her on the neck and cheek. He didn't make a scene about it, he just gave her small kisses of affection that made her smile and twist her neck as though it tickled. It was past 3.

I got up and Rafael thought I was leaving, but I told him no, I'd be right back, and I walked near Elle's table where I knew she'd see me. I went into her café's toilet. When I came back out I walked past again and sat down at my table, and not long after she glided past and I called out to her and she acted surprised and came alive like she did with the two young Swedes and the man in the gray suit. She squeezed herself between the tables and we kissed three times—left cheek, right cheek, left cheek—and she sat down and playfully hit me in the arm.

"I've been looking all over for you!" she said. "And here you are having a beer without me."

Rafael arrived and she made a production about the beers they served, asking him to not just list them all, but describe them in detail. None seemed adequate, so I said I'd order for her since I was a brewer, after all.

"You lush," she laughed, hitting me in the arm again, jumping in her seat. "I must have gone around here ten times. How long have you been here?"

"I don't know," I said. "Twenty minutes, maybe. I didn't see you, I was dying of thirst, so I decided to have one here where I could watch for you. I don't know how I missed you."

"Twenty minutes my ass," she teased.

"If that," I said. "I just sat down."

Her beer arrived, a German Dunkel, and we clanged glasses, making the dull sound, and drank. In her dark sunglasses and red hair and clinging blouse and short shorts and big white teeth, she seemed twenty-five years old. I had to remind myself she was nearly twice my age.

"Don't you just love this country," she said, sighing.

"I do. That's why I'm here."

"I could stay here forever. We don't have places like this in America."

"Not many, anyway."

"None—there are none," she said. "And I thought Leuven was beautiful."

"The glory that is Leuven and the grandeur that is Bruges," I said. She didn't get it, the way Julia would have, which irritated me slightly.

"No, seriously, we don't have *any* place like this. This was here before America was even discovered. We'll never have something like this."

She became melancholy, briefly, and stared into the Markt. But then she snapped out of it, as if suddenly waking.

"So," she said, "you know that I've been back from Ireland for a while."

"I know," I said trying to sound amazed, "you told us all about it that night. How was it?"

"How was it? Oh, you know—wonderful, amazing, unbelievable."

"Glad you had a good time," I smiled, then took a drink. I watched her over the rim of my glass before setting it back down.

"It was such an amazing experience, James," she said. "I didn't want to come back. I mean it—I didn't."

"Sounds like a blast," I said.

She took the liter of beer with one hand, but it was now too heavy for her after the alcohol she'd already drunk, and so she used both hands. She stared into the beer, then turned to me sullenly.

"You really don't understand, do you."

"I'm not sure what you mean."

"I think maybe you do, but you're a gentleman."

"I still don't know what you mean."

"Oh, James," she said, and placed her hand on my arm. There was no easy way to move it off, so I pretended to sneeze and then dropped my hands casually to my lap. "Don't you see I'm trapped? No matter where I go, I'm trapped."

"By what?"

"Oh, James," she said, "I can't. . . *move*. I feel like I'm stuck in quicksand and I can't move."

I took another drink. As I set the glass down her hand moved to my thigh, not sitting still, but flitting from there to midair and then back again, as she spoke.

"So tell me what happened in Ireland," I said. "I talked to Rick."

"That liar."

"He's a wreck, you know."

"James, whatever you do, whatever you think, don't believe that lying son of a bitch. He lies. He just lies."

"About what?"

"Promise me," she said, gripping my thigh, "that you won't believe all the shit he tells you. He's a drunk. A boring old drunk."

"He just said he was concerned about you. He misses you."

"I won't go back," she said vehemently. "I won't."

"You're not living at home?" I asked, feigning surprise.

"You know I'm not."

"I thought you were," I said. "I mean, I assumed you were."

"Of course, I'm not. Is that what he told you? Just lies, lies, lies."

"Elle," I said, "Rick didn't say anything about what's going on between you two. Only that he misses you and it's killing him."

"It could have been *you*," she said, nearly flopping herself on the table, then reluctantly bringing herself upright again. "Harry's not in the same league as you."

"Harry? I thought it was the Irish musician." I took another drink. My throat was tight. Everything now was tight.

"It was," she said casually. "But when I came back, I don't know, Harry was so nice and sweet. He seemed to sense things weren't going well for me. I think it was the night we all went out that he decided to break it off with Marta. But wasn't that a riot? What a fun night that was."

"Is that where you're staying, with Harry?"

She ran her finger along the sweating liter of beer.

"Marta doesn't seem too put off by it. They were ready to split, anyway. She's not around much anymore."

"I see."

"It's not like we're really seeing each other. I just need a place to stay. He's been very nice."

"What's Rick got to say?" I said.

"What do you mean, what's he got to say? It's not up to him."

"You're still married, aren't you?"

"It's not up to him," she repeated.

"I think you need to be clear about your intentions. You owe him that."

"I don't owe that liar anything," she said, grasping the liter for another drink.

I said nothing and looked away. The beer and the hot afternoon and now this had given me a mild headache. I wished I was back in Leuven looking out my window, or with Julia. I'd have given just about anything to be with her.

"What do you want, Elle?" I said.

"Can you tell him?"

"Tell him what?"

"James," she said falling against my shoulder, tapping her head there. She lifted it, wiping away tears. "Why are you making this so hard? Why are you torturing me?"

"Rick's my friend."

"And I'm not?"

"You're something altogether different," I said.

"Don't be cruel. You're not a cruel man. *Please,*" she said. "I don't want to break his heart, but I need time away." She leaned into me. "Tell him that you've talked to me. That I'm all right but I need to, well, sort things out. It's better for the both of us. Tell him I won't be coming back for now. Tell him not to look for me; if he sees me on the street, don't stop, don't make it harder than it needs to be. Tell him I love him, but I can't be with him anymore, not just now. Oh, please, James."

She began to cry. I let her cry on her own, but then allowed her to lean against my chest. I thought about Rick and what he must be going through, but I couldn't think about it too long because there was nothing to do about it and it made me anxious without any resolution.

We wandered through Bruges, stopping often to look down at the canals and the medieval stone buildings and their steeply pitched tile roofs. She said she'd give anything to live in one of the houses. Swans floated by down below. She tried to get their attention but we had no bread to drop, and so they went past, silently, like submarines on patrol. Tour boats went out regularly. One boat was smaller and available. I didn't want to, but she pleaded with me, asking me when I would get another chance to ride the canals of Bruges. I paid the man a good deal to take just the two of us out. She bobbed in her seat as the boat set off.

"Isn't this exciting?" she said, clinging to my arm.

The man started in on his spiel about the history of Bruges, but she didn't listen to him. She leaned into me and lay her head against my shoulder, and then she had me move to one side of the boat so she could lie on the seat with her head in my lap. She took my hands and pulled them close, cradling them. We watched the buildings go by. They were more ornate than Leuven's and the canals were real canals for use by boats, not mere slithers of water. I tried to think of Julia, and I could do it, but the rising and falling of her stomach made it difficult.

"I'm not Rick's wife anymore," she said.

"I think you are," I answered.

"Does our age difference bother you?"

"That's not what bothers me."

"But I'm not his. I'm free."

"That's for you two to work out," I said. "It's none of my business."

She sighed, reaching her head back so the sun hit her face more directly. "You don't approve. I know what you must think of me, James. I know what everyone must think of me. I would have cared not too long ago. But I don't care. You see, I just don't care." Again she rested her head in my lap and closed her eyes.

"What happened?"

"Over in Ireland or you mean between Rick and me?"

"Between you and Rick."

"Ireland was wild," she said. "Ireland was everything I wanted and more. It's amazing how much attention a woman of my age can get when she doesn't behave like a professor's wife."

"But you are a professor's wife," I said. "So, what happened between you and Rick?"

"You know what happened."

"I don't. That's why I'm asking."

"You don't know *exactly* what happened in Ireland, but you have the general idea," she said. "It's the same with Rick and me."

"Maybe you'll go back," I said.

"Maybe I will. You never know. I haven't filed for divorce yet.

What's the point right now?"

"He's a friend, you know."

"Oh, shut up," she said giving me a feeble elbow in the leg.

"I shouldn't be here, not like this."

"Oh, James, just don't."

We got off the boat and stopped in a couple cafés, but I drank only half a glass in each since I was driving. She asked if she could ride back with me instead of taking the train and I told her of course. At the second café, after ordering drinks, she went into a small boutique next door that sold summer clothing and perfume. She came out wearing a new pair of faded jeans: tight, frayed, with a belt made of interconnecting loops. She was nothing but red hair and dark skin and big teeth and an aggressive, hungry walk. She sat down and took a drink of her beer.

"Up until two years ago I'd only been with Rick. Faithful for over twenty years."

"Are you talking about Ireland again or Harry?"

She eyed me from behind the sunglasses. "It's just a comment, James, because I can see how uncomfortable you are."

"Me? I'm fine. Rick's a good man." I lifted my glass of beer. "Santé, Rick."

"Cheers," she said, lifting her glass. "To Rick."

"He really is a good guy."

"Aw, shit, I know he is," she said. "That's the killer. You think I like doing this to him? I hate it. And I hate myself." She leaned forward, gesturing with an upturned hand as if pleading with herself. "But what can I do? Our marriage has run its course. It's not his fault. It's not my fault. I didn't try to pull away from him. It just happened. There was nothing I could do. I'd played that role for most of my adult life. We had a lot of good times, Rick and me. But those are memories, just plain memories. You can't move forward on memories, now, can you, James."

"I haven't had to try. But I imagine not."

"You can't. I know you can't. The only thing to life is what's up ahead. The past is done and buried. You can't live off the past. You can't *love* off it, either." She put her hand on my wrist and rubbed it leisurely.

"I know in five or ten years someone like you wouldn't spend time with me like you are now. That's not *why* I first broke away. But once I had, I understood that there's only so much time left before I'll become something desperate. I don't want to be one of those women. I hope I've found love again by then. But right now, I feel as if I'm running, just running trying to catch up—to what or who, I don't know. I can't stop myself. He's tried. You can try." She shook her head. "It's like going through another adolescence—it's painful—but it's going to happen. It's not something I can avoid."

I decided to have another beer. I figured, why not. The sun was shining and the air smelled clean and fresh and I was in a beautiful city I'd probably never see again. There was nothing pressing I had to do back home.

"Tell me about Julia," she said. "She sounds like a nice girl."

"Julia? Oh, yes," I said. "She is."

"How long have you two been seeing each other?"

"Not too long."

"She seems very smart, from what you've told me."

"She is that."

"And a gorgeous girl, too?"

I nodded, looking into my beer.

"You don't have very much to say for a young man who's just won the lottery. What is it? You're uncomfortable talking about her with me?"

I looked up to her. "It is a little weird."

"Only if you feel we're doing something wrong. You don't think we're doing anything wrong, do you?"

"No," I said, though I felt a nagging guilt.

"I mean, we're just having a drink in Bruges like any two people would do. I've asked you to meet me to discuss my marital problems and you've been more than kind enough to oblige. That seems pretty innocent to me."

"Sure," I said. "Sure, it is."

I drank some more of my beer and watched the tourists go by. Some days in Leuven I'd sit for an entire afternoon just watching people. It made me feel good knowing they had things to do and places to go, that they'd be there a year from now after I'd gone. I suppose it was the continuity they represented. As I watched, I felt her eyes on me. I knew what she wanted. I can't say I wasn't attracted to her, but I really wasn't interested, for many reasons. I thought how Julia would get a good laugh out of it. She'd probably laugh herself to tears when I told her.

We finished our beers and she suggested we get another, just a half glass each. As I sat there I thought about what she'd said, how we weren't doing anything wrong and there wasn't anything to feel bad about. The thought of driving back loomed. I'd have to wait a few hours to let the alcohol work out of me before I could drive. It didn't make much sense. Julia was busy studying—we weren't going to see each other tonight anyway.

"I don't feel like driving back tonight," I said.

"Oh."

"I don't mean anything by it, I just don't feel like it. It's not like I have to be back."

"You don't have to explain," she said.

"I mean, there's Julia. I don't mean anything by it. I just don't feel like driving back. I feel like sitting here and having another beer, and I don't want to get pulled over for drunk driving, not in a foreign country."

"That makes sense."

"We can get two rooms, or I'll sleep on the couch. Or you can go back on the train if you want—you'd probably rather sleep in your own bed, anyway."

"You're giving me the option of riding the train all the way back to Leuven or spending the night in Bruges?" She rolled her eyes.

"Well, whatever you want," I said.

We finished our drinks, and then I asked the waiter for a good hotel. There was one a few blocks away. The only rooms left were suites. I paid, and we went up to take a look at it. It was on the third floor overlooking an alley with a dumpster, but one window had a view of Bruges and one of its church steeples. She stood at the window looking at the better view. She remained at the window, her back facing me, until I suggested we go out and see more of the city.

We walked a long time, then had dinner. The sun was dropping below the crenulated profile of the old buildings and it made me think how tired I was. She agreed that we should head back to the hotel for a brief nap, then go out again later on if we felt like it.

There were two beds. I let her have one of them while I lay down on the couch in the other room. It wasn't long before I fell asleep. When I woke back up it was dusk. The room had turned gray and timeless. I lay a while, thinking, then sat up to look at the street down below. It could have been a hundred years ago, or a hundred years in the future. I stood up and walked to door of the bedroom, which was open. Elle was asleep on her back, on top of the bed, not underneath the covers. She'd taken off her clothes, all but her underwear. I approached the bed and looked down at her. I reached out and moved my hand above her contours, but didn't touch her. I don't know what I would have done if she'd have woken just then. I'd like to say that I wouldn't have done anything, but I really don't know. I left her and went back to the couch. I removed my jeans and sat looking out the window. I was both pleased and disappointed with myself.

I was about to lie down again when I turned back to the bedroom. Elle was standing in the doorway. We gazed at each other, but then I turned my head to look out the window. She approached and stood next to me, saying nothing at first. I didn't look, but then I had to, my eyes traveling all the way up to see her, waiting. She didn't sit down beside me, or move to the front of me. She remained where she was, standing.

"It was one of Rick's students," she began. "A boy of twenty-two. He saw my confinement. He was a lot like you: sensitive, quiet. I was shocked when he first tried to kiss me. It was at a Christmas party, we were upstairs just outside the bathroom. I laughed, I thought it was cute. But then he kept calling me. I didn't even know I was unhappy. We met for coffee and I still thought it was all too cute. When he kissed me for real, I knew it wasn't a game anymore. I resisted, but then found myself kissing him back. We met a few days later and. . . finished what we'd started. My whole life exploded before my eyes. He shattered my fears. I didn't know I'd been imprisoned—a self-imposed imprisonment having little to do with Rick—but he led me away to freedom. I saw Rick and our marriage plainly for the first time in years. I cried—for who I'd been for so long, and for knowing I would never be her again. I'd been dead but hadn't realized it. It took the boy to show me. He gave me another life. What I thought was a great risk was no risk at all; the risk was remaining cocooned in the wings of death.

"I know you're probably thinking it's just a midlife crisis, and maybe a part of it is. But it's much more than that. I'm not a whore, James. But my time on this earth is over half over. I want true happiness now, not the appearance of it."

I saw her hand from the corner of my eye reach toward me.

I had no ill will toward her, and in fact empathized with her situation. But I couldn't take it. It didn't matter if I had three months to live or a full lifetime—I loved Julia. I said nothing and waited. She finally walked back into the bedroom. I put my jeans on and left the hotel. I drove home, comforted by the temptation I'd resisted, but frightened that I was tempted at all.

Confessions

A thick mist hovered above the fields, gray and sluggish, reluctant to move, blanketing the crops in an endless sheet. It was a pleasantly warm morning. Birds were slow to glide across the landscape, and those that did appeared and disappeared like silent celestial sentinels scouring the earth. The faint yellow mass of the sun throbbed behind the mist, slowly soaking up droplets from each blade of grass and every dandelion petal.

Philippe leaned against the right front panel of his Volkswagen Jetta, hands on his cane, wearing a light jacket. Around his neck hung a stop-watch. Julia stood beside him with a clipboard in her hand. They'd come out to time me on some hill repetitions. I was already on my bike, coasting back and forth, warming up. I pedaled thirty meters down the road, then came back again, moving my knees in and out to get my legs used to any angle.

"A fine morning for training," said Philippe. "How do you feel?"

I glided toward them, then stopped, standing with my feet wide. I took a drink from my water bottle. "I feel pretty good."

"I can't tell you how excited I am," said Julia. "Gosh, Eddy, are those really your legs? I never realized how massive they were. You think you can really go all the way up that hill without a jet pack?"

I reached out and tapped her nose. "Watch me," I said.

"Couldn't ask for a better morning," said Philippe. "But you'll be hurting before you're done, make no mistake about it."

The hill was outside Aspelare, where he grew up. He'd ridden it many times as a youth when he was training to become a cyclist himself. It was nothing to be laughed at. Only serious riders climbed it, and surely none but the very serious trained on it in succession. I gazed up it as I took a final squirt from my water bottle.

"Got your pencil ready?" I said to Julia, then turned my bike and pushed off.

"Go get 'em, Eddy," she said.

I went thirty meters away from the hill, came back around, and started pumping my legs, head down, my hands gripping the handlebars low. The base of the hill came at me fast but I was ready for it. My head bobbed left and right, not excessively, not wasting energy, but to the cadence of my thighs. The middle section leveled slightly and briefly, giving me a mental pause if not a physical one. I felt relaxed and strong and when the second and more difficult half of the hill came I attacked it, gearing down to move the burden off my legs and onto my lungs. I lifted my head slightly as I neared the crest, and when I arrived I peddled ahead for a while shaking the lead from my legs, then coasted down the hill past Philippe and Julia and came back around.

"Very nice," said Philippe. "3:47."

"Is that good?" said Julia.

"That's good," said Philippe. "You didn't go all out, did you?"

It was a warm-up; there were plenty more to come and he didn't want me to get gassed on the first one.

I shook my head. "I took it easy, but there's only so much you can back off when it really gets steep."

"No, it's more a matter of leaving a bit left so you're hungry, so you know you can improve on the next one."

"There's plenty left," I told him.

Philippe drank some coffee and reset his stopwatch. "Ready for number two?"

I nodded.

"It's a fine morning," said Philippe. "It's a fine morning for riding."

On the second ascent my legs were warmed up and used to the nuances of the climb. It was easier than the first and I arrived at the top barely breathing, curled back around, and coasted back down.

"3:42," said Philippe.

"Bravo!" said Julia.

I took water, loitering in figure-eights longer than I had on the previous two runs, then let my legs fly. When I reached the top I knew I'd found my groove, and as I glided down past Philippe and Julia he shouted out the time of 3:34.

"That's the way," encouraged Philippe. "Like a scythe laying down summer wheat."

I went up the hill with times of 3:26, 3:25, 3:32, 3:40, 3:35, 3:38, 3:38, 3:36, 3:40, and 3:35. By the time I finished, my legs felt it and they burned. Philippe offered to take my bike on his bike rack but I said I wanted to ride the few miles to Aspelare. It would be a good cooldown.

"Come on," I said to Julia. "Hop on."

"But where are you going to sit?"

"We'll do like kids. I'll stand, you sit."

She held my waist as we rode into town. I heard her feet skimming the road playfully as we went and I told her she was slowing us down and making it harder on me, and then I really heard it, and we nearly came to a stop as I started laughing. The pub was across the stream. We turned into the gravel parking lot, which had dozens of dips that needed filled, and glided on down to the low white building. Philippe wasn't there yet. We stood waiting for him, but when he didn't come we walked around. We went along the tree line that shadowed the stream, then came back through the overgrown soccer field. The field was unmown and the grass waved languidly in the light breeze. We sat down on the bleachers and I extended my legs to let them stretch. Not long after, Philippe arrived and sat down on the bleachers with us.

"Where've you been?" I asked him.

"Just taking a quick tour," he said.

"Oh yeah? See anybody you know?"

"I didn't stop. Believe it or not, I haven't been back for several years.

My aunt lives just around the corner, but I didn't want to bother her."

He sat looking out over the abandoned field. He said he and his friends used to roam the field and surrounding woods as youths—he lived in a house just behind us on the other side of the pub. His mother and father were no longer there.

We went into the pub, which was more like a reception hall with a long, simple bar along one wall.

"My dear?" Philippe said to Julia.

"O.J. with a straw," she said. "Heck—it's barely noon."

"An amateur," I said to Philippe. "I'll have a Witkap."

"One Witkap, an orange juice, and a cava," he told the young woman behind the bar. We went back outside and sat at a small table between the building and the field. There was no breeze there. Gnats congregated in small clouds near our heads. The sun baked the faded, yellow stucco wall of the building.

"It's such a deserted place," I said.

"It didn't used to be," said Philippe, his eyes as optimistic as ever.

"Did you play soccer here?"

"Oh, yes, of course. This was where we all played."

"Does Aspelare have a team?"

"It did. I believe it's been absorbed by another team in the area."

"Where do the kids play now?"

"I think there are newer fields on the edge of town. I don't quite know."

Julia was quiet. She listened to us and looked at the field and seemed deep in thought. I kept my beer in the shadow of my head, but still it grew warm quickly. It was good when warm, but not as good as when it was cold.

"Did you hear Eddy went up to Bruges and ran into Elle?" Julia said.

"Really?" Philippe turned to me. "James, you've been withholding vital gossip."

"Isn't that some coincidence?" she said. "Think of the odds."

"It wasn't a *coincidence*," I said. "I told you I met her up there."

"Think about it, Philippe—of all the cafés in Leuven, not one of them had just the right table for the two of them. They had to go all the way up to Bruges."

"Of *course* she wanted to meet away from Leuven," I said. "She didn't want Rick to see us. And I didn't know that until I got up there."

Philippe, who'd been listening with mild amusement, placed his hand on Julia's arm. "My dear, I'm sure you have nothing to worry about."

"I don't know," she said. "I'll need to pierce my nipples just to keep up."

"One," I said, not knowing whether she was having fun, whether I should bust out laughing, or tread lightly. I couldn't help myself and laughed. "She only had *one* pierced nipple."

"Was it the right or left, honey? I can't remember which one you said it was."

I pretended to think hard. "I'm pretty sure it was the left. . . No, let me think. . . No, it was the right. Yeah, it was the right."

She made a face to Philippe and then elbowed me in the ribs.

Philippe didn't know what to think. I leaned to the side and tried to give Julia a kiss, but she swerved away from me. She got up and sat down next to Philippe.

"I think I'll sit here," she said. "Philippe and I are going to decide which nipple I'm going to get pierced."

I lifted my glass and took a drink to hide in it while I chuckled. I didn't know what else to do. I told Philippe all about Bruges. He was philosophical in his response.

"I judge no one for following the trail of love," he said, "or lust, for that matter. Be prudent. Avoid hurting friends if you can. Knowing when the time is right—that's the key. Love is pure luck and don't let anyone tell you otherwise. We believe ourselves to be in control of our own destinies, when it's the same as it's always been—it's in the stars."

Philippe went inside to get us another round. I tried stuffing a bill in his hand as he went by, but he wouldn't take it. I moved my chair next to Julia's. She stood up and moved into Philippe's chair. Laughing, I came behind her and started kissing the side of her neck. She went to get up, but I put my arms around her, keeping her there. I held her breasts, then pulled on her nipples through her T-shirt. She took in a deep breath.

"You fucker," she said.

"They're perfect the way they are," I whispered.

I kept on doing it, slightly pulling them. She took my hand and put it down between her legs. We could both see Philippe through the dirty window at the bar. We knew we didn't have much time.

I took her hand and pulled her up and ran with her across the derelict field into the trees. She went to get down on the leaves, but I told her to turn around. She did, putting her hands on the nearest tree trunk. I pulled down her shorts and pulled my bibs to the side and made love to her quickly, trying to beat Philippe. We ran back to our table, but Philippe had already come out with the tray of drinks. He knew what had just happened and he smiled warmly at each of us and made a toast to our love.

"Tell us, Philippe," Julia said a while later, now with a glass of red wine, "about your first love."

"My first love? Why do you want to hear about that?"

"I don't know," she said. "I bet you were quite the Romeo."

"And what makes you say that?"

"You're a romantic. Everything you do and say says you're a romantic."

He paused, considering it. "I'll tell you if you both tell me yours."

We looked at each other and shrugged in agreement. We were sitting beside each other now, her right leg over mine. I rubbed it absently, openly, moving my hand wherever it wanted to roam.

"So, you want a love story," Philippe said, licking his lips. "Make of it what you will, but it's the truth and so at least it has that to offer." He took a drink of his cava. "I told you I was from Aspelare, just right back there, in fact. At times it seems so far in the past, as if it were someone else's history. But this small village once was my entire universe. It was along this now abandoned soccer field that I spent my youth, and beside which, just behind us, I first felt the tremors of love.

"The field was well-maintained in those days. My mates and I loitered here when games weren't being played. We'd sit in a circle on the ground or on bicycles, conspiring to perform heroic deeds, whispering about older, mysterious girls, or discussing a recent soccer match or cycling race. It was not uncommon for us to trudge between the creek and the field several times a day. We'd sit on the bleachers straddling the benches playing cards and eating lunches our mothers had packed for us. Older boys who smoked and drank sometimes brought girls to the field, forcing us to vacate it. We hid behind the bank leading to the creek, fascinated at what went on between the two sexes, and wondered how we could ever get from playing cards on the bleachers to performing similar acts.

"One day we stumbled upon a young cyclist and his girl on the far end of the field beyond the fence, in the tall grass. The cyclist was a budding champion and had just signed on with an important club. His whole life, up until then, had been cycling. You would see him in early mornings leaving Aspelare wearing a light jacket, and then returning before noon sweating in his short-sleeved jersey, his face pink, his big bullfrog thighs throbbing on and off as he pedaled. After lunch or in evenings, he would go out again. No one knew where he went, not precisely, because no one could keep up with him. He did nothing but eat, cycle, and sleep. He became the pride of Aspelare and there was talk of big things ahead for him and for the town's reputation.

"The things the cyclist did with the girl confused us, but also enticed us. He appeared stripped of his dignity there with his riding bibs shoved down to his ankles, moving against the girl in rough, non-fluid movements so very unlike his fluid movements on the bike. I pitied her. It seemed as if the cyclist were doing her harm. Yet, she too did things we found remarkable. I. . . knew the girl and could not believe she willingly performed acts I had only heard rumors of girls doing. The cyclist rode out on his training ride the following morning just as he always had. Nothing about him seemed different. But to me and my mates, the prior day had been a revelation."

He took a sip of cava, absently biting his lip in thought.

"As I've said, we lived here adjacent to the soccer field. The fronts of the houses were plain, crowding close to the road, but in back there was much space, even small pastures inside ramshackle wooden fences or stone walls. Our own yard was compact, with a soccer net for my brother and me, a compost heap, a row of flowers tucked neatly along the edge of the house, two trash cans, and a round, concrete table where we sometimes had meals, and where I often sat reading or staring dreamily onto the other yards. The table was like a center of things. All questions my young mind had ever encountered seemed to converge there. I would lose myself in the pages of a book and succumb to the warmth, dissolving into a sudden sleep, thinking of dozens of things at once."

He took a drink of cava and wiped his mouth with his wrist.

"Through the wire fence were goats and a cow. The cow was aging and no longer gave milk. The three goats twitched their ears, begging me with their marble eyes for clumps of fresh grass. I obliged them and tore big handfuls and stuck the grass through the square holes in the wire fence. The goats chewed the grass methodically without any expression, though they twitched their ears faster and nuzzled their horns against the fence, expressing their happiness. When the wind blew it moved the tufts of coarse hair caught on the rusted fence and turned time into floating carpets of hope and pleasure.

"The goats belonged to a family who seldom came out back, other than to check on the vegetables that grew along the fence near the soccer field. There was chicken wire around the vegetables to keep the goats out, which was not always effective. The mother had a foul mouth when she discovered a half-eaten plant. She never let this other part of her personality out at any other time. Her son was younger than me, around my brother's age, and those two often went off on their own together, looking for adventures. Then, there was the girl."

"About time," I said.

"Ah, you Americans expect instant gratification." He smiled from the warmth of the cava. "Yes, the girl. She came to her back yard as I came to mine. Whether she too was experiencing the toothache of adolescent loneliness or came merely to enjoy the sunshine, I did not know. She had her own table, a wooden one, where she always sat with her back to me. I could not fault her for this. I could not fault anyone for choosing solitude over unwanted contact. She would nod if we happened to make eye contact, or give a weak flit of the hand before taking her seat with a book. Whenever she curled her legs beneath her, or shifted her position, or turned a page, the muscles of her shoulders and back exploded with life. There was a light spritz of freckles on the round knob of each shoulder. She possessed freckles on her nose and a few on her cheeks as well. She read quickly. I, myself, was a slow reader, often having to reread pages. I knew I had to speak to her, to bring her into my world. I was in love. The pain of not having her was agonizing.

"I devised a strategy to bring her closer. Each night while the town slept, I quietly slipped over the wire fence between our yards. Moving quickly, but with precision, I nudged her wooden table closer to our own yard. I moved it exactly the width of three closed palm. I'd lie on my back, press the table upward with my legs, and gently maneuver it the small distance. This was not an easy accomplishment. If I scraped the grass, exposing the dirt, she would discover what was happening. I also had to ensure that the alignment of the table remained the same.

"The girl did not notice the table moving. Each day she came a little closer to me. It was like slowly reeling in a large fish from the ocean. One day, I was able to discern a light brown mole on the back of her arm. The next day, that she had downy, fuzz-like hair at the base of her scalp. The day after, I witnessed the expansion and contraction of her ribcage, prompting wild conjectures of various kinds. Then, a few days later, I heard her breathing. How it hurt to hear this so close through the rusted wire fence. I watched her expanding form, listened to the rhythmic breathing, caught other wheezing sounds, or, occasionally, the soft humming of a song I knew. When the table was ten feet away I determined it to be close enough. If she came too close she surely would notice the change.

"The day came when I knew I had to speak to her. I had the idea of reading an excerpt from Shakespeare or William Blake, gradually increasing the volume of my voice until she heard me. On that day I had meant to bring my copy of Shakespeare's sonnets, but instead I took a small book of Grimm's fairy tales. They were similar in size—I had mistakenly grabbed the latter in my haste—and I panicked, not sure what to do. I had read the sonnets so many times in preparation I felt I did not need the book. I decided to recite the poems from memory—a feat surely more impressive than reading them. I began in a low voice, not a whisper, but as you normally would when reading aloud for purposes of clarity. Gradually, I increased my tone, growing more confident—and was soon reciting at a volume loud enough to be heard at three times her distance. The girl placed her book on the wooden tabletop. There was no mistake, she was listening to me. She turned her head slightly toward me, revealing her ear. Though outwardly calm, inside I felt the dull pressure of pent-up emotion in my chest and throat. And then, she brought her chin around and her eyes met mine."

Julia let out a gasp.

"She asked if I was speaking to her. I told her I was. She asked why. I said because goats don't understand our language. She chuckled, which is what I wanted. Make a girl laugh and you're well on your way. She paused, then asked what I wanted. I stood up and walked toward her. I lifted my hands to the fence, clutching the wire squares with my fingers. I told her, quite boldly, that I wanted to kiss her. She said I was just a boy, though she was a mere year older than me."

"Did you tell her that?"

"Of course. I'd hooked the quarry—you think I was about to let her wiggle free with such a feeble effort? I did tell her. I said I was a year younger, but eight inches taller, twice as strong, and three times as determined to get what I wanted. To this, she fell silent, eyeing me. My mouth went dry and I felt the nausea creeping up my throat. Then, as if in a dream, she rose from the bench and came forward. 'All right,' she said. She gave a glance toward her house, and another to the soccer field. The wire fence was too high to lean over. Instead, we turned our faces in opposite directions and kissed through one of the squares. I smelled the musk of the goats and the rust of the wire and the ripe sunshine of her skin as we kissed. Her lips were warm and soft. She gave a little moan, and then she pulled away and we stood there with the slight breeze and gnats hovering around our faces."

"And then?" said Julia, leaning forward.

Philippe sighed, his eyes squinting as he remembered. "She was the girl with the cyclist. We met several more times, kissing through the wire fence. We were planning to meet at the far end of the field, to lie in the grass, to become lovers for real. But instead, a day or two later, she lay with the cyclist, on the very same spot we were to meet. When I saw her with the cyclist, it crushed me. She was not a malicious girl; I don't think she intentionally led me on or meant to deceive me. She said she liked *me*, but her mother—because the cyclist was more or less a budding celebrity—pressured her into dating him. However, the result was the same, regardless of the motive. I'd learned what a young girl's heart was capable of."

"That's awful," said Julia, visibly disturbed. "That's just awful."

"Must have been a brutal thing to see," I said.

"It was like she'd cut open my chest," said Philippe.

"I'll bet."

"When you're that young, such an act of betrayal is quite traumatic. It took months for me to recover."

"You ever wonder where she is? What she's doing now?" said Julia.

"Her? Oh, heavens no. I haven't thought of her for decades until just now."

"So, she was your greatest love?" I said.

"You asked me for my *first* love."

Julia placed her hand on his. "That was a nice story," she said. She squeezed his hand, then turned to me. "Okay, Eddy, your turn."

"My turn?"

"Ladies first, but I defer. Your turn. Come on, tell me."

"I don't know," I said.

"You do have one, don't you?"

"A first love? I have a first encounter," I said. "I wasn't in love with the girl."

"A first encounter will suffice," said Philippe. He waited as I gathered my thoughts, trying to find the right beginning.

"The ending's a lot like yours," I said.

"Quit stalling," said Julia. "Out with it—or I'll get my nipple pierced this very day."

I said nothing, but put my chin in my hand. Though I hadn't thought about it for many years, it came back to me sharp and crisp.

"I was a teenager. I guess around sixteen or seventeen. It was after one of the surgeries. There was always a long rehab after the surgery. I hated it. I'd done it enough to know it wouldn't be fast or easy.

"Like I said, my mom and dad weren't around much for it. My dad was working, and Mom just didn't want to deal with it. I was out of the hospital, at home in my bedroom. A nurse was always on hand, and for the first several weeks there'd be a rehab therapist working with me. It's easy to say he was a sadist, but that's not true. He was just doing his job. I had to get up several times a day and walk, or stretch, or use these ultra-light dumbbells. The only time I could really rest was at night. During the day I'd either be doing rehab or thinking about it. I hated the daytime. I couldn't wait for evening when I could rest without anyone bothering me.

"It was summer, and after a while I was able to go outside and sit in the sun. We have a vast amount of land on the estate, it's really quite beautiful. I'd sit on the veranda—the *veranda*, not porch—reading, maybe chatting with Harold, one of the groundskeepers, just idling my time. Anything was better than being in that room. When I became strong enough, I walked through the gardens. The estate was old and there were secluded areas where no one went, except me. One place was beyond the rose garden near the cliffs. There was a small pond. To get to it you had to push through some tall brush and walk over some boards that had been laid down years ago over a marshy depression. The pond had marble benches around it, and big goldfish. To this day my parents don't know about the pond—I always made sure they never saw me enter or leave through the brush. Not that they ventured far from the house very often."

I took a big breath and a long drink.

"We often had visitors staying with us. There was a family from the West Coast. Some business friend or acquaintance of my father's from years ago—I didn't know and didn't care. But they had a daughter around my age. We were both shy and avoided each other at first, but then we realized we had something in common—we were both very lonely. So, we began spending time together. Initially at the house, but then I took her to the pond where we could be alone. We had the best time talking. We'd smuggle six-packs in and keep them cold in the pond. I was still weak. I wasn't supposed to exert myself, other than the walks I took around the grounds. She liked taking a piece of grass and teasing my cheek with it as we talked. Or, she'd sit with her bare legs over mine, casually, telling her funny stories about friends back home, acting as though her closeness shouldn't have any effect on me. But of course, it did. We were *friends*, but she was still a girl and I was still a boy."

"Yeah—*friends*, my ass," chimed Julia. "Fucker. Go on."

"We started to fool around. What I mean is, we kissed. That's all we did. She'd sit practically on my lap and tease me with a blade of grass, and then we'd kiss. She'd press herself against me and moan, wanting me to go ahead. But I didn't know what to do. Plus, I was embarrassed. I'd never kissed a girl like that before and I didn't want her to feel how excited I was. But it was impossible—it was so obvious. She whispered things in my ear, asking me if I was going to wait forever to do it, asking me if I liked her, and how much, and how if I did I should show her. My head was spinning, and I thought I was going to explode any second.

"This went on day after day. Each time, all we did was kiss, but she became more aggressive with her hands and her legs moved against mine more forcefully. Then, she started coming into my room at night to say goodnight. She wore this thin nightgown, barely coming to her knees, practically nothing at all. She'd cup my face and kiss me with her soft lips. Sometimes she'd lie with me for a little while as we kissed. She dropped her hand beneath the sheets and took hold of me, briefly, her hand moving in a frenzy between my chest and legs as a thin disguise of her intent. She'd leave me with the smell of her perfume to tease me the rest of the night.

"One day she cut her knee. I was already at the pond waiting for her and she came limping through the brush, her knee bleeding. She leaned toward the pond and splashed water on the small gash, and then sat down on the bench before me, putting the wounded leg up. As I looked it over I noticed that having one leg up and one down left her completely exposed. I was stunned. She wore these short shorts and the thin material pulled to the side with her leg lifted. I tried not to look, but I couldn't help it. But then I saw her watching me, smiling. I knew she wanted me to look, and there was a good chance the whole thing had been a ploy."

"My God—your deductive powers are astounding," gasped Julia. "Continue."

"I reached out and touched her. It surprised me, how soft and wet she was. . . You sure you want me to go on?" I said to her, her eyes bulging big and white.

"Are you kidding me—and leave me hanging? Get on with it, cowboy. My jealousies apply only to the last five years."

I tapped her on the leg and began stroking it again.

"Anyway, I finished her off."

"Nice synopsis."

"That night when she came to say goodnight, she didn't hide what she wanted. She leaned over, kissing me, then climbed in the bed. She began stroking me, and then she disappeared under the sheets. She rose up, straddling my hips, and I had to cup my hand over her mouth to prevent others from hearing. I was pretty sure she'd done this before—"

"Brilliant conclusion," said Julia, fanning her face dramatically. "Go on—on with it, before I faint."

"She came to my bedroom the next few nights and we did the same thing, always with a brief prelude of her kissing me, ending with her above my hips and me cupping her mouth.

"Eventually, she wanted to see my scar. She hadn't seen it up to this point; it had always been dark when she'd come to my room. I didn't want to show her, but she kept on asking. We were at the pond on one of the benches and she unbuttoned my shirt. She pushed the shirt away and jumped back when she saw it. She didn't know what to do; she was in obvious shock. She tried to act casual about it and ran her fingers along my chest, touching every part but the scar itself. It was exactly as I'd feared. She thought that by seeing the scar, she'd bridge some gap between us. She thought she'd be drawn to me even further. But the opposite happened. She saw how weak I was. I wasn't a wounded soldier, but a sickly patient.

"Her family stayed another week. We still went to the pond and she still put her legs in my lap. We still talked as before. But the spell was broken."

I gave Julia's leg a squeeze.

"I haven't told anyone about my condition until you two, and haven't shown anyone my scar except that girl and you, Julia."

I went inside to get another round. I stood at the bar and breathed heavy. I brought the drinks out and set the tray on the table.

"Thanks, Eddy," said Julia as I handed the glass of wine to her and sat down. "Hey. I'm sorry about before."

"Before?"

"Giving you the old needle about Elle. I didn't mean anything by it. I know you wouldn't do anything to hurt me, at least not on purpose, which is about all anybody can ask."

"I think what she's trying to say is she loves you," said Philippe.

"Well put, Philippe," she said. "Thank you."

"You guys are too much," I said. "You think you can make me sob or something?"

"Aw, Eddy, come on."

I told them I appreciated it, I really did, but I wasn't about to cry for anybody. I told Julia it was her turn. She didn't answer at first. The wine was beginning to affect her, slowing her down and shifting her mood from lightheartedness to melancholy. Philippe and I waited patiently, gazing out over the billowing field. I wasn't expecting to hear what she was about to tell us.

"All right, Eddy," she said. "But just like you, I've never been bitten by the love bug—ask Lily, she'll vouch for me. And, just like you, I do have a rather sweet and sad story of a first experience. Tap out any time you want. Here you go. . .

"I went to a Catholic school, all through grade school and middle school. The family I was staying with was kind, but they were strict

Catholics. I wouldn't call them fanatics, but the woman in particular thought the devil was hiding behind every tree. We went to church on Sundays and every morning before school." She stopped herself, then started again. "Oh, I know this is more than you need to know. I'm trying to give you some idea of the kind of upbringing I had. . . I didn't mind any of it. In fact, I liked my school and my teachers and pretty much everything about my religious life up till then. I enjoyed wearing our school uniform—heck, I thought it made me look pretty. I liked how we all looked the same, though we were all different. It was all I knew until high school, and I never had any reason to give it a second thought. I knew how expensive it was to send me there, and that made me feel special.

"It was a hot day, like the kind we just had. Just unbearable. Well, there was this quarry not far from our town. It was abandoned. Men went there to fish, though I don't think the fishing was that good, and kids went to jump off the high wall at night."

"Like you?" I said.

"Sure, why not? The high wall was up there, crazy high. If our parents knew. . . We went at night, like I said, but this time we went during the day. We all just wanted to get cooled off. We always skinny-dipped. It was exciting to strip our clothes off in front of those boys, while still not showing too terribly much. But this time, in daylight, it was more serious. We started out wearing underwear, but eventually everybody took everything off. You could really see things, if you know what I mean. A real thrill, but embarrassing as all get-out for some of us. We didn't loiter around any, or who knows what might've happened. As soon as we came out of the water, it was back up the hill again. A more taxing workout, I never have had."

She took a drink of wine, rubbing her finger along the stem of the glass.

"There was this boy. I don't remember his name, but I knew it then. We all knew him. He was a friend of the other boys, sort of a tag-along, but a nice kid. He wasn't a very good swimmer. When he jumped, we'd watch to make sure he made it to shore all right. We all got busy jumping, climbing back up, and jumping again. Then, we didn't see him. We looked to the top, to the path, the water, but he wasn't there. Everybody started calling out—at first, like we thought he'd pop out from behind a bush or something, but then in panic. We all got out of the pond and looked as the water settled and became still. He wasn't there. We jumped back in and started looking for him, feeling with our hands. Some dove underwater. It was all so surreal and crazy, like it wasn't really happening."

"You found him," I said.

She nodded slowly. "Yeah, we found him. We pulled him out and set him on shore. He looked the same, but he was limp and his eyes stood open. He looked like he was sleeping, except for those eyes. They tried doing CPR and mouth-to-mouth, but it was too late; he was gone.

"For a few days, none of us got together. It was too sad. I remember staying in my room. I don't know what I did, I can't remember, but I barely came out except to eat. My friend Gina and I were surprised when a couple of senior boys asked us if we wanted to go for a ride. We were only freshmen. Where we lived, there wasn't much to do and going for a ride was like going on a date. It seemed like going for a ride would wash away the pain and confusion of the kid's death. They picked us up and we drove around. We went through town, out on the back roads, and then to the coffee shop, which had ice cream. I was up front and Gina was in the back seat. I felt so big and important riding around town with a senior. A tad bit afraid, a little awkward, but quite mature. You have to remember—I'd never been on any kind of date before. If my foster parents knew, I'd have been in some real trouble."

"Foster parents?" I gave her a look.

"Well, of course," she said. "You didn't think I learned to speak like this back in Italy, did you? After dear old dad really started hitting the bottle, things got a little crazy at home and I was shipped off to small town America. I was about ten, I think. I say foster parents, but they were a relation of some kind, I'm just not sure how, exactly. But that's another story for another time, Eddy."

"So, you went to school *here*?" I said, trying to piece her story together.

"Didn't I just say that?" She looked at me, then Philippe.

I waved her off. "No, it's all right. I got it; go on."

She gave me a smile.

"The boys decided to drive down this road, and then in between two corn fields. The corn was high, way over the car, and when we parked we were totally secluded. They had some beer, which I'd never had before. It was lukewarm and bitter. I thought it tasted like burnt toast, but I sipped it anyway. Peer pressure—ha! It was pretty clear what they wanted, but we thought they were nice and we didn't want to blow it—I mean, we were with *seniors*. We started making out, me up front with my date and Gina in the back with hers. We both came from the Catholic school, but Gina was always more the extrovert than I was. She talked about guys all the time and could be blunt, even crude, in terms of male-female biological interactions. So, it came as quite the surprise when she pushed back the guy she was with and said she wanted to go home—pronto. I couldn't believe it. I was stunned and, frankly, pretty upset. We went outside the car and we had this huge fight. She was crying, and kept on saying how she just wanted to go home. I saw there was no choice but for us to leave. When he pulled the car near Gina's house, she got out and started home without looking back or saying so long. I thought that was it. I thought I'd be dropped off next, but the guys told me we could go back to the corn field and finish the beer."

"Here we go," I said.

"Ha! 'Sure,' I said. 'Let's go.' And that's what we did—we drove back to the same spot, parked the car, and started drinking beer again. My date asked if it would be all right if his friend joined us in the front seat so we could all talk and be together. He joined us and we went on like that, just drinking and talking. I felt the beer start to take effect. My feet seemed like they were floating over my head. It was scary, but exciting."

"I'll bet."

She gave me a sharp elbow.

"Oh, just stop. We started kissing."

"Didn't see *that* coming."

"First, just like before, but then it got steamier. He started moving his hands along my arm, then down to my leg, then up again like that. It was like a fickle fly landing on one place and then another. I pushed his hand away when he got to my chest. A girl's got to put up some kind of defense, but really I wanted him to. He was so nice and cute. I pushed him away a second time, but not a third. He unbuttoned my blouse. I felt fingers at my bra strap and realized it was his friend, and pretty soon I was naked from the waist up.

"My date kissed me and touched my breasts, while his friend reached around and touched them, too. Their fingers mixed together so I couldn't tell whose were whose. My head was floating, just floating. He kissed my neck and my breasts as his friend held them up like fruit to his lips. I was the one who reached for his pants. I unzipped his jeans and took hold of him. I couldn't believe how big and hot it was; my hand couldn't get enough. I noticed the more I stroked him and squeezed him, the more he groaned. I kept doing it, like I was trying to start a fire against him, and he groaned like I'd never heard anyone before. It happened suddenly—it started spurting. It went as high as the roof of the car and came back down on my hand and on his jeans and my shorts and the car seat. It was everywhere, like hot drops of rain. I was shocked, but I liked it. He groaned like some wild animal when it happened, then went into these strange convulsions. I thought I'd really hurt him!"

"Sweet," I said.

"You're not jealous, Eddy, are you? Don't be jealous. You wanted to know."

I reassured her. "Of course not."

"We didn't have sex," she said. "I was a virgin until I was twenty-one."

"That's some self-control after a start like that."

"That's not all. I thought it *was* it." She paused. "A few days later, my friends told me they'd heard things. As in details about the things we did in the car. I couldn't believe it. I was crushed. I never thought he'd go tell his friends, but that's exactly what he did. Before long the whole school knew. I felt so dirty. Something that at the time seemed natural and sweet turned into this set of dirty acts. Those two guys snickered every time I went by. They pointed at me to their jock friends. They made up all sorts of lies about what happened, and then of course other kids added to it so that I became this major slut in the eyes of the entire school. I couldn't wait for the rest of high school to pass."

She placed her hand on my arm. There was a sharp vulnerability in her eyes, in her voice, that was totally new.

"I haven't told anyone this, but now you two know. It's the secret I've held all these years. I don't know what it explains or doesn't explain. It's there all the time, like a piece of food stuck in my throat that won't go down. Like you, Eddy, I've never really loved anyone before. I've been afraid of boys, of men, yet succumb quite easily to those with certain persuasive talents. I find it troubling how the past dictates the future, but there's nothing I can do about it. I don't know that any of us can. Like Lily Lolimper says, the best we can do is see what's coming ahead and brace ourselves, if it's a train wreck, or, if it's something really wonderful, dream about it every night until it gets here."

It All Falls Apart

It was a stunning morning, crisp and clear. I'd ridden out beyond the cemetery and then, on the way back, stopped and shuffled between the headstones, reading the dates, but understanding nothing of the cursive in Flemish. Whenever I went there, my eyes lifted to the fence and beyond. I half expected Philippe to be there leaning on his cane, transfixed as he followed the muscular triumph of the horses galloping across the green field. I went back home to my flat, showered happily humming a song I recently heard, dressed, and then hopped on my town bike and cycled to the university hospital. I sat in the lobby browsing through magazines I couldn't read, looking at the pictures, unconcerned, feeling slightly put-off at the inconvenience.

The tests took longer than expected. When I ran on the treadmill I felt sure they were discussing my unusually superior condition. I was about to intercede into their whispering and describe my training regimen, when all but one of the doctors left, scurrying in their white coats like rats from a sinking ship. The remaining doctor was small in stature, but direct. Her nose seemed disproportionate to the rest of her angular face; I focused on her nose as she went over my history, the unusual patterns from the stress test, and the results of my X-rays. She was a perfunctory, sallow-complexioned doctor not prone to beating around the bush, and told me my condition had worsened, severely. Seemed that my heart was limping along. Without an operation, I had a month, maybe two, to go.

I suppose it shouldn't have been a shock. I'd been increasingly fatigued, the sweats had occurred more often, and I'd begun having palpitations now and then. Nothing too bad, but enough to signal that my condition was changing. Still, I sat stunned listening to the rest of her diagnosis. I felt sorry for her; it was her nose. A nose like that shouldn't have happened on an otherwise normal face. She was a doctor, but that didn't mean she didn't have feelings, it didn't mean she lacked the normal desires of a woman her age.

I didn't ride home directly. I stopped at Philippe's, but he wasn't there. I went to Harry's flat, but he also wasn't home. I ended up outside Het Moorinneken where I parked my bike, and then went inside St. Peter's. I sat in a middle pew where I felt I'd be most isolated, put my face in my hands, and wept. I leaned my head on the pew in front of me; tears dripped onto the old floor in big splotches. I'm not a praying man, but I prayed for something; I'm not even sure what. I suppose for the courage to do what I had to do. Yet, I wasn't sure what that was.

I left the church and went home. There, I made toast and coffee and sat in my chair staring out the window. I watched the girl on her balcony, who was on her phone texting, moving her body to the music. A year from now, she'd still be there bouncing in place, living free in her own world, but I'd be gone. I wouldn't see the birds in their tidy flocks passing by, or the tops of the trees billowing against the wind, or the canal dark and still as people strolled along its edge. These were but a few pedestrian moments, the familiar lily pads keeping us above life's swamp, that I'd no longer experience. I wept sitting in the chair, looking out the window, gazing at the girl and her beautiful freedom. The girl soon shifted my thoughts to Julia, the elephant in my mind I'd been avoiding. I thought of how I'd soon be gone, never to lie with her again and feel her smooth skin against my face or lose myself in the scent of her hair. I thought of her on the bed beside me, touching my face, kissing me. I pictured her mother back in Italy, how I'd promised to help her. It hurt to think about. Like any tragedy, I tried imagining ways around it, and for brief moments my fantasies came to life and I believed them, but they dissolved quickly, and the pierce of reality grew more acute each time a door of fantasy closed.

She was over doing homework in the living room, lying on her stomach on the floor. I took some pictures of her. She heard me, looked up, then went back to her book. She was over more often and stayed the night a couple times a week. I didn't realize how much studying she actually had. She had little time for anything else, but we did go out for an hour here and there to photograph or have a quick bite to eat. I'd taught her how to develop film and make prints, and she helped me in the darkroom. She was quick to learn and I never had to tell her something twice.

I'd begun photographing couples almost exclusively. Usually, they were sitting together in a café, but sometimes I'd catch them walking the streets, or gazing at a shop window, or just standing beside some interesting piece of architecture. It had been a gradual shift. It wasn't a conscious decision, though I suppose seeing all her photographs of young people, including children, had a subconscious effect on me. When we put new photographs on the wall we often couldn't remember whether she had taken a given picture or I had. Not only our subject matter, but our styles merged, as if we had a single point of view.

She closed her book with a loud, definitive snap and lay her head on the floor in overdramatic exhaustion. I began rubbing her shoulders.

My father, strangely, hadn't gotten back to me yet about the money I'd requested for Julia's mother. I was very clear in my email about why I needed it and how important it was to me. He didn't know why I'd come to Belgium or why I was staying for so long. I didn't tell him about my last visit to the doctor's, but now I thought maybe I should have. I'd resisted telling him for several reasons, the most obvious one being that he'd want me to come home. I had no intention of ever returning to America and didn't want to get into an argument about it, but I had to have the money. I decided to follow up with him in a couple days if I still hadn't heard anything.

I was leaning toward going ahead with the surgery before the recent trip to the hospital. The shock of my diagnosis forced me to reevaluate things, and I was anxious to tell Julia that I'd decided to go ahead with it. It was a decision I wasn't completely at peace with, but I knew I couldn't willfully leave her.

My hands, having rubbed her shoulders and upper arms, moved to her back. I pulled her shirt from her shorts and pushed it up. She helped as I pulled it over her arms and head, then unsnapped her bra, and she lifted herself and tossed it aside.

"I want to tell you something," I said, my hand moving over her skin.

"Do you?" she said in a low voice, having settled in for the back rub.

"Yeah. So, I went to see the doctor the other day."

She immediately raised herself up on her elbows. "And?"

"And they did some tests. The usual stuff."

"And? Come on, Eddy—out with it."

I furrowed my brow. "Do you know you have red spots all over your back?"

"Eddy," she pressed.

It was the strangest thing. She had bright pink spots across her back. They weren't spread evenly, but were in random groupings as if she'd brushed something and contracted a rash.

"I. . . ran on the treadmill," I went on. "They had me hooked up to these wires. . . Really, Julia, you should take a look at your back."

"It's probably from the wax," she said. "Come *on*—what did they say?"

"The *wax?*"

She sighed impatiently. "My God, Eddy, yes—the *wax*. If you must know, Nico likes pouring hot wax on our bodies."

My hand stopped.

"What was that?" I said.

She sighed big. "It's not all that unusual. Lots of people are into that sort of thing. He's a sadist at heart, a very benign sadist if you want to know the truth. He doesn't go for whips or belts or anything terribly dangerous. And it's not like he has to have it all the time. He gets in these moods, and when he's in one of those moods he likes to use the wax."

"But I thought Nico was with Valentina now. I don't understand."

"Eddy, I told you, Nico's about as fickle as they come. Do you really think one of us is going to keep that man content?"

"But the wax," I said. "Why did he pour wax on you?"

"We all line up for *that*," she said, "so we can keep an eye on him and make sure he doesn't take things too far. He once covered Valentina's nipple in so much wax it peeled for days and days. I thought she was going to lose it. From then on, it's all of us or none of us."

"But. . . Julia, is Nico still with Valentina? Is he with Valentina or is he with you again?"

She gave another big sigh. "Eddy, I'm pretty sure I told you about this."

"You didn't," I said. "I'm positive you didn't."

She looked up at me in surprise, then turned on her side to face me.

"Well, I can't help it if Valentina doesn't give him what he wants, can I? He's always had a sweet spot for me, I suppose because we go back the longest. I thought I told you, Eddy," she said, "but maybe it did slip my mind. Black mark for me if I didn't, but now you know."

I felt my heart thumping. I just looked at her, numb, fighting my emotions.

"Eddy, what's wrong?" she said. "You're not upset, are you? Why on earth should you be upset about a trifle like that when you know very well the arrangement we have? *And* that it means no more to me than washing the dishes."

"Washing the *dishes*?" I heard myself utter.

"Even less. It's more like taking out the trash, if you must know." She shifted position, putting her head in her hand. "But who cares about that? You went to the *doctor*. What'd they say?"

I stared past her until she touched me on the arm.

I made up something about how I was doing all right, and that things were stable for now. I got up and went into the bathroom and held my hand over my mouth, telling myself it wasn't true, it just couldn't be true. But it was true. I pushed my face into a towel to suppress my anguish. I felt like a fool, and I wanted to be anywhere but there. I collected myself enough to walk out of the bathroom, grab my wallet, and leave the flat. I didn't know where to go. I wanted to hide from the world.

I left her a note when she was at school and briefly explained my feelings. I told her that I still didn't have any right to place judgement on her, but I couldn't accept her arrangement with Nico. I asked her to remove her personal items from the flat while I was away. I told her I didn't want to talk about it and to please respect my decision.

I packed a bag and, without knowing where else to go, headed for Bruges. I booked a room, which had a good view of the canal, and laid on the bed. I didn't know what to do. I told myself I could do anything I wanted, but nothing seemed appealing. I went down to the café where I'd sat with Elle. I was able to get the same seat as before. Rafael saw me and smiled as he approached, quickening his step.

"Ah, James," he said. "Welcome, my friend."

I'd given him a fifty-euro tip before, not thinking I would ever see him again, and was embarrassed at his effusive greeting. He motioned for another waiter to come over, who immediately went off to fetch me a beer while he remained.

"I am so happy to see you again," he said. "Are you staying in Bruges for some time?"

Though his friendship had been bought, he brightened my mood.

"I really don't know," I said. "I just arrived."

"Well, welcome back—you are always welcome here. And, if you ever need this table, all you have to do is call and I will make the necessary arrangements." He stood with his heels together, erect and attentive.

The beer arrived and I sat looking at the Markt. I gazed up at the bell tower and remembered the scene from *In Bruges*, and thought half-seriously about climbing to the top and letting myself fall down to the cobblestones below. It was a passing thought, not a real urge, and it humored me and made my spirits rise. I only had one beer, then strolled the great circle of the Markt. I'd noticed the Dalí Museum the last time, but hadn't gone in. I bought a ticket and entered and spent several hours inside. It was a small museum containing some of his more obscure and personal works. As I was examining the pieces I thought of Elle, how she'd probably enjoy them and find them interesting. She'd left several messages on my machine since the last time I saw her, but I hadn't returned any of them. I thought about her as I lingered in the museum, until the growing urge to call her became something undeniable. I hurried back to the hotel and made the phone call.

"What are you doing?" I asked her.

"You mean right now?"

"Yes, right now."

"I'm doing laundry," she said.

"At Harry's?"

There was a pause.

I told her she should come up to Bruges this instant. I told her all about the Dalí Museum, and Rafael, and the seat at the café where we could watch the tourists, and the flocks of pigeons around the bell tower, and before I was finished she said she'd be on the next train. I said I'd be waiting at the café.

I showered and put my things away. I called the café and told Rafael I'd like the table reserved and he said he would make sure no one so much as looked at it. She arrived around three o'clock wearing a dress much shorter than most women her age could pull off, but she pulled it off brilliantly. She leaned over and gave me a kiss on the cheek before sitting down, and when Rafael arrived to take her drink order she insisted on him giving her a hug. She looked stunning. After a short time she put her hand on mine, rubbing it.

"How's Harry?" I said. I couldn't help myself.

"Who's Harry?" she said.

"That guy you've been sleeping with."

"Say the word and *poof!*—no more Harry."

"How's the Irish singer?"

"The Irish singer's in Ireland, and you're here."

I was waiting for her to ask about Julia, but she didn't. I think she knew enough and didn't need the whole story. We were both here and that said plenty.

When she was finished with her beer I took her to the Dalí Museum. Neither one of us was a Dalí expert, but everyone knows Dalí and surrealism and it was something to say that you looked at some of his lesser-known works. Some of the images weren't only surreal, but overtly sexual in nature. They were the thoughts and fantasies of the artist without the filter of propriety.

"To think," she said, "there are some people who can be as free as this. He's so free, it's not a choice. It's just who he is."

I thought it a strange thing for her to say. I couldn't imagine her ever having to decide whether she ought to do something or not; she seemed the living embodiment of a free spirit.

She asked if we could go on another boat ride. She wanted the same boatman as before, but he must have been out. I rented another one and she leaned into me as I held her, my arms folding around her slight frame. My face pushed into the side of her neck. The scent of her perfume was different from Julia's and it struck me. When my hands moved even the slightest bit, her body reacted as if she were on the verge of extreme arousal. I wasn't consciously comparing her to Julia, but I couldn't help but notice these differences. I gave her light kisses on her neck and she reacted by reaching her hand up to hold the side of my face; her body shifted on the bench restlessly.

I'd moved my hand down to feel the slope of her hips, and then her bare thighs, which were almost entirely exposed the way she was sitting. The boatman remained facing forward, never turning back. Her thighs parted, not slightly, but wide, and I nudged them back so it wasn't so obvious to those onshore what was occurring. She wore nothing beneath the dress. Her legs kept wanting to part and I kept moving them back with my knee. A few moments later her body shuddered. For the rest of the ride I sat with my hands holding hers on her knees. She would have abandoned herself completely if I'd let her.

We walked the old cobblestone streets, stopping in some shops, and talking little. Her eyes were sluggish whenever she leaned up to kiss me, as she did often. When she kissed me her leg reached up in an attempt to clutch the back of my waist, and I had to settle her down and get us moving again. She whispered how she'd abandon everyone—the Irish singer, Harry, this waiter she'd recently met—everyone—if she had me. I believed that she meant it, at the moment, but I also knew that she couldn't help herself; she was a vessel without a captain being steered by whoever climbed aboard and seized the wheel. This bothered me little now. My time was so short, I didn't care.

We got back to the room and she went to the window to look at the view. I waited for her to turn around and then kissed her. I took her into the bedroom and undressed her, kissing her as I went, then I undressed, leaving my T-shirt on, and kissed her again, down her neck, between her breasts, and on her stomach, and on down. I held her legs aloft, pinning her bare softness to my lips. I gazed up to see her watching me, her eyes shocked, almost fearful. Without warning, I turned her over, brought her up, and made love to her hard, without asking what she wanted, sinking my hands into the taut halves of her cheeks. We made love several times, always with me taking what I wanted, never asking, knowing that this was what she desired.

We lay exhausted on the bed facing each other, our hands still caressing and exploring our damp bodies. She had several black tattoos—one on her upper arm and two on her upper back near her shoulder. They appeared to be names.

"Who are they?" I asked her as I rubbed my hand along the one on her arm.

"Why do you want to know?"

"Just curious."

"I know you won't judge me," she said, "so I'll tell you. This one here, the one you're touching, was the first. It was the lead singer of this band back home."

"A lover, then?"

"No, not him. You've heard of the band, but I'm not going to tell you who it is. It doesn't matter and so I'm not going to tell you. I only got his autograph—he signed my arm and I decided to get it made into a tattoo. The other two—they're also singers. The bigger one on my shoulder is the Irish singer—I just had it done."

"What's Rick think about those?" I asked her.

Instead of reacting the way she normally did when I brought him up, she surprised me.

"I suppose it is a kind of slap in the face, having other men's autographs on my body."

"Sort of."

"But in each case, it wasn't something I'd really intended to do. I was caught up in the whirlwind of the moment. I've met lots of people at the concerts I go to. There's this whole community of followers, different groups for each band, and I've gotten to know them, I've become friends with many of them. They all have these tattoos. I felt I needed to do this," she said. "I'm more like them, I'm more *part* of them, than I am a wife to Rick."

"You have plenty of room," I said. "How many more do you want?"

She thought about it more than I expected her to.

"I'm quite selective," she said. "I'll get them until I look like a fool, or someone I care about tells me to stop."

We stayed in Bruges two more nights. By the end I'd squeezed everything I wanted from what our time together could give. Elle made it known she wished to continue on together when we returned to Leuven. I told her I didn't think I could. I told her I wanted to be alone for a while. She didn't know the details about Julia and me, and she didn't know how brief my time was. I felt no compulsion to tell her of either.

Passing Time

I was outside The Carousal at one of the small tables. It was evening and the sun was behind the buildings, and the air coming up from the pinched alleyway was thick and smelled of the pizza shop nearby. The pizza shop delivered, and scooters maneuvered between pedestrians making a nasal, caustic noise, but I was used to it and it didn't bother me. Nothing much bothered me anymore. I felt as if all my senses had been numbed. The city, and my life in it, was like one of my black and white photographs— a frozen representation, a fraction of what it truly was, as I sat immobile, nothing more than some unnoticed observer.

I hadn't seen Julia in two weeks. I oscillated between not thinking of her at all and obsessing over her. More than once, I'd picked up the phone and dialed half her number, only to hang up before finishing. I'd written her letters, but never sent them. Several times I'd ridden close to Nico's while out training, once passing in front of the house, but didn't stop. I'd gathered the few items she'd neglected to take with her—an extra toothbrush, a phone charger, some clothes that were in the laundry, and put them in the corner of the closet. They remained there, like burning black embers, reminding me of what we'd had, but had no more.

A delivery scooter went past, snaking between people until there was an opening, and then it zipped off and was gone. Derek came along. His bush of curly brown hair gave off hope, but when he sat down and ordered a beer, there was no hope in that.

"Coffee?" said Derek, leaning forward, giving a surprised look. He sat back and held himself the way fat men do. It was an unusual thing to do since it wasn't cold.

"Why not?" I said. "It's a stimulant, you know."

"So I've heard."

I eyed him as he took sheepish sips from his beer.

"What's with that?" I said.

"What, this?" He held up his beer.

"You all right?"

"What do you mean?"

"Okay," I said, "if that's how you want to be."

"It's just one beer, James," he said. "A man could get more drunk having a swig from the chalice at church."

"It's none of my business," I said.

"Damn right, it's not," said Derek, taking another, longer drink.

"If you're looking for Emma, she's right over there." I gave a nod to Het Moorinneken a few cafés over.

He waited, then took a quick guilty look.

"Come on," I said. "Let's go say hi."

I went to get up, but he held my wrist.

"Not right now, James. I just don't feel like it."

"Let's go back to my flat," I said. "I've got some new photographs to show you."

"Naw. I just stopped in for a quick beer. I have to get back to work."

"I thought you couldn't work after drinking."

"Come on," he said. "Give me a break."

We both waited, but neither of us said anything more. He finished his beer and sat for a minute, then abruptly got up and hurried off. I decided to switch to beer and ordered a Belgian sour. I thought about Derek, but then my mind wandered back to a memory of Julia I'd been reliving.

"James," came a voice. "James, what are you doing?" It was Emma. She snapped her fingers in front of my face. "Wake up, you fool."

"Emma," I said, coming out of my daydream.

137

"I'm working—I don't have much time. Did you talk to Derek?"

"Who?"

"Derek. I saw him heading this way. Did he stop by?"

"Derek?" I looked left and right acting confused. "No, I haven't seen him."

"Are you sure? It looked like he was walking toward you."

"Well, Emma, he may have passed this way, but he didn't stop by. I'd have known if he stopped by." Her eyes were red, and gray underneath. "You look tired. Are you all right?"

She slid into the chair Derek had been in, halfway. "I can't stay—*I'm working*. Will you let me know if you see him?"

"Sure, Emma," I said. "Are you sure everything's all right?"

"What do *you* think?"

"I don't know what you mean."

"He's drinking. The fucker's drinking again."

"Oh. I'm sorry to hear that."

"You sure you haven't seen him?"

"No," I said.

"That stupid, stupid shit." She pressed her curled hand to her forehead.

"Maybe he'll come out of it. Maybe it's just a crisis. We all have them."

"I want to talk to you later," she said.

"Okay."

"Promise?"

"Emma, I said I would."

"I don't know what to do, James," she said. "I'm worried."

"It's bad, then."

"Of course, it is."

"If it's bad, sit down."

"I can't. I have to get back to work."

"Where do you want to meet?"

"My place."

"Your place? All right." I could see how desperate she was. "I'll see you after you're done working."

She stood up and rushed away from the table. I thought about going to see Derek right then, but it was quite a walk to his flat and I didn't know if he'd be home. There was a good chance he was still out.

I went back to thinking about Julia and one of the last times we cycled into the countryside. We'd gone to the cemetery near the picnic. The grass was taller than before and hid us completely. I lay alongside her and unbuttoned her blouse, carefully pushing aside each half. I placed my head on her chest, cupping her breast, rubbing it with my thumb. My eyes faced the grass, but hers were above in the clouds skating past. When we rode back, she talked of her mother's failing health and the helplessness she felt:

"She's getting much worse, Eddy," she'd said. "My aunt phoned last night and told me. "Her feet are going numb. She can barely walk now."

"I should have the money soon," I said.

"I hope so," she said. "She's really going downhill fast."

"It takes a little time to get that much, but I should have it soon."

"You're a doll, Eddy. I don't know what in the world I'd do without you."

It hurt to think about that ride home. It gave her an emotional lift knowing that her mother would soon be taken care of. But the delay in receiving the money had, I'm sure, given her doubts about my assurance. Our breakup hadn't changed my resolve. I hadn't told her, but I was going to see her mother get well no matter what happened between us.

I sat without ordering anything for a while, writing in my notebook. I wrote for an hour and afterward felt drained, but refreshed. I ordered a Stella and watched Emma working at Het Moorinneken. She glanced up now and then, but didn't acknowledge me. She worked the table without her normal ease, the way a new girl would.

Rick and Elle came along. It seemed they were looking for me. Rick gave Elle the chair opposite me and then pulled another over for himself.

"James," he said eagerly, shoving out his hand for a shake. "I haven't seen you in a while. Where have you been? I guess I've been hitting the wrong cafés." Rick looked tanned and healthy. Elle smiled, but I couldn't read it. She wore a blouse unbuttoned to mid-chest; her hair was wild, swept over the right side.

They ordered drinks. Elle told the waiter she'd have whatever I was having, but then changed her mind and asked for an IPA. On top of the tan, Rick had a week's worth of facial hair.

"What's in the book?" Rick pointed to the notebook.

"Nothing, really," I said.

"Nothing?"

"Not really."

"You a writing man now, James?"

"Isn't everybody?"

"I guess you're right," he said pushing out his lip in agreement. "Especially these days. I like to scribble down thoughts myself. Like to doodle, too. I could compile a whole book of doodles I've drawn while my students were taking exams. Some of them not fit for their parents to see, if you know what I mean."

"Must get awfully tedious during exams," I smiled. I made eye contact with Elle to keep her in the conversation. She hadn't taken her eyes off me since they'd arrived.

"About drives a man to drink," said Rick. "Speaking of which—I heard about Derek. Gee, that's too bad. That's just a tragedy. Have you seen him since he fell off?"

I shook my head slowly, then took a hard sip from my beer. "Nope."

"It's just a tragedy. He was doing so well, too. Jesus."

"It isn't necessarily a tragedy," said Elle without the emotion of a conviction. "Who's to say being an alcoholic is the worst thing in the world?"

Rick nodded in agreement. "That's true, honey. If he can still produce a high quality of art, who's to say it's all that bad? History's full of artists just like Derek. Without the booze, maybe they would have been just like us."

Elle narrowed her eyes and the slightest smirk appeared at the corner of her lips.

"Ah, well, what can you do? How about you, James—anything new with you? I hear you've been seeing one of Nico's models. How'd you manage that? Wow. If that's not something."

"Oh, you know. The usual. I used my charm and wit."

"What's her name?" asked Elle.

"Her name?"

"Yes, her name. Nico's model does have a name, doesn't she?"

"Her name is Julia."

"*Lovely* name," she said.

"Well, you know, what's in a name?"

"Is she a professional?"

"A professional?"

"I mean a professional *model*," said Elle.

"I don't know," I answered vaguely, a bit put-off. "What does it matter?"

"It doesn't *matter*, oh—not at all. It's just that she looks the part. So sleek and tight. Quite a little package, you've got yourself there." She sipped her drink, then turned to Rick. "Don't you think she looks like a real pro?"

Rick put his chin in his palm. "I hadn't really thought about it," he said. "I suppose so. She's a pretty girl, for sure."

"When did you two see her?" I said.

"Rick and I were walking through town not too long ago and spotted you. I said to Rick, 'That must be James' new girlfriend. Isn't she just gorgeous? Leave it to James to find himself a gorgeous new girlfriend, and a model at that.'"

"You should have said hi."

"We didn't want to disturb the new lovers, did we, honey?"

"Wouldn't think of it," said Rick.

"Really, you should have said hi. I could have introduced you to her."

"Oh, that would have been fun," said Elle.

"Next time."

"Yes," she said dreamily, facetiously, "next time, indeed. Next time."

She stood up, nearly knocking over the small table. Rick and I grabbed our own beers and then Rick grabbed hers. We chuckled as she strode off to the toilet.

"What's up with her?" I said.

As soon as I set my beer down and had my hand away from my glass, Rick seized it. "James," he said in a low voice. "I know about Harry."

"Harry?"

"Don't be coy, James. I thought we were friends. You've seen what she's been doing to me. Why didn't you tell me?"

I hesitated, pulling my arm free. "I thought you knew."

"Of course, I knew," said Rick. "Everybody knew after that night at the café, the way they were making eyes at one another. But you didn't have to remain silent. You didn't have to."

"I didn't want to get in the middle of things. You understand."

"Look—we don't have time. I'm not going to hurt anybody. I'm not even that mad at Harry. Hell, I don't blame him."

"I'd be upset, too."

Rick leaned back, suddenly at ease. "You might think I'm a real chump," he said.

"No, you just have a difficult situation."

Rick eyed me as I fidgeted with a spoon lying on the table.

"I guess you could put it that way," he said.

"You two seem better, other than that outburst. But you look good— both of you."

"That's because I've decided to play the game," said Rick. "You know, I really hate them—games, I mean. I always thought you shouldn't have to play games. But I *have* been a real fool. I thought your spouse was supposed to be the one person you didn't have to play games with. I thought you could just be yourself, that it was a dance together instead of a chess match for winner-takes-all." He leaned in. "It *is* a chess match, and we men are completely outclassed. We're not wired for it. Our secrets are of things we've done, not schemes four moves ahead." He smiled wickedly. "But it doesn't mean we can't learn, now, does it." He looked left and right, then lowered his head over the table. "I thought I'd let her do what she wanted and eventually she'd get it out of her system. She'd see the stupidity and narcissism of it all. Even have some guilt. I could not have been more wrong. She's become an addict. And not just a private addict, but one who cares nothing about making a fool of herself or me. I must hurry—she'll be back soon. . . I've decided not merely to allow her these indiscretions, but to encourage them. Yes, that's right. Instead of being hurt, I'm playing an active role. Do you know how many times I've helped her pick out something to wear before she. . . well, went out on the town, as they say? When she comes home I ask her about it—I force her to tell me what happened, in detail mind you, in detail. This has resulted in the effect I've hoped for."

"Shame."

"Precisely. Not guilt, but shame. No woman, no matter who she is or what acts she commits, wants to feel like a tramp. *That's* been the turning point, James. And why I need *you*."

"Me?"

"I need you to finalize what's begun. I want you to make sure she never goes back to the way she was—and, if she does, it will be brief and discrete."

"I don't know, Rick," I said. "I think you two might want to think about heading in opposite directions."

"Listen," he said. "I want you to seduce her."

"Rick. . ." I shook my head.

"Or more accurately, allow her to seduce you. She obviously goes for you. We've talked it over. You're her next conquest, as it were. She's been reluctant to pursue you, only because she fears rejection. But she won't be denied—whether I'm in on it or not. I want you to do whatever you want with her. Treat her the way you would if she weren't my wife." Rick sat back with satisfaction. He appeared sure of himself to the point of arrogance. "Meanwhile, I have made it clear that for each one of her dalliances, I shall have two. This arrangement is retroactive. I have a lot of catching up to do, James."

I smiled uncomfortably. "I thought you looked healthy. I figured you went to the Mediterranean for a week."

"It's amazing how a woman who presumes to care nothing for her husband can be enraged when she sees him drive off with a beautiful, *younger* woman."

"I don't know, Rick. I don't know."

"There she is. *Shhhh.* No more about it. She's quite the tornado. You'll enjoy it."

"But Julia," I protested. "What about Julia?"

Rick bolted up in his chair, blinking. "I hadn't thought about that."

"I couldn't do that to her."

His mind churned quickly. "Better yet—lead her on. Get her to the very point of seduction and then—*poof!*—drop her like a leaf."

"Rick," I said.

"Here she comes. Do it. Come on, now."

Elle sat down. No one spoke, and then we all broke out laughing. When they left, Rick gave the waiter fifty euros to cover the bill.

I walked the streets without a purpose or destination. I was along the canal when I saw Marta sitting on a bench. She was well-dressed, one leg crossed over the other, looking ahead. I sat down with sufficient space between us, my fingers underneath my legs, casually swinging my feet back and forth.

"It's a beautiful evening," I said to her.

"Leuven is Paris on a smaller, more personal scale," she said.

"You look nice." I pulled back, playfully giving her a once over. She pretended to ignore me, then cracked a smile looking away.

"Oh, James."

"Well, you do."

"Of course. But you are silly. Too silly for your own good."

I continued with the play until she turned and pushed on my shoulder, but I barely moved.

"Hot date?"

"You know," she shrugged.

"No, I don't believe I do. Is there news I've missed?"

"You have been too busy with the model. A whole decade has passed."

"Has there been a war?"

"A war, a depression, and a revolution by the working class."

"If the result is *this,*" I said, nodding toward her, "then it was worth it."

"Oh, James," she sighed.

"No more Harry?"

"We are in the middle of the iceberg breaking away."

"I can leave, if you want." I began rising.

"Sit down," she said smirking.

"You're meeting someone here, in this darkened corner of Leuven?"

"It adds to the mystery."

"Do you have your mace?"

She shook her head and looked away so she wouldn't laugh.

"How is Harry taking it?"

"He is taking it the way all men take it when a beautiful woman decides she no longer wants to be with him. He has calculated all the fantastic sex he will be missing, and now he suddenly finds he can't live without me."

"I'd be crushed, too, if I were Harry."

"He made his bed," she shrugged. "He must lie in it."

"Are you going to stay in Leuven?"

"I don't know." She furrowed her brow in thought.

"Where would you go?"

"There are many places, James. I have many friends."

"I'm pretty sure he does actually love you."

"I know he does, as much as any rich young man can at this point in his life. It helps that he and Elle flaunted it."

"She's not so bad," I said.

"She's wonderful. It is refreshing to be in the company of someone so honest with her desires."

"Are you sure you need to leave?"

She waited, turned to say something, then hesitated. "There is so much you don't know, James. I will miss Philippe. I will visit, of course. But visiting is not the same thing."

"Stay a while. We'll all miss you." I said this sincerely, and put my palm on the ball of her knee. She took my hand and removed it.

"Oh, James." She looked away.

I saw that she was tearing up. I didn't think it possible that she could be hurt enough to cry, though this was a silly, primitive thought. Her date would be arriving soon. I didn't want to be there when he did, and so I said goodbye, kissing her on the cheek.

"You're as sweet as apple pie," I said.

"I don't know what that means. Go away."

"It means look at yourself from a thousand feet. You're the envy of millions. See what others see."

I made my way to Het Moorinneken and sat down outside, but didn't order anything. I waited, but didn't see Emma. I finally asked another waitress if she was still working and she said no, she'd left an hour ago.

Her flat was near Philippe's, on the second floor above a shoe shop. I trudged up the short, sagging, parallelogram staircase and knocked on her door. She answered and let me in. I hadn't been in her flat in some time. Much of her furniture was gone, having been moved to Derek's. Her roommate sat on a couch eating a bowl of granola, her feet curled beneath her. She waved and said hello, and then went back to the book she was reading. Emma took me to the balcony in the back of the flat over-looking a small courtyard where no one ever went.

"You all right?"

"No, of course not." She shook her head. "He's a mess. Have you seen him?"

"No."

"I thought you might have seen him."

"No, I haven't. When did he start?"

"It's awful," said Emma. "Just awful. You have no idea." She held her fingers to her temple.

"Do you know why?"

"Why? Because he's an alcoholic, that's why," she nearly shouted. "I'm sorry. I've never seen anyone behave this way. He starts drinking at seven o'clock in the morning. He's nearly destroyed his studio. He can't paint anymore—that's what he says. He begins a painting, and I don't see how it's any different from any of his other paintings. He's already

146

drunk, of course. He never paints drunk. He'll be halfway through the painting, and then he'll throw it across the room and start shouting. I try and stop him—I've asked him what's wrong—but it only angers him." She touched my arm. "He's not Derek at this point. He's someone I don't know—someone I *fear*, James. I don't think he will hurt me. That's not the kind of fear I have. I fear he will destroy himself. He is possessed. All kindness leaves him. He is not rational. Do you know what he said? He said it's left him."

"What's left him?"

"The magic. The confluence of the stars that creates great art. I told him that's crazy—his paintings are wonderful—I don't see the difference, James, I really don't see any difference. But he told me I was a fool, a stupid fool, if I could not see how uninspired his paintings have become. I told him, so what? So for now you don't paint exactly the same as you did before—what difference does it make? He looked at me so bitterly—so horribly, I wanted to cry. He said he had no reason to live if he could not create art at the highest level."

"Oh," I said. "That's not good."

"I know. I know it's not. But in his current state, he does not see clearly. You see why I am so afraid? Who knows what he might do? I can't talk to him. He doesn't listen to me."

"I could try," I offered.

"Would you?"

"There's no time when he's sober?"

"Only in the early morning, and then he is hungover. He has stopped once or twice for a period of a few hours, but it is not something you can rely on. The morning is the best time to talk to the real Derek."

I glanced back into the flat. "Have you moved back here?"

"I'm sleeping here some nights. There are times I have to leave, I cannot take it. You will talk to him, then?"

"Of course."

"Tell him you want to meet for coffee or breakfast."

"Will he want to leave his studio?"

"Perhaps not," she said. She crossed her arms to think. "It might be better if you drop by. Do not tell him you are coming. Stop by around 7. Try and get him out of the studio. Get him in your car where he cannot escape, or go for a walk where there is no alcohol. Try and talk to him, James, the real Derek. Take him to a hospital if you have to. Do something."

"I will. Do you want to come with me?"

"I will not be there," said Emma. "I would not help. I would only cry and make it more difficult."

"I'm sure he'll pull out of it," I said.

"You must help him, James. You must do everything you can. Make him see what he is doing to himself, or I am afraid he will not have a future."

I was beat. I left Emma's with my head buzzing. I should have gone straight home, but I kept walking. I walked along the canal where it was darkest and I could think. I didn't really want to think so late at night, but there was much to think about. I walked into the night. The streetlights glowed bright when I walked past.

Two Minotaurs

I arrived at Derek's before 7 with two large coffees, one in each hand. I knocked on the lower part of the door with my foot for some time without an answer, then decided to go around back to the courtyard. The wooden gate was latched from the inside. I took a stick and slid it in the crack and unlatched it.

The first thing I noticed were the missing tomato plants, and then I saw them shriveled and brown in spaghetti strands on the brick of the courtyard. Derek had taken the tomatoes themselves and thrown them at the wall. There were faded red-brown spots where the tomatoes hit, then streaks where they dripped down. The orchids were gone, and the small ceramic planters that had hung on the wall were in pieces. I didn't knock, but tried the back door, which was unlocked. The studio, just as Emma described, was destroyed. I stood looking at the mess in disbelief. There wasn't a single painting that wasn't ripped or broken in half. Whole shelves had been pulled down. Paint was flung on the walls like feces, some of it hardened, and some still glistening. Cans and bottles were strewn everywhere and the place smelled of stale beer. Gnats hovered above uneaten plates of food.

I made my way through the debris, stepping over heaps of twisted canvases. Derek was on his bed facedown, an arm jutting awkwardly off the mattress. I kicked the mattress near his head.

"Hey," I said. "Der."

He twitched, but didn't change position. I lifted my foot and pushed it against his arm.

"Derek, get up. . . Get up. . . Hey—get *up*."

He swatted at me and rolled onto his back, giving off a long wheeze. I waited, but that was it.

"Come on," I said.

I dragged him out of bed and took him to the courtyard where we drank our coffees. Derek stared silently with a bemused expression. His hair stood up stiffly, looking like it hadn't been washed in days. He chuckled to himself, never looking at me directly, slumped back in the chair as though he had no worries.

"You look like shit," I said.

"That's because I haven't had a beer yet. You want one?"

He stood up. I stuck my leg out to block his path.

"Sit down, Der."

"It's getting late for the first drink of the day," he said. "You sure you don't want to start the day off properly?"

"Maybe later," I said.

"Yeah, sure, later. But why wait when we can start right now? Isn't that the beauty of being an adult? Nobody around telling you what to do all the time."

"Are you trying to be funny?"

"I'm trying to be *hospitable*."

"No beer for you today, I'm afraid." I winced looking at him. "Jesus, Der."

I took him inside and made him shower. I waited outside the bathroom until he was done, then followed him into the bedroom and waited while he dressed. He held out his arms and asked if the clothes suited wherever we were going.

"You look like a movie star," I said.

We got in my convertible and drove away.

I didn't know where to go, so I went to this old abandoned orchard I'd seen. We pulled some fallen limbs close together and sat down. I'd brought a large jug of water and urged him to drink.

"I'm not thirsty," he said.

"Drink it."

"You don't have any beer in your trunk, do you, James?"

We didn't talk for some time. I knew the heat would start to work on him, and sure enough a while later he asked for the water jug and from then on he wanted it continually. He began to sweat and said he was getting nauseous. I told him that was good, it meant his body was starting to fight with the alcohol.

"Hey, man, I really appreciate what you're trying to do," he said. "I do. But you're wasting your time."

"You think so."

"Yeah, I do," he said. "It's really sweet and all, and I know it comes from your heart. But there's so much you don't understand."

"You want me to take you back home? Let you finish off your flat? Destroy everything you own? See you dead?"

"I'm just saying—it's a valiant effort, but one doomed to failure."

I shook my head looking into the dirt. "I just don't get it."

"Get what?"

"Why you feel the need to be so self-destructive."

"I'm pretty much this way, James," he said. "You happened to come along during the one time in my life when I've been clean, fairly well-adjusted, and productive."

"Keep it up, then."

"Keep it *up*?" He constricted his face at me.

"Don't you have a choice?"

"I don't know, James," he said. "Do you?"

"I'm not a drunk. I drink a hell of a lot, but I'm not a drunk."

"Not yet."

"That's right—not yet."

"Do you have a choice about who you are?" he asked me. I didn't feel like answering. "We all have choices. *I* still have choices. But we only have choices about the things we don't need." He leaned forward gesturing emphatically. "You think I wake up and I have a choice about wheth-

151

er to open a bottle of beer. I say, I don't see a choice. It doesn't register that way at all. I wake up, and I *have* to have a beer. You drink. You should understand."

"But I can stop. If I get drunk it's not because I can't stop. I don't understand why you can't stop."

"If I knew that, I would stop," he said. "You keep going the way you are and you'll be sitting right here with me. Then you won't have a choice, either, and maybe you'll wreck somebody's life."

"I don't need to drink to do that," I said.

"No, you don't. But it sure helps."

"Look, can't you not have a drink until three o'clock in the afternoon?"

"Pretty unlikely," said Derek. "I'm not being a punk. That's just the honest truth."

"I covered for you. She came over to my table yesterday after you left. I told her I hadn't seen you. I didn't think you were really as bad off as she said. I thought you could pull yourself together."

"Big mistake, James. Never, ever believe in a drunk."

"What am I going to tell Emma? She loves you. She loves you, Der. She's too good to see you like this."

I got up. I was frustrated because I didn't know what to do. I wanted to do something, to make him see what he was doing to himself and to Emma, but I wasn't getting anywhere.

"What does it matter?" I said.

"What does what matter?"

"Whether you're a great artist? Whether your paintings are going to be looked at by people a hundred years from now? What the hell does it matter? You'll be dead. You have this beautiful girl who loves you, who'll do just about anything for you except see you destroy yourself because you don't think you can lay paint on a canvas quite the way you should. What the fuck, man. I mean, Christ."

He stood up and wandered beneath our tree, kicking at some fallen apples.

"I've been trying to find an answer to give you," he said softly. "I'm not one man. I'm two, or three, or four. It's a constant struggle to keep them all in one sphere where they appear unified and I can function in a normal way. What you see is the spokesperson, the salesman." He paused, then turned around, his hands in his pockets with abashed humility. "You're not that different from me," he said.

"What do you mean?"

"We're Minotaurs, you and me. We don't want to be, we try and deny it, but there it is. We spend our lives hoping the world won't notice. But we might as well have a sign hung around our necks." He opened his arms as if surrendering. "I have one foot in darkness and the other wanting light. I don't want to be like this, but it's who I am. If I reject who I am, then I reject my existence. Nobody can do that and still find a legitimate reason to remain breathing. So, I embrace this train wreck at times, and merely accept it at others. I'll always have this side, and as long as I do I have to defend it. James, there's no solution. Not if I'm going to remain alive. And, at least for the time being, I want to remain alive."

The water jug was empty. I'd often wished for Derek's ability to see the world in ways most can't, for that's where true artistic greatness arises. But there's a price, and most of Derek's life had been a Herculean attempt to pay it.

We drove back in the convertible as the sun fell. There were birds in concert over the crops. There were men on tractors, children in soccer fields, women tossing scraps to pigs, old couples holding hands walking along the road, dogs jousting with teeth bared in play, fences overgrown with grass, church steeples having stood through world wars, closed lace curtains, automobiles parked side-by-side, bridges, and telephone poles, and advertisements, and standing stacks of concrete block, and planted pots below windows, and men at work patching the road. There were so many beautiful things. We saw them together. We saw them as we would not again.

The Heart Gives Way

I was standing in the middle of the room taking my pulse. I'd just finished a ride and, during the last stages, had a strange feeling in my chest. It wasn't a sharp pain and I didn't feel faint, but there'd been a heaviness. It lasted only a few minutes and then vanished. By the time I was home I felt fine, though my pulse now seemed high at sixty-five beats per minute.

I made myself a sandwich and sat on the balcony. The air was dry and smelled particularly sweet. I finished the sandwich and waited for the girl from across the canal to come out onto her balcony, but she didn't emerge. I waited for the birds to swing by in their chaotic clouds, but they too failed to show. It was all right. The air was good-smelling and I'd assured myself there was nothing unusual happening with my heart. I took a shower, staying under the hot water a long time after washing. It was moments like these, now, that I'd begun trying to appreciate. Things like the smell of the air, the sound of the birds, the taste of a sandwich, and the feel of a hot shower after a long ride that meant everything to me. There was nothing big I wanted to experience. Anything big I could have already done. The big things were mirages, anyway.

Julia was calling and leaving messages on my machine. She was often in tears when she talked. It hurt to listen to them and I didn't always do so on the day they were left. Whenever she started talking on the machine, I'd go to the balcony and close the door behind me so I wouldn't hear it. I had to be in the right frame of mind to hear her voice. I thought of her while in the shower, standing under the spray, letting it pulse at the base of my neck. I pictured her lying on the floor, her legs kicking absently in the air as she did homework, and the strange humming noises she made. I'd sometimes caress her as she studied, or I'd kiss her on the base of the neck. I liked to see how long it took her to stop what she was doing. I'd either continue or leave her alone, depending on how much work she had to do. She never got upset when I distracted her, even when studying for a big test.

I forced myself not to think of her anymore. I finished up and dried off, then set the developing trays back in the shower. When I stepped out of the bathroom, Elle was standing in the middle of the room.

"He's crazy," she said.

Her eyes dropped and became big. I went and took a towel from the bathroom and wrapped it around my waist.

"Who, Elle?" I said, folding it over and tucking it in tight.

"My husband, of course." She smirked, still looking below my waist, but then she raised her eyes.

"I won't argue with you there," I said.

She began pacing across the room, arms folded. I couldn't tell if she'd been drinking.

"He wants *you* to seduce *me*?"

"That's what he said."

"Ha!"

"Or you can seduce me," I said. "Either way. It doesn't matter to him."

"What does he think we are—animals?"

"I'm not sure he gave it a whole lot of thought."

"Well?" she said, suddenly stopping.

"Well what?"

"Don't you think that's the most ridiculous thing you've ever heard?"

"It's pretty crazy."

She strolled over to the table of pictures, fluffing through them, and

155

then looked at the ones on the wall.

"He thinks that if I sleep around enough, I'll grow tired of it and run back to him?"

"I guess so." I was trying to keep it light. I didn't want to upset her, or say something that would make her probe deeper.

"He's nuts." She picked up a photograph, blinked twice at it, then tossed it down. "He's been pushing me off to Harry's, you know."

"Yeah, he told me."

"What kind of stupid idea is that? The more time I spend away from *him*, the more I'm convinced I never want to see him again."

"Yeah. I bet."

"Harry's been his usual generous self—but for Christ's sake, he won't leave me alone. It's all I can do to walk out of the shower without seeing him standing there like some idiot holding a bunch of flowers."

"So, you're still. . ."

"Screwing him? He won't leave me alone—what can I do? I mean, he's not unattractive. I've been so upset lately with Rick's craziness—I need *something* to help me keep my sanity."

"Does it work?"

"Ha-ha, very funny. Besides, he and Marta are done. God, James," she said, still browsing through the photographs, mostly of Julia, "are you obsessed or what?"

"That's a coincidence."

"Ha-ha. You think it's too funny." She picked up some photographs and tossed them aside, as if she were looking for something.

"Sort of."

"I wouldn't have to see Harry if you made yourself available. But no—you have a thing for this *student*. How old is she—ten?"

"Eight."

"Ha-ha."

"She's nice. I like her," I said.

"I'll bet you do. I'll bet I know what you like about her."

"Oh yeah?"

"Yeah, wow, that's a real shocker," she said.

She approached. Her hand went to the towel and she tried to give it a tug. I stopped her, backing away.

She'd been so absorbed in looking at the photographs, she hadn't noticed my scar. She saw it and gasped. It shook her, but she said nothing and turned away. She clutched herself as if cold, staring out the window.

"Is that why you wouldn't take your shirt off?" she said.

I went to my bedroom and put on a T-shirt and some underwear. When I returned she came up to me. She looked me up and down, touching my arm with her fingertip.

"I was hoping we could. . . you know." Her finger moved over my shirt, along my sternum.

"I'm not your type, Elle," I said. "Not really."

"But you are. I'd drop everything and everyone for you." Her hand moved to the elastic of my jockeys, pulling them away from my waist. She gazed down. She went to reach her other hand inside, but I pulled back.

"Look," I said. "How about we go have a cup of coffee?"

"Why don't you drop those shorts, we'll make sure everything's still working, and *then* we'll go have a cup of coffee."

I gave her a smile. "I'll be back in a sec."

I went into my bedroom, closing the door, and put on a pair of jeans and changed shirts. When I came back out I was half surprised to see that she was still there, sitting in a chair, waiting for me. We went to a café in the Oude Markt where she sat perched on the edge of her seat, holding the tiny cup aloft with her long, thin fingers. When she wasn't holding the cup she took my hands, which I let her do, and tried rubbing life into them. I remained friendly, but firm in my intent.

"I really do think he's going to lose it," she said. "He keeps calling and calling—asking if we've done it yet. I'm half temped to tell him of our little trip to Bruges. It would make his day." She leaned toward me. "Don't you want to make his day, James?"

"Tell him whatever you want," I said.

"Maybe I will," she said dreamily. "Just to see how he'll react."

"There you go."

"And how is she?"

"She's doing fine," I said.

"But you haven't seen her in what—a week? Two? Three?"

"Well," I said, fingering my cup of coffee, grinning noncommittally.

"Call her. Quit being such an idiot and call her. Whatever happened, forget it. You're not Rick and she's not me. You two were made for each other. If there is a God, He molded the perfect couple and out came you two. Don't fuck it up, James. God wouldn't be happy about it."

I'd ordered some toast so I'd have my hands back. I ate it slowly, breaking off a piece at a time, applying butter and jam meticulously. I chewed until it melted in my mouth and went down with barely a swallow.

When I was done with the toast I told her I had to go back and get ready for a long training ride. She suggested she come up and help me change, but I laughed and said I was old enough to do that for myself. We hugged goodbye, briefly, and I left. As I was walking back I wondered what would have happened if we'd met before she married Rick, and if I never had heart problems, and we were closer in age. I had no answer, but it was interesting to think about and it occupied me the whole way home.

The next day I walked the streets for about two hours, taking pictures. It was a warm, comfortable morning and I found myself wandering far from my flat in areas I'd not been to in some time. I developed the film, but didn't make a contact sheet. It was heating up already and I wanted to get a ride in before it grew oppressive.

I'd intended to go well beyond the cemetery on a long, steady ride. The morning commute was over and the roads weren't too bad with traffic. I was moving along well enough when suddenly I felt strange. It seemed as if I were moving effortlessly, as if I weren't on a bike but floating through the air like a bird. It was pleasant, this unusual sensation, and for a moment I wondered if I was dreaming. Then the road moved in languid undulations. My breathing quickened and I couldn't see where I was going. I pulled off the side of the road and stood strad-dling my bike, waiting for my equilibrium to return. I opened and closed my eyes, then tried focusing on a tree. I expected the two images of the tree to merge, but they continued vibrating as though I'd crossed my eyes. When nothing changed, I turned around and began walking the bike back toward Leuven, but I didn't get far. A few paces later I stumbled and fell. A series of small lights hung in the air. These, as I was to find out later, were the eyes of the paramedics.

I woke the next morning to find Philippe standing by the window with his back to the bed. I knew I was in a hospital, but I didn't know why. I didn't move or speak. I pulled the covers around my neck in fright, trying to remember what had happened. Philippe, hearing the rus-tle of the bedding, turned around.

"You're awake," he said, smiling so that his lips parted.

"Philippe?" I inched myself upright. Tubes and wires followed me like limp snakes. "What the hell?"

"The worst part about being in the hospital. No, the worst part is the catheter. But once it's in, ah well, nothing to worry about."

"Why am I here?"

Philippe described, as best he understood it, what happened. Once I fell unconscious a motorist spotted me, stopped, and called the ambu-lance. I may have been there for some time by the way the motorist de-scribed dried blood on my lip and cheek. Since I had no identification on me, it took a while to decipher who I was and who to call. By chance, a friend of Philippe's was a medical assistant in the emergency room and recognized me and called him.

"You've had a mild heart attack," Philippe said, now seated in a chair beside the bed. He smiled stiffly and bravely.

"A *heart attack*?"

"The tests confirm it."

"But. . . How?"

Philippe raised his eyes affably and his smile turned over in worry. "Well, you know."

I went to say something, then stopped. I slowly shook my head. The last thing I remembered was turning my bike around and feeling as if I were running along the side of the road. I didn't remember any pain or falling.

"God damn," I said through gritted teeth.

"You're lucky. There doesn't seem to be permanent damage. You'll be out of here in a day or two."

"Yeah, I'm a lucky guy, all right," I said flatly.

"I know you don't think so."

"God damn, Philippe." My eyes filled with tears.

Philippe, who couldn't bear to see me tear up, gazed out the window.

The doctor and a nurse came in and he left the room. The doctor asked how I was feeling, and then went on to explain what had happened in more precise detail. My heart attack had, as Philippe said, been very mild. There was no permanent damage, but the fact that I'd had one at all indicated I was in bad shape. He didn't know about my full history, though he saw that I'd been in recently for tests. I gave him a brief summary of the various operations I'd had. He listened, and when I was finished he said they needed to do further tests. I was ambivalent about it and shrugged.

The doctor left, and I sipped some soup from the tray over my lap. Philippe came in soon after.

"I can get out of here tomorrow," I said. "Well, more or less."

"Marvelous!" Philippe clapped his hands.

"Yeah, tell me about it. This food isn't bad. You try it?"

"You're the patient," said Philippe. "It's yours."

"I figure I'll be back on the bike in a few days. I'll need some rest, and I'll take it easy the first couple times out, but I'll hardly miss a beat." I churned spoon after spoon of the soup into my mouth. "I mean really, this soup is great. I'd pay for this in a restaurant."

Philippe watched me, patient as ever. "Is there anyone you want me to call?"

"You didn't, did you?" I stopped eating and looked up.

"Not yet. I know how private you are."

"No," I said. "I don't want anybody to know."

"Your parents?" he asked delicately. "Do you want me to call them?"

I shook my head without looking up.

"Julia will be wondering where you went," he said in a voice even lower.

"No she won't," I said. "That's over."

"I know you haven't spoken in a while," he said in a near whisper, "but. . ."

I fed more soup into my lips. All my focus was on the soup.

"No," I said.

"It's your decision. I'll do whatever you tell me."

"Philippe, I'm going to order another bowl of this so you can have some. You really need to try it."

"I don't disagree with your wish to keep matters tight-lipped. But Julia is different. She would want to know."

I looked up from the bowl. "What?"

"Julia. I'm saying she would want to know about your situation."

"Funny thing, but I haven't heard back from my father yet," I said. "I thought he'd have wired the money by now. I don't know what the holdup is." I went back to the soup and broke a piece off the end of the baguette.

"I understand why you don't want the others to know. You and I are much the same in that regard. Don't you think she might be hurt if she found out and knew you kept it from her?"

"I told Julia I'd have it by now. Her mom needs it right away. She probably thinks I made it up. But why would I make it up? Remind me to call my father to see what's going on."

"She loves you. Of course she would be hurt."

I stopped and stared into my tray. "I'm not trying to hurt her," I said softly.

"No," said Philippe, "but you will if you keep this from her."

I put down the spoon and baguette and eased myself back against the pillows. I closed my eyes hard, fighting it, shaking my head. "She's moved on. We've both moved on."

"She's been calling you," he said. "That doesn't sound like someone who's moved on."

"I told you about her," I said. "I told you what she does."

Philippe cocked his head. "Yes, and she didn't deny it for a second."

"That makes it all right?"

"That makes her honest about her own less-than-ideal situation."

"She doesn't have to do that," I said. "I see lots of girls who don't do that. Just open your eyes and you'll see thousands of them."

"I can't explain her motivations," he said. "But I do know she's a sincere girl with a heart as big as the ocean. Whatever it is, I'll wager she struggles with it every day. She told us some of it. I'm sure that's not all of it."

"You don't understand."

"I'm sure I don't, not exactly. Give the girl a call and she'll be here in ten minutes. She loves you, James. That's what I'm trying to say. And you love her, too. There's no need to continue this needless separation. There's no *time* for it. I think you're afraid."

"You're a mind reader," I said.

"Of course, you're afraid of what's just happened," he said. "But I think you're using her arrangement with Nico as a reason to keep her away. As much as you do love her, you remember when you were a boy, all those surgeries, and all the times your parents neglected to console you. Who wouldn't be afraid of returning to that? But James, Julia is not your mother or your father. She's a young woman who's deeply in love with you—*you*. She's not going to abandon you at your neediest hour. She's not going to think you're weak. She's going to help you, as anyone would, as I would, as I *will*, James, because you are dear to us."

I closed my eyes. I felt weak and slightly dizzy. I'd listened to Philippe more than I would have anyone else, but I was fading.

"Are you all right?" he said.

"I'm just tired."

"Do you need a nurse?"

"No, I'm all right," I said. "I'm just very tired."

"I don't mean to upset you, James. It's the last thing I want to do."

"I know." I offered my hand. I fought to keep my eyes open. "You've been a good friend."

"Why wouldn't I be?" he smiled.

"Do you know why I first spoke to you? I thought any man using a cane who moves as fast as you did, without a hint of self-pity. . . That's somebody I want to know."

"I thought it was I who first approached you."

I shrugged weakly. "You've been good to me. I came to Belgium a real punk. There's no reason you should have spent two minutes on me, but you came right up, sat down, and told me I looked like a thoroughbred waiting for a worthy challenger. You have a way of putting things."

"You stood out from half a mile away," said Philippe. "A thoroughbred, you are."

"My father never said anything like that to me."

Philippe leaned forward, squeezing my hand tight. "Then I pity him."

I closed my eyes and grinned.

"You'll be up and out of here in no time," Philippe said. He went to let go, to pat me on the leg, but I held on.

"I am afraid. I pretend I'm not, but I am."

"How couldn't you be? I would be. Anyone would be."

"I'll get the money, don't worry. You tell her not to worry. Her mother—what a sweet, sweet woman. I've never met her, but she's the sweetest old woman you ever saw. . . Call my father, will you? . . . It's the strangest thing. I know it's a lot of money, but I promised to return soon. I can lie when I have to. . . Lies are all right sometimes, aren't they, Philippe?" I breathed deep, but then held my breath listening. "Do you hear it?"

"What, James?" Philippe whispered.

"She's playing. . . The girl on the balcony is playing her music. . ."

When I woke, Philippe was seated beside me with his typical bright expression.

"How long have I been asleep?" I asked him.

"A couple hours."

"That's all?"

"That's all."

"It feels like days." It took some time to gather myself. I eyed the tray and turned to Philippe. "You try the soup?"

"Horrid. Simply horrid."

The nurses came and went and I tried to be polite, but I didn't feel like talking. My eyes kept going to the phone. Each time I went to reach for it I wrapped my arms around myself and sighed big. I looked to Philippe, but received no help. Finally, when one of the nurses was about to leave I told her I wanted to make a private phone call and I'd like to be left alone.

"I'll wait outside," said Philippe.

I called Julia. I told her I was at the hospital but not to worry, I was going to be fine, but I missed her and would love to see her. She began to cry, then gathered herself and left immediately. When she arrived my door was cracked. She peeked her head in and was told by one of the doctors present to please wait in the hall. I called out to her saying they wouldn't be long. The doctors stayed another fifteen minutes.

"Oh, Eddy," she said, and fell against me.

She cried when I told her I'd had a mild heart attack. She held my hand, rubbing it manically, tears streaming down her cheek. I explained how I'd had no permanent damage, and I'd be released from the hospital very soon.

"But Eddy," she said, "how can someone like you have a heart attack? You're so young and strong. You cycle fifty miles a day. You're the last person on earth that should be having a heart attack."

I gave my shoulders a weak shrug. "I've been trying to figure that out my whole life," I said.

She burst into tears.

"What did they say—those doctors who were just in here—what did they say?"

"I guess it's worse than I thought," I said. "Don't cry. Please, Julia, don't cry."

"Eddy," she said, lifting her head from my chest, "how bad is it?"

"Pretty bad, kiddo."

"Tell me."

I stroked her cheek. It was so good to see her again. I'd forgotten how beautiful she was and how different I was when she was with me.

"I thought I had a couple months," I said. "That little powwow we just had was to inform me that a couple months is vastly optimistic."

She cried, asking if something could be done, if surgery could fix things. I remained silent. I pulled her up and she lay beside me. She nudged a finger down the collar of my hospital gown, trying to reach my scar. A nurse came in and asked her to sit in the chair, not the bed. I raised an eye as if to admonish her further and she smiled. A while later, Philippe returned with some flowers, some cheese and crackers, and a container of lobster bisque.

"*This* is proper soup," he said. "Feed that dishwater to the dogs."

I insisted that Julia have some first, and then Philippe and I tried it.

"Doesn't he look well?" he said brightly. "For a man who's just had a heart attack, I think he looks remarkably well."

Julia couldn't speak. She nodded tentatively and then burst into tears and left the room.

"Philippe," I said. "The doctors were here."

"Yes—what is it? What did they say?"

"It seems I don't have much time."

Philippe's eyes squeezed down. "How long?"

"A month. Maybe less. It seems this old ticker's a lemon. I should get my money back."

Philippe received the news stoically, blinking. "I see," he said. "And does she. . ."

"I just told her."

"Good," said Philippe firmly. "That's good. That's very good."

"Philippe?"

He stared into the bed, his face flat, his glasses drooping down his nose to reveal tired eyes. "Yes, James?"

"Nobody else."

He shook his head. "Not a soul."

Julia entered the room. She stopped halfway to the bed and held up her hand like a traffic cop. "There'll be no more crying in this room," she said. I clapped my hands in thanks. Philippe leaned over, kissed me on the cheek, and left in a hurry. I watched him, somewhat bewildered, looking to her for an answer.

Julia sat down, her face gray and flat. "Even Philippe has his limits."

We Choose Life

I was home in two days, not one. She wanted to move my bed into the living room as we did during the heat wave, so I'd have a better view of the canal and I'd be with her as she did her homework, but I told her there was no point. I wasn't going to be spending a lot of time in bed and besides, I could always lie down on the couch. She moved in full-time. She went to her classes, but other than that she was home with me.

For a few days I sat around reading or sitting on the balcony writing. I went through all my photographs and organized them—both the ones I'd taken with her and the older ones. Many of the latter, however, I decided to throw away. She asked me why and I told her they seemed so lifeless.

"But Eddy," she said, "I don't want you to throw them away. You're just about the only photographer around who cares two ticks about those old men. They're important."

I went to get my bike down a couple days later. She was on the floor doing homework when she looked up at me. She said nothing, but watched as I checked the air pressure in the tires, filled my water bottles, and got into my cycling gear. I told her I'd be back in an hour.

I took it easy and felt great. I'd been off the bike less than a week and hadn't lost much, maybe just a very small bit on the hills, but in some ways the time off had reenergized me. When I returned she was in the shower. I stripped off my clothes and pulled back the shower curtain. She gave a loud shriek.

"Eddy, don't *do* that to me," she said. "Come on in here and let me scrub that sweaty body of yours. I'm sure you have layers and layers of filth on you."

I stepped in and she did start scrubbing me down, but, not long after, we started kissing and then I sat down in the chair she'd put in the shower for me and she climbed on top of me and we made love, frantic at first, then slowly. I clenched my legs, which was enough to move her up and down just a little. Our lips never parted.

We lay on the bed, caressing one another. She cried. At first she tried holding it in, but then she broke down, sobbing uncontrollably on my chest.

We had dinner on the balcony. I broiled salmon, with sides of asparagus and hot rolls. We dressed up for it. We decided we'd dress up every evening for dinner from now on.

"I missed you," I said. "I wanted to call back but, well, I don't know why I didn't, exactly."

"Oh, Eddy—I about died without seeing your handsome mug, I really did. I've never missed anything so much in my entire life, and that includes my first dog, Chocolate. That might sound rather juvenile, comparing you to a dog, but you didn't know Chocolate or how much I absolutely adored that boy. Plus, I missed you even *more*, which says volumes for your temperament and personality."

I squeezed her hand. "It's none of my business what you do when we're apart. I'm sorry I reacted the way I did."

"No, it is very much your business when you love somebody, so don't apologize for *that*. I guess I figured you wouldn't care. Now, before you blow another fuse, let me finish and then that'll be it—we're never going to talk about this canker sore again. You see, I just look at Nico as this clown—when he's not painting, of course. When he *is* painting, I think he's one of the most gifted souls on earth. I can't believe what I see appear on a canvas from nothing at all—just his mind and not a speck more. It's fascinating and amazing and I'm way beyond in awe. The other side of him, the clown side, is something totally different. He's the most ridiculous man on the planet. I can't take him seriously. So, when he asks for ten minutes of meaningless nothing to help keep his motor running, I've never seen it as a big deal. I'm sure it's quite unconventional and if I were on the outside looking in, I might pee my pants in shock." She paused for a moment, then went on. "But I've been a real dingbat thinking it wouldn't matter to *you*. The last thing in the world I'd ever want to do is hurt you, Eddy. Good God, I don't. So, no more Nico."

"You're leaving?" I said.

"I'm not leaving the artist," she said. "I'm saying adios to the drooling fat man. Even when you're. . . Even when you're not around anymore—it's going to be strictly professional between the two of us."

I leaned across the table and kissed her. I didn't want to hear anything more than what she'd just said. Not because of any leftover jealousies, but because I'd been such a fool.

She was taking an art class as an elective and had an assignment where she had to use papier-mâché. She said she wanted to make an impression of my chest. She said I had a beautiful chest and she wanted to have it with her for the rest of her life. She was going to keep the impression, and then when she saved up enough money she'd have it cast in bronze. I told her I'd let her do it if I could make one of her chest at the same time. She didn't understand why I'd want such a thing, but said it was okay by her.

We had a hard time coming up with newspapers—I finally had to go down to a nearby shop and buy several copies. We cut them into strips and mixed up the solution of flour and water. I put down a sheet so we wouldn't mess up the floor, and then we began. She'd lay a strip on me, then I'd lay a strip on her. In less than an hour we were done. All we had to do now was wait for it to dry. I'd brought a small fan out and aimed it toward us. We sat side-by-side on the floor against the couch, her hand in mine.

"Eddy?" she said.

"Yes?"

"What do you suppose it's really like when we die? I mean *really*. Everybody talks about heaven and hell and all that stuff, and who knows—maybe it's all true. I mean, who am I to say? But I've got a hunch it's not like that at all. And if it's not like that, then what is it like?"

"I've actually given this a lot of thought," I said. "Hard to believe, isn't it?"

"Very."

"I'm not sure why you're thinking about it, though. A healthy young girl like you?"

"I'm a healthy young girl with a dark and morbid inclination, and a boyfriend who's got one toe dipped into the River Styx."

"Good point," I said. "*Two* good points."

"So, what do you think?"

"What do I think? I think the answer's so far out there, so beyond what I'd be able to understand, it's not worth thinking about."

"Sure sounds like a cop-out to me, Eddy."

I laughed. "It may be. But, other than I'm afraid, because I don't really know what's going to happen, I'm looking forward to finding out."

"Get out," she said. "You are not."

"I am," I said. "Part of that's bravado, but part of it's sincere. Who knows what's out there?"

"What if there's nothing?" she said. "What if there's absolutely nothing—doesn't that just terrify you to pieces?"

"I'll never know," I said.

"Well, that's definitely not an option in *my* mind. Now that I've found you, my stardust companion, I'm not letting go for anything. You know what Lily Lolimper says? She says it's the cosmic bonds of love that really hold the universe together. Forget your electrons. Forget your protons. Toss quantum mechanics in the garbage disposal. Those are nerd-based answers to non-nerd questions. That's why it's so important to find your true one and only. When you form that cosmic pair bond, you're adding to the strength of the whole shebang."

"I guess that makes sense," I said.

"You guess? Why, it makes such obvious sense—I don't know how anyone could think otherwise. Eddy," she said, rubbing my hand hard, "I was nearly ready to pack it all in when you wouldn't see me."

I turned to her. "What do you mean?"

"I mean I had the old razor blades on the stool—right beside my bath. There I was, ready as can be. I put the pointed corner at my wrist. . . when I said to myself, you're not done with me. You might think you are, but you're not. It's in the stars—Lily never saw anything so clear in all her life. You don't fuck with the cosmos, and if I'd have done the slash-and-squirt, that's just what I would have been doing. Who am I to stick a middle finger at infinity? Like you said—it's way too complicated for *me* to understand. I knew I had to abide patience and wait for you to come around. And, well, here you are. Here *we* are—slathered in flour and water and yesterday's news. It's frightening to think how close we were to remaining floating bits of frightened, shivering Brownian motion for probably the rest of eternity." Her thumb ground into my palm fiercely. "But it's done, Eddy. We've sealed it. Our love is forever now. We're part of the cosmos."

I told her I was sorry she'd come so close to doing that, and made her promise—no matter what happened in her life from here on out—that she wouldn't ever consider harming herself again. She promised wholeheartedly, squeezing my hand again. I felt a tightness in my throat thinking about it. The more I did, the more frightened I became and the more ashamed.

"I love you, you know," I said.

"I know you do, Eddy. And I love you more than you could possibly understand."

"It tore me up when we were apart. I thought that if I put you out of my mind I could live out the rest of my days in some kind of calm, orderly way. Why I thought that was so important, I don't know."

"Fear," she said. "It'll make you do all sorts of wacko things."

"I've been thinking," I said. "I've been thinking a lot. There's something I want to talk to you about."

"Uh-oh."

"Nothing bad."

"Well *that's* a relief."

A feeling of peace passed through me. For the first time in my life I felt completely naked and glad for it. There was nothing left to hide.

"I've decided to have the operation," I said.

There was a pause and then she began to cry.

"I'd give you a great big hug, but I don't want to mess up these nice papier-mâché boobs." She dropped her head against my shoulder. "Aw, Eddy, I don't know what to say. Me and Lily have been praying for this day to come. Every night before I go to bed I pray for my mom back home, my sisters, and for you. I know it's not going to be easy. And we've got a long road ahead before you'll be back to your old self again. But I'll be with you. Me, and Philippe, and all your friends—we'll be there every step of the way."

She asked when the operation would be and I said I didn't know. I told her I'd talk to the doctors about it. Considering how bad off I was, it wouldn't be too long.

"Gosh," she said, "maybe you can have it tomorrow? Oh, I know that might seem soon, but maybe you could, huh? I mean, why wait?"

I told her there was a problem with that. I hadn't been able to reach my father about getting the money for her mother. I'd initially thought he was just busy, then that he was thinking things over. But he'd emailed and said that he didn't think it was wise to send that amount of money. He said I'd been negligent in my responsibilities, and as much as it pained him he was thinking about cutting me off entirely. He said I'd had plenty of time to do some soul searching, if that's what I'd been doing all this time, and it was pretty arrogant to ask for that kind of money for someone he didn't even know. As far as he was concerned, I was going to use the money for a new car or a trip.

Julia fell silent.

"Well," she said. "I'll figure something out."

I told her there was another way.

"I can get it from the race," I said.

"What do you mean?"

"I'm going to bet Harry. He's got as much money as I do—his father wouldn't blink an eye if he asked for that amount."

"But Eddy."

"I won't lose."

"You've just had a heart attack."

"I won't lose. I know Harry. I could take him with one leg."

"But if you do," she said. "Where will you get the money to pay him?"

"Look," I said, "I feel fine. I'm in great shape—I won't have to push it that hard."

"No," she shook her head. "I don't want you to."

"I'll be fine—I promise. It'll be a walk in the park."

"He might not even agree to the bet," she said.

"Harry? Are you kidding? He'll snatch it up."

"But. . . when will you have the surgery?"

"Right after the race," I said.

"But why don't you have the surgery first, and then do the race?"

"It'll be half a year before I'd be ready." I shook my head. "You know your mom can't wait that long."

"I love my mom," she said, "but I love you more."

I gave her thigh a squeeze. "Then that tells me I'm doing the right thing."

We peeled off the molds and set them aside on the table, then took a shower. We didn't talk about the race. We talked about my decision to have the surgery. She cried for a while, then she was all right, then she cried some more. She cried uncontrollably. There were many things expressed in those tears.

Baking Bread

"Hey," I said as I pushed on the door to the flat and stepped inside. "Why do you have the door open?"

"I'm in here, Eddy," she said from the kitchen.

I'd been out for a ride. It was a long, medium-tempo ride because of the heat, but I'd felt good.

"Christ, it's hot in here," I said.

"I know," she said. "That's why I have the door open. Leave it open."

She turned and came toward me carrying a small pan of water, nude except for my gray, cotton running shorts.

"Hi," she said and leaned up and gave me a kiss, wrapping her arms around my neck. Her breasts were hot and wet with sweat. There was sweat on her face and on her thighs, and collecting at the top of the running shorts in back.

"Lord, it's hot," I said.

"Tell me about it," she said rubbing her thighs together.

"What are you doing, anyway? You have the laundry running?"

She nodded, leaving me and returning to the table where she'd been working. "And the oven's on. That's why it's so hot."

"But—" I started, watching her breasts swing back and forth as she kneaded dough on a cutting board. "But it's almost ninety out."

"I know," she said in a strange, drugged-like monotone.

174

"Aren't you dying?"

"I'm burning up. God, I'm on fire—can't you tell?"

I looked at her curiously, watching her knead the dough. She seemed to be in a trance. It was so strange.

"How was your ride?"

"Pretty good," I said. "I felt great."

"That's nice." She answered as if not hearing me. She watched me. Her eyes moved between me and the dough.

"What's that?"

"Bread," she said.

"Bread? You don't know how to make bread, do you?"

I watched as her hands pressed and folded, pressed and folded, and when I looked up she was gazing at me, her cheeks ruddy, almost feverish. Slowly, she wiped her temple with a forearm. She kneaded, added more flour, and then kneaded some more. Sweat ran down her brown skin.

"Here," I said, and I picked up the small fan that was on the floor and held it up in front of her. The fan wasn't on, it was unplugged. "You need to get this thing going. Where do you want it?"

"There, right there," she said, nodding to the counter.

I plugged it in and turned it on. Flour from the table blew onto her skin and she quickly became white, and then the sweat from her body soaked up the flour. She didn't care.

"Oh, that feels good, Eddy," she said. "That feels so good. I'm so damn hot."

"Can I get you anything else? Water?" She looked as if she was going to pass out.

"Water."

I went to the sink and ran the water until it was cool, and then filled a glass. I added three ice cubes and handed her the glass.

"Thanks," she said, taking it with both hands. She drank the water in one breath, her Adam's apple bobbing up and down her neck like a man's. She handed the glass back. "You know, I talked to your mom this morning."

"Did you? What did she have to say?"

"I said I talked to your mom today," she repeated, her eyes wandering around drunk-like. "I asked her how to make bread. Do you know why I asked her how to make bread? Because when I asked her what you loved more than anything when you were growing up, she said you loved her bread. You loved your mom's homemade bread."

"Sure," I said, "the one or two times she made it."

"You love your mom's homemade bread, don't you, Eddy. I know you do. I called your mother, I know you do. God, I'm hot," she said, closing her eyes. She leaned against the fan with her arms resting on top. Her eyes opened and closed. "We talked about you. About her baby boy. Her little baby boy. . . I have something to tell you. I bet you were the cutest boy ever born. I wish I could have seen you. I have the best thing to tell you. I bet you were so cute. God," she said and she cradled the fan so that her breasts pressed the grating. "She told me how you used to lie awake at night and they'd walk past your room and you'd be there with the covers pulled up to your face, and you'd wave and smile goodnight. I don't know how she could walk past without stopping to hold you and kiss you." She brought her face up from the top of the fan and looked at me, though her mind seemed to be somewhere else and I didn't recognize her. Her lips were full and glimmering, her eyes half-open. "She said you rode your bike everywhere, all summer long. Every day you'd get on it and go over the estate and come back with a handful of wildflowers for her. I know you don't think she took very good care of you, but she loved you so much. I bet you didn't know how she watched you. She said you'd be on your bike hours and hours by yourself. But you weren't a lonely little boy. She said you weren't." Her eyes, sluggishly, looked up. "You weren't, were you? Maybe you were, but now you have me and you're not lonely anymore. . . I need more water. I'm just so hot. I've never been this hot before. I feel like I'm on fire. Get me some water, Eddy, please?"

"Sit down," I said to her. "And turn off the oven and the washer and dryer—"

"No," she stopped me. "Leave them alone. All I want is water." She pushed me toward the sink. I got the water and handed it to her. She drank it down and went back to kneading the dough. Sweat dripped from her face, down her chest over her breasts, then fell off her nipples as they shook forward and back. She added more flour to the ball to keep it from sticking to the cutting board.

"Are you all right?" I asked her.

"I'm fine," she said.

"You don't look all right. Why don't you step out on the balcony for a minute. At least there's a breeze out there."

"I'm fine, really."

"You look like you're going to throw up."

"Maybe I am," she laughed weakly. "It feels wonderful."

"Can I at least help you? Do you want me to finish up?" I said.

"No, I'll do it. You go take a shower. You need one."

"You want to get one together?"

"No, I'll do this. Not now. Later. Tonight we can get one together."

In the shower, I wondered what was wrong with her. I thought it was strange how she'd called my mother, and even more surprising that they'd had a lengthy conversation.

When I came out she was sitting on the stool, panting, drained, soaked in sweat, her arms listless between her legs. I asked her if she wanted to lie down. She said she was with child. I said, what do you mean, you're with child? She said I mean I'm pregnant. When she said that she turned and slid from the stool and stood on my toes. Her hands slipped over my chest up to my neck, anchored themselves behind my head, and she pulled herself up to me. She coiled her left leg around mine, pressing against me. She moved up and down, and then I felt her fingers instead of her leg.

My mind seemed to explode. We made love on the floor traveling across the room, coupled, as I rocked against her. A while later we bumped into the dryer, my head banging it, her own head thrown back, shining from the light cutting through the window.

· · ·

Evening came. We'd fallen asleep on the floor. The room glowed pink with dusk. I showered with her and then we got dressed. We went down to Het Moorinneken. Emma was working and she stopped and chatted with us, but Julia didn't say much, looking tired but content. I ordered a beer and she went to order a glass of wine, but I reminded her of her condition now and it made us both smile with happiness. Her face looked full and ripe in the fading sun and the artificial lights from the cafés. I leaned over and kissed her, then had a sip of beer, and then kissed her again. I moved my chair so I was beside her instead of across from her.

"How long have you known?" I said.

"I just found out. I went to the doctor's this morning. I thought I was—I took a test and it was positive—but I wasn't sure until I went to see the doctor."

"And how far along are you?"

"About a month." Though tired, her eyes brightened. "Can you believe it, Eddy—our baby is growing inside me right now, right here. Isn't it the most wonderful thing in the world?"

I let my head fall against hers, then turned to kiss her neck. I kissed her behind the ear and on her shoulder. She smelled as good as she looked. "It is," I said.

"You're happy, aren't you?"

"Of course," I said. "Can't you tell?"

"I think so."

"Julia," I said, looking down at our clasped hands, "now, no matter what happens, you'll have the baby with you."

"Oh, Eddy," she said, "what are you talking about? You're going to have the operation and you're going to come out of it just fine."

"Sure, but you never know. You'll be taken care of," I said. "You don't need to worry about that."

She gave a deep sigh. "We'll have to start looking at names. What names do you like?"

"I don't know. You can decide."

"Don't you care?"

"I'm sure you're better at picking out names than I am," I said.

"Well of course I am," she said, "but that doesn't mean you shouldn't be part of it."

"How about you come up with a list and I'll tell you what I think of them?"

"Wonderful. That's wonderful."

"Anything but James."

"I love James," she said.

"James is out," I said.

"Maybe it'll be a girl. What if it's a girl, Eddy?"

"I'd love a girl."

"Isn't it exciting thinking it could be either one? Oh, Eddy, I don't know if I want to find out. Do you? Wouldn't you rather be surprised?"

"Sure, I love surprises. I got one a few hours ago."

She gave me a light elbow. "Don't even. I'm serious."

"Whatever you want," I said. "If you want to keep it a surprise, then we'll keep it a surprise. And if you want to find out what it is, then we'll do that."

"Let's wait," she said. "Yes, let's do that."

She barely touched her drink, a Coke, just as I neglected my beer. I didn't want to do anything but feel her beside me, her body expanding and contracting to the rhythm of her breathing.

Loose Ends

We decided to have a party. I'd given parties regularly my first few months in Leuven, but I hadn't had one for quite some time, and none like the kind we were planning. This was to be a celebration of our life together, of our friends, and the child Julia was now carrying. It was to take place a few days before the race.

I wanted to talk to Elle beforehand. We met at a quiet café just down from the Grote Markt. I invited her to the party and told her, briefly, how Julia and I had reconciled.

"It's your life," she responded evenly. "She's a gorgeous girl."

"You're not upset?"

"Of course, I'm upset."

"She doesn't know about, you know, you and me," I said. "I'd tell her, but I think she'd rather not know."

"You're an astute observer of women, James," she said. "And you're quite right." A cold pint sat before her, barely touched. She fidgeted with the rim of the glass. Finally, she took a sip. "I don't suppose I really loved you," she said. "I don't mean to be blunt."

"No," I said. "It's all right."

"It's just that, well, we only had sex a handful of times. You can't really love someone after such a short window of intimacy now, can you?"

"I guess not," I said.

"And you didn't really love me. Not *love* me the way you do her."
She took two more sips. "Are you two going back to America?"

"I'm not sure what we're going to do," I said.

"I know what you mean," she sighed, hanging her arm over the back of the chair. "I think it's time I finally move on, too. It's getting to be such a bore. I think I'd like Spain. Or France. I hear Marta's in France. She really is a wonderful person. It turns out we have a lot in common."

"Elle, *you're* a wonderful person," I said. "Actually, I might be leaving soon."

"With her?"

"It's sort of a goodbye party." I paused thinking about it. "Yes, that's what it is."

"Italy? Off to see the motherland?"

"Italy would be nice."

She reached up and pressed the back of her hand to my forehead. "James, are you sick?"

"What?"

"I've never seen you so pale," she said.

"I'm all right. I've been having trouble sleeping."

"I'm sure you have."

"So, you will come, won't you?"

"To your party?"

"She wants you to. I want you to."

"Can I get a goodbye kiss?"

I leaned forward; she laughed.

"I mean at the party, Romeo. I'd ask for more than that, but you're a gentleman at heart. I wouldn't put you in that position."

She finished off her pint, smiled at the waiter, and soon had another one. I put my face in my hands and looked at her. "I sure am going to miss you."

"Then don't."

"I mean it, Elle. You're a good person."

"Then don't."

I smiled. "You and Rick never had a chance."

"It took twenty years to figure it out," she said, "but we were toast from the start."

"But now you know," I said.

"Yeah. Now I know."

"I'm going to invite him to the party."

"Be my guest. He won't come."

"Still. Will you be civil?"

"Me? I'll be as cool as can be."

We finished our drinks, and then I went to Emma's flat. Her roommate said she was staying with the drunk. I stopped by Het Moorinneken to see if she was working, but she wasn't there. I continued on to Derek's studio. I knocked but there was no answer, so I walked to the back and unlatched the gate as before with a stick. Emma was sitting in a chair reading a book. The courtyard was cleaned up. Orchids were again hanging on the wall. The tomato plants were gone, but flowers had been planted where they were torn out. When she saw me her face lit and she set her book on the table facedown.

"James!" she said. "What are you doing here?"

"Wow," I said. "The place looks great."

I sat down, and when I did she took my hand and squeezed it hard.

"I haven't seen you in ages," she said. "Where have you been?"

"Oh, you know."

"Yeah, I know," she said shaking my hand excitedly. "How is she?"

"Amazing," I said. "Wonderful."

She stared at me with wide eyes. "You wear love very well, James. Though you could afford to eat more often. You're as thin as a cracker."

"I've come to invite you to a party."

"Another one of your famous parties?"

"A dinner party."

"My James is all grown up," she said.

"Something like that. So, will you come?"

"Of course," she said, squeezing my hand. "When is it?"

"Next Saturday. I hope you're not working."

"If I am, I will find a replacement. It will be no problem."

I lifted my eyebrows and gave a nod to the studio. "And him?"

"Sleeping."

"I thought he'd be up by now smashing plates. How is it?"

"Better. He has agreed to keep his temper under control. He does not drink before noon, usually."

"I guess that's something," I said.

"Yes, it is something. He is trying."

"Well, tell him he's invited, too. Drunk or sober. I want him to come."

She squeezed my hand. "Thank you."

"It sure is good seeing you," I said. "I mean it."

"You hardly ever stop by the restaurant anymore. I wish you would. It's not the same without you."

She made coffee and we enjoyed our time together talking about the days with Victor, when the three of us roamed the countryside shortly after I arrived in Leuven. She'd dated Victor for a while before she met Derek. It hadn't ended well, but before that we had some good times together.

I tipped my head to the bedroom again. "He might have problems, but he's a good guy," I said.

She narrowed her eyes. "James, are you drunk?"

"No," I answered.

"You sure are acting strange. What's going on?"

"Nothing," I said.

"You're a bad liar."

"Don't you like parties? I thought everybody liked a good party."

"Good friends don't keep secrets," she said, eyeing me.

I stared into my cup, absently trying to fit a finger into the hole of the handle. "Some secrets are too big for anyone to know," I said.

"Is that the kind of secret you're not telling me?"

"It's the kind of secret that needs a party like this."

"But I don't understand."

"That's all right," I said. "I just want you to enjoy yourself."

She took a sip of coffee. "I'm not sure that I can enjoy myself now that I know you're not telling me something."

"Just come. Come, and have the best time."

I gathered our cups and saucers to get more coffee. I stayed a while longer. We talked more about the early days with Victor, and she was able to laugh about it without getting sentimental or bitter.

I was near Philippe's flat; I walked the short distance over. I stood outside looking up at the second-story balcony with its array of potted flowers and debated whether to stop in and say hello. I hadn't seen him since leaving the hospital and had never been inside his flat. Then his head appeared over the balcony railing.

"James!" he called down. "Why are you standing there? Come, come," he waved.

I went up the stairs where Philippe was waiting for me. He was without his cane, and showed me into the flat, bearing down on his bad leg with his hand. The flat was spacious and neat and was furnished expensively, with paintings on the beige walls, mostly of nudes. Fresh flowers rose from a metal vase in the center of a table, and an entire wall was nothing but books and trinkets. He had on classical music, which he turned down so we could hear one another.

"What brings you here?" His eyes lighted.

"I was over at Emma's and thought I'd stop by," I said, still looking the place over.

"Ah, and how is Emma? Has she tamed the beast?"

"A little," I said.

"I fear she stands in quicksand and thinks she is on solid ground. Such is love and obsession. Ah, well." He rolled his eyes behind his head. "What can we do but hope for the best. And you," he said, smiling broadly. "You look well."

"I feel pretty good." I patted my ribcage.

"You look it. . . Yes. . ." Philippe examined me more closely, his eyes narrowing. "Thin still, and your color hasn't fully returned, but I see expectancy and vigor in your eyes. Have you ridden today?"

"I went out for a while this morning. No problems. It's like nothing happened."

"Excellent," he said. "No need to push things too fast. Do what you feel you can." He placed his hand on my wrist. "You don't have to do the race. You know you can beat Harry, and now with what's happened, it might be best to hold off. At least for now."

"You mean let Harry have the satisfaction of winning by default?"

"I understand," he said. "I would probably do the same if I were in your shoes. But keep in mind, I won't think less of you if you decide not to, and Harry—who cares what he thinks."

I told him I'd decided to have the operation and he jumped up and down on his good leg. I'd never seen him so excited. He actually cried and hugged me. He wanted to know when it was going to be because he was going to make sure he was with me at the hospital. I told him I wasn't sure yet, I had to schedule it, but very soon.

"Yeah, but I have a slight problem," I said.

"A problem?" he said pulling back his head. "What kind of problem?"

"Money problems."

"*You* with money problems? Unthinkable! Did you lose your debit card? I have two hundred euros I can loan you, if it would help."

"Two hundred euros isn't going to do a whole lot," I said, "but thanks."

"How much do you need?"

"It'll be all right," I said.

"James," said Philippe, taking my arm. "How much?"

"A hundred thousand."

"A hundred thousand—" He cut himself off. "For the surgery?"

"Well, there's that, too, but no. Remember Julia's mother? The money I've been trying to wire her?"

"Ah—yes, of course."

"I didn't think it would be an issue. I figured my father would ask some questions, I mean, that's a lot of money, but I didn't think it would be a real problem. I told him I'd be coming home soon."

"Yes, yes—I remember. Go on—what did he say?"

I shrugged. "I thought in the end he'd come through. Guess I was

185

wrong."

"Oh, James," said Philippe, "I'm sorry. I know how much you wanted to help. I'm sure Julia will understand. Have you talked to her about it?"

"She knows," I said.

"Well, that's good to hear."

"I can still get it." I grinned mischievously.

I told him about my plan to bet Harry on the race. As he listened his face grew skeptical and worried.

"But James, do you think that's a good idea considering what recently happened?"

"I'll be fine," I said. "It shouldn't be any problem. I've already called Harry. He swallowed it up in two seconds."

"But. . . You don't have that kind of money. What if you lose?"

"I'm not going to lose."

"You just had a heart attack."

"A very mild heart attack," I said. "I'm fine. There's nothing to worry about."

He shook his head. "As your friend, as someone who cares deeply about you, I ask you to reconsider. I think you should postpone the race until after your surgery."

"Philippe," I said, "I know you're trying to help and I appreciate it. But I have to do it now—her mother can't wait. It would be months before I could race and by then it would be too late. If I win, and I *will* win, everything will be fine. Harry can cover the bet no problem. If I lose, I'll explain things to my father. I'll tell him everything. He may pity me enough to pay Harry *and* wire Julia's mother the money."

"I thought you didn't want pity," he said.

I gave him a playful fist on the arm. "I don't, but I'll use it if I have to."

We sat on the balcony looking down on the small plaza. A stream of students flowed from one end to the other on foot and gliding on bicycles. We watched them the way you do flocks of birds at the sea.

"How is the party coming along?" said Philippe. "Do you need anything?"

186

"Actually, we could use those two guys from the picnic. We need a couple bartenders."

"Yes, yes—I'll call them today. They might already be booked on such short notice, but I am friends with one of their mothers. It should not be a problem. Anything else—anything at all?"

"I don't think so. It's not going to be complicated."

"Do you have enough chairs?"

"Chairs?"

"You can never have enough chairs. I'll bring some. If you don't need them, we'll put them in the bedroom."

"Sure," I said. "Bring on the chairs."

"Anything else?"

"Not that I can think of." I fidgeted with a small potted succulent. I held the clay pot in my hand, turning it one way then the other. My eyes went from the pot, to Philippe, then back. "I stopped by Nico's the other day," I said.

"Uh-oh," he said.

"No, it's all right. We're fine. He doesn't know I know, and I'm going to keep it that way."

Philippe brightened. "Well, good—good. And how is the photographer-turned-painter?"

"He's all right. I was on my way back from a ride. I stopped to see if he was back doing photography."

"And?"

I shook my head. "Still painting. I don't think he's going back to photography anytime soon."

Philippe waited. I kept fidgeting with the pot, barely looking up.

"We went out back, the two of us, and had a beer under the trees." I cleared my throat. "We got to talking. We talked about Julia. We talked about the other two. He told me about Valentina and him and how they broke up. Broke up. That's a funny way of putting it—Nico must be fifty years old." I was having trouble getting to the point. "*Anyway*. . . He said that you two were at university together. He said you were in art school with him. And he told me. . . some other things."

Philippe became somber, but defiant, his face falling flat. "Did he, now?"

I nodded. "About you two. And, cryptically, something about you and me."

"You and me?" he said. "I don't understand."

"I don't either, that's why I'm asking. He just laughed. Every time he started to tell me, he started laughing. I finally grew irritated with him and left."

"I see." He looked away.

"Do you want to tell me about it?"

Philippe, noticeably red in the face, got up from his chair and stood leaning against the balcony railing looking down on the plaza. He gave a long sigh.

"Oh, James. . ." he said.

"You mind telling me what's going on?"

Philippe rapped his fingers along the railing, then abruptly stopped.

"You must know," he said.

"Know what?" I waited. "Philippe, you mind telling me straight, because I'm pretty much at a loss here."

"I suppose I am being somewhat circumspect," he said. "Let me see if I can clear it up: James, my boy, I was once like you. Frighteningly, like you. I wanted to be a cyclist as a youth. You know that, I told you. I trained for it from the time I was twelve or thirteen until I was twenty-one. There was nothing else I wanted, but to be on a professional cycling team. I had talent and I had the desire—but too much of the latter and not enough of the former. My whole day, my entire existence, was cycling. I venture to say that you possess talent that I never had, even with your gangly legs. That's a joke, James, and I expect you to laugh.

"Once it became clear I had hit the ceiling of my athletic prowess, I was lost. I didn't know what to do with myself. I enrolled at university here in Leuven and studied art. Again, I possessed talent, but not of the noteworthy kind. I so desperately wanted to be exceptional at something, as I think every young man does. . . Youth is a time for discovery, isn't it, James. That's what makes it so wonderful. That's why we look to the young for inspiration. It can also be a period of profound change. Nico and another artist, Peter, were seeing each other. Neither was serious about the relationship or about young men. They were artists, and what do artists do but take giant leaps outside the circle of what society expects from them? I, on the other hand, had come to the slow realization that I much preferred young men to women. Nico, you see, was my first crush. I stole him away from Peter, if you could call it that. It lasted a few months and then it was over. He had no real interest in me or in men, and we remain great friends to this day."

Philippe pushed himself to and from the railing, gazing down at the throng of students.

"That day in Aspelare, I intended to tell you. But age does not lessen the anxieties of the heart. And Julia was there, making it rather difficult." He looked skyward, shaking his head. "I am not a naturally open person, James. It is difficult even now to express my feelings. I thought you might have guessed by now and come to realize what I could not say directly."

"Which is?" I waited, still baffled.

He turned to face me. "Oh, James," he said. "Really?"

We looked at one another. I thought I knew him well enough to read him, but for quite some time I sat there. My eyes narrowed. My mouth slowly opened as I began understanding what he was trying to tell me.

"Jesus, Philippe—why didn't you say something?"

"I wanted to."

"You could have said something," I said. I grew anxious, and then angry.

"I wanted to. I really did."

"All that time—you just remained silent? You could have told me any time."

"I intended to," said Philippe, "on many occasions. That evening at Nico's—I was going to suggest we have a drink afterward, but then you and Julia went into the house. I waited, thinking we would still have time."

"Why didn't you?" I said through gritted teeth.

"I've seen you many times in the presence of young ladies," he said. "But the expression you had after being with Julia for the first time was totally different. You had the quiet reflection of someone who's finally found what they have been looking for. I did not feel I had the right to interfere."

"You didn't have the *right*?" I said. "What about my right? Don't I have the right to know how you feel?"

"It wasn't easy. I did what I thought was best. I was thinking of you."

"You coward," I said, hitting my fist on the table.

Philippe swallowed hard. "James, I may not have always made the right choices, but my intentions were sincere."

"As a father! But you're not my father, are you?"

"No, James, I am not."

"I have a father—thank you—I don't need another."

"That was my mistake, I see that now. I wanted to be both protector and. . . more. I felt, however misguided, that you needed someone looking after you more than you needed my affection. James, my thoughts were always of you."

My fist slowly tapped the tabletop. I couldn't look Philippe in the eyes.

He sighed. "It was folly from the start. I assumed you didn't like men. It was complete fantasy. Being so much older, I did not want to make a fool of myself. I have done so on many occasions, but I'm getting too old for it." He paused. "There is a certain amount of narcissism in it, too, I think. In you, I see myself of twenty years ago. I am drawn to you because in you I see all that I was, and all that I could have been." He smiled. "This can't be a complete surprise to you; things like these never are, not in retrospect. The thing I could not bear was losing you. I erred on the side of holding back and assuring our friendship remained intact, rather than making my feelings known and possibly losing you entirely."

I'd listened carefully. My face was hot. Instead of anger, I felt loss, a hollowness I knew I would never fill.

"Why would you assume that?" I asked. "Do you think so little of me?"

"James, I think more highly of you than anyone."

"Then you must have known I wouldn't have reacted badly. It makes no sense."

"Once that cat's out of the bag, it can't be put back in," said Philippe. "You may not have rejected me entirely, as a friend, but that friendship would have been forever altered."

"You could have tried," I said gazing up at him.

"And presume I had the power to change the design of man? No, James, that was not a possibility. And now. . ." He choked up. "I project an appearance of calm, of stability, but inside I am an utter mess. I knew in the back of my mind some day you would leave Leuven and return to America. It has been something I have dreaded. But when I face the prospect of losing you forever, not to another continent, but to the cruel hand of fate. . . It's not fair," he said bitterly. "It is an affront to God's divine social contract."

We remained silent. A flock of pigeons sped past and then exploded just before the building at the far end of the plaza. I watched them, and in watching my emotions cooled and I was able to think more clearly and rationally.

"All this time," I said, "and you never said a word."

"No," said Philippe, "I couldn't."

"I'm sorry."

"Sorry?"

"For losing my temper."

He smiled. "Quite all right, James. It's a lot to throw at you, especially with all you have going on."

"It's just a shock. I had no idea." I sighed and slowly shook my head. "What if you had told me, early on, say, after our first few meetings. What might have happened?"

"I imagine you'd have politely told me you weren't interested."

"Maybe."

"Maybe?" Philippe cocked his head in surprise.

"I don't know what I would have said. You never gave me the chance to find out."

"But you don't like men."

"I'm a dying man who's never loved another human being," I said. "I like *you*. What body you happen to be in would have made little difference."

Philippe narrowed his eyes. "So, I gambled on the wrong horse?"

"We're still good friends, aren't we?"

He nodded slowly. He put his hand on my shoulder and squeezed it affectionately. "Yes," he said. "And that means everything."

Smashing Fate

We stood before the mirror in the bathroom, Julia painstakingly applying mascara, leaning into the counter, standing on toes, while I checked my hair. She wore the blue dress. I moved behind her, pressing my weight against her. She smiled and took my hands as I slid them around her. I closed my eyes with my chin on her shoulder. I wanted to feel her and smell her. I wanted to forget the party and lock the door. She was patient, as she always was, and did not try and push me away.

I knew she needed to finish getting ready, so I moved away from her and stood beside the door jamb, arms folded, watching her in the mirror.

"I can't believe Marta is coming," she said. "Where has she been?"

"France. England. Prague, unfortunately."

"Have you seen her since she's been back?"

"No, I haven't," I said. "She hasn't been back long. She may have come specifically for the party, I don't know."

"She and Harry?"

"Oh, I don't think that's going to happen," I said. "She's cut the cord. Once a woman cuts the cord, that's pretty much it."

"Is that so?" she said, eyeing me in the mirror.

"From what I can tell."

"But Harry may not see it that way."

"Harry's been spending time with Elle."

"Your friends do get around, Eddy," she said.

She leaned farther toward the mirror, emphasizing her curves.

"Have you heard from Derek?"

"I don't think he's coming," I said. "I'd be shocked."

"But there's no reason Emma can't. I hope she comes. She's a sweet girl."

Along with my friends, she'd invited many of hers. Gia and Valentina took the opportunity to pass the word to their circle, so that the flat became speckled with young, beautiful people dressed as if going to a formal event, many of them in black. The two mustached bartenders were set up just outside the kitchen and in the light of the room didn't look as identical as they had outside. Two caterers laid food out in the kitchen and served it to guests, moving swiftly and professionally, weaving between the throng holding plates of food above their heads. We'd cleared off the table of photographs and returned the bathroom to its former state.

Philippe, Emma, Julia, and I stood on the balcony in the early evening sun, along with two of Gia's friends, who sat on metal chairs sipping wine, looking down on the canal. They, as with everyone who came to the balcony, watched for signs of life in the water, and were vaguely disappointed when they saw only ducks.

"Is that Victor I see?" said Philippe, nodding into the flat. "I didn't know he was coming, Emma, did you?"

"I heard he might be." She shook her head dubiously.

"I wonder how Ukraine was? Shall we call him over and find out?"

Emma blocked his path with her arm.

"Don't you dare."

"But don't you want to hear how things in that part of the world are doing?"

"Philippe," she warned.

"He looks so dark and wild. The last time he was here, I heard he and James had a pissing contest right on this very spot." He leaned into Emma's ear. "Word has it their streams made it all the way to the canal. Isn't that right, James?"

I nodded, prompting a curious look from Julia. "Impressive, Eddy.

Wow."

"Can you imagine. I mean, can you *imagine*?" said Philippe.

"If I want a king pisser all I have to do is wait near the university after the bars close," she said.

"Is Derek coming?" said Julia.

"I hope so," said Emma.

"I hope so, too," said Philippe. "He livens things up wherever he goes."

Harry spotted us from inside. He sliced his way toward us, carrying a plate full of food.

"You guys try this spinach dip?" he said with a full mouth. "Amazing."

"We were just discussing who can piss the farthest from this balcony," said Philippe. The two sitting in the metal chairs listened in. "Do you think you could make it as far as the canal, Harry?"

Julia cleared her throat. "On that note, I think I'll go check on the ice," she said. "I have such a fondness for it." She gave me a wink and left us.

"Well, now," said Harry, "that depends."

"Depends? Depends on what?"

"The wind, for one."

"Ah, the wind," said Philippe. "Yes, you're quite right. That would make for a substantial difference."

"Sure. I mean, if it's behind you, I think you have a pretty good chance after a few beers, or maybe first thing in the morning. If it's coming toward you, you'd have a tough time making it to that tree right there." He pointed with his pinkie since both hands were holding the plate.

"Do you think size is a determining factor?" said Philippe.

"Size? Size of what?"

"Oh, goodness." Philippe laughed into his hand.

"Oh, *that*. Oh, sure. Why wouldn't it?"

"Size doesn't necessarily imply propulsion," said Philippe. "Some of the smallest jet skis can zoom across the water at tremendous speeds."

Harry placed a cracker into his mouth, chewed, and thought about it.

"This conversation is terribly compelling," said Emma, "but I must excuse myself. Call me when you begin the vomiting discussion."

She left us. Philippe inspected Harry's plate and then took two crackers and scooped some spinach dip onto one and made a sandwich.

"Are you two ready for the race?" asked Philippe.

"Sure," said Harry with his usual confidence.

"James is a formidable competitor," Philippe said.

"He's a pussy cat," said Harry.

"Oh?"

"But I'm sure you'll bring your best game to the race, won't you, James?" Harry grinned at me, chewing with his mouth closed.

"I'm going to give it my best shot," I said.

"Do you think he's been showing all his cards?"

"Oh, I don't know," said Harry. "I've seen enough of them to feel pretty good about my chances. No offense, James."

Philippe eyed him carefully. "The world is full of surprises."

We left Harry and walked inside to Marta, who hugged me first and then Philippe. She held his face in her hands for the longest time. She was tan, her hair had been tinted a slightly darker color, but still blonde. Her dress revealed an ample, though not garish, cleavage, and even Philippe glanced down when he believed she wasn't looking, merely to appreciate her beauty. She said she was modeling again, or as she put it, dipping her small toe in the water to see what sharks were lurking about. He asked her what city she was currently residing in, and when she answered *Prague* he acted surprised, but happy for her.

"You look wonderful," he said. "Prague suits you."

"I miss Leuven."

"Ah, who wouldn't? It is the city of lovers—forget Paris."

"I miss you," she said. "Oh, how I miss my Philippe. And you too, James—I miss you both. Won't you come to Prague for a while?"

"Me?" said Philippe. "What would I do in Prague?"

"I have many interesting friends. You would be my agent. You come to Prague, and that instant I fire my agent."

"Isn't your old boyfriend your agent?"

"What? Of course, I have seen him—I do see him from time to time—but he is not my agent. He is not a real agent. He was my boyfriend posing as my agent, which caused tension. I now have a regular agent, *not* my boyfriend."

"My darling, you know I could never leave Leuven. I've never been to Paris, so why would I visit Prague?"

"To see *me*, of course," she said, patting him on the cheek.

"But I'm seeing you right now. I would rather remain in Leuven and have you visit me all tanned and beautiful and full of wonderful stories. Have you met anyone?"

"I have no time," she said. "I am trying to inch my way back into modeling, and even inching is exhausting."

"Harry's over there, you know," he said.

"Philippe," she said, "you are such the matchmaker."

"Talk to him. He won't bite."

"It is because of Harry that I am modeling again," she said.

"Harry? What's he got to do with it?"

"Harry was this rock, remember? Remember me telling you this? You and Harry—my twin rocks after my breakup with the loser boyfriend. Harry and I were friends trying to mold ourselves into lovers. It worked sometimes, but mostly it did not. We remained together because, well, I am not sure why. Both of us are insecure, I think, in different ways. When I left Harry—or rather, when he had his affair with Elle—it freed me. Not just from a dull relationship, but from the rut I was in. I love Leuven. I love you. I loved all that I did here—but it took my period with Harry to refocus my future. I don't know if modeling is my future, but it is the first step on my new journey. It is exciting, yes? Are you happy for me?"

Philippe took her by the hands, his cane on his wrist, and squeezed them. "I am very excited, and very happy for you. Promise me something?"

"Anything—I will promise you anything."

"Don't go back to the loser boyfriend?"

He said it as a question, a plea. She didn't answer. Her eyes glistened with moisture. He placed her hand under his arm and walked her to the bar, where they had cava to celebrate her new beginning.

I met Victor in the middle of the room and listened as he talked about his adventures. He didn't make it to Ukraine. Instead, he visited Greece and the surrounding countries, including much of the coastline of Croatia, then flew to Mongolia. He would have stayed longer, but he ran out of money. He was stuck in Mongolia without a way home until I wired payment for his airfare.

"God, the water, James," he said. "I didn't know there was water like that in the world. You see pictures, but it doesn't tell you anything. When you get there and see it for yourself and immerse your body in it, then you know what purity is. It's biblical. Epic. You have to see it. As soon as I drum up some cash, I'm heading back. You need to come along. It'll knock you back a hundred yards."

Elle and Emma approached as he was finishing.

"See what?" said Elle, smiling with big teeth and a toss of her hair. Emma demurred, glancing up at Victor.

"Victor's been talking about Greece," I told them.

"You've been to Greece?" Elle lighted.

Victor nodded and raised his eyes to Emma. "Hello."

"I've always wanted to go there—how was it? I bet it was gorgeous. God, I want to go—are you going back?"

"Not any time soon," said Victor.

"Why not? I'll go! Let's leave tomorrow."

"He's a little short on cash," I said.

"Hell, I've got money," said Elle. "Come on—let's go!"

Victor grinned and nodded, but didn't answer.

"Elle," I said, "you need a refill?"

She lifted her beer glass, which was half full. "I will in a minute."

"Bet you can't down that thing before we make it back to the bar."

"Ha! Right," she said, and drank it down on the spot.

We headed for the bar and along the way I told her about Victor and Emma, and she said she felt like a fool. "Next time kick me, will you?"

We returned and the conversation, in our absence, had come to a halt. Emma gazed around the room, not at Victor, waiting for him to say something.

"This is different," Victor finally said.

"Different? What do you mean?" said Emma.

"You've never had parties like these before, have you, James?"

"You mean adult parties?" said Emma.

"I guess you could say that. What's with the twin mustaches?"

She turned her body to look, then turned back around. "Those are called bartenders," she said.

"Is *that* what they are?"

"Yes. They are a new invention. You see those two women carrying plates of food? Those are called caterers."

"Well, I'll be," he said with some sarcasm. "And here I thought they were just drunk mothers looking for the way out."

"You would," she said under her breath.

He took a drink, bobbing his head, waiting. "You look nice," he said.

"Gee, thanks," said Emma. "So do you. I love the belt."

"You don't like my belt?"

"I just said I loved it, didn't I?"

"Yeah, but I can never tell when you're joking."

"No, seriously," she said, her eyes darting down, "it's amazing. I've never seen anything quite like it."

He took another drink. He didn't know what to say.

"I'm going to get another beer," he said.

"See you," she said, and walked away.

Nico held court in the corner, doing animal impressions solely with expressions he made. No sounds. No hands. Just using the contortions of his face. His audience was young and mostly female. Gia hung at his side as his dark, puffy face danced with grimaces. He wore baggy khakis and a white cotton shirt unbuttoned to his chest. Valentina, who was standing to the side of the bar gazing across the room, spotted Elle, Philippe, and me and made her way over.

"Enjoying the party?" I said.

"I have come to the realization that Nico is a bore."

"A bore?"

"Yes, a complete bore."

"Well, Nico is many things, but being a bore isn't one of them," said Philippe.

"He is a bore. He defines the word, bore. He is like a plump sausage with no flavor. I thought he was something more than he is, but he is not, he is just a bore. A horny old bore."

"He does like his young women," conceded Philippe. "Still, who doesn't have their flaws?"

"I have no problem with him liking such young women, his fickle nature, but what does he offer in return? He paints. For this I am to deny that he is a bore? Just because he is an artist, I am to pretend he has a heart to match the size of his sexual cravings? He is like a shark, a hungry, cunning shark swimming the ocean in search of his next meal."

Elle and Valentina had never met, so Philippe introduced them.

"Ah, so you are the famous Elle? Julia speaks highly of you," said Valentina.

"Does she?"

"Oh, yes. She says you are a woman who gets to the point, you do not pretend to be something you are not."

"Spot on," I said.

Valentina continued watching Nico. "James is the opposite of Nico. He is quiet and shy, but he is not a bore. Don't you agree?"

"I would," said Elle. "He's a lovely young man."

"What a bore, this Nico! I can't imagine James ever becoming so fat and boring, and if he did I do not think he would pursue young women so comically the way Nico does."

"Don't you know," said Philippe, "he's our hired entertainer for the day."

"You joke, but it is true; I have never been so bored with a man. I don't know what was wrong with me. James would not turn into such a clown. He would make a good father, indeed."

"He would be a good husband, a good father," said Elle. "He's good all around."

"All right, you two," I said. "Knock it off."

"James," said Valentina, turning toward me. "Have you picked out a name?"

"A *name*?" said Elle.

"I hope it is a girl. I love boys, but I hope it is a girl. I know I have Gia as a younger sister, but she can be difficult. I would love to spoil a little girl."

Elle gasped. Philippe twitched, then leaned forward.

"James," he said, "are you and Julia pregnant?"

"Yes," said Valentina. "Isn't it wonderful news? They are so happy. It is the most wonderful news!"

Philippe hopped on one foot, unable to contain himself. "Wonderful, indeed!" He clenched his fists and bounced in place. "The best news I have heard in quite some time."

"But, *shhhhhhh*; it is still a secret."

Elle, eyeing me over the edge of her glass, took a drink. "Congratulations," she said. "Secret is an understatement."

"We wanted to be sure," I said. "You know, before we broadcast it to everyone."

"James, I'm just beyond excited!" said Philippe. "It's joyous news."

"How far along is she?" asked Elle.

"Not very. We just found out. It was a surprise to us, too."

"But a glorious one," said Philippe. "Oh, James, I'm so happy for you."

It was nearing dusk when Derek walked in. I spotted him and waved and made my way toward him through the crowded room. He had on a light overcoat and was sweating. He stood with drooping eyes, hands in the pockets of his coat, staring at me.

"What's up, man?" he said sheepishly.

I seized him by the hand, then embraced him.

"I was hoping you'd make it."

"I smelled the food," he grinned.

"I'm really glad you're here," I said, still holding him by the shoulders, then finally letting go. "It's about time you get out of that coal mine."

"It's Emma," he said. "She's a slave driver. Ties me to the chair and forces me to paint. I tell you."

"I'm going to have to have a talk with that girl," I said.

"Nice spread," he said, looking around.

"You hungry?"

"I'm not kidding," he said. "I smelled the food and followed my nose. Hell yeah, I'm hungry."

"Come on, there's plenty left."

I took him into the kitchen and asked what he wanted. I made a plate for him the way a parent would for a child. We stood there as he attacked the food like he hadn't had a real meal in quite some time. He wasn't drunk, but he'd been drinking. At least he was up and socializing and keeping it together.

"So, you missed the big news," I said.

"Big news? What big news?"

"Julia's pregnant."

"Wow," he said. "That is big news." He paused only briefly before shoveling more food into his mouth. "Good thing? Bad thing?"

"A very good thing."

"I'm impressed. You don't mess around, do you?"

"Not this time."

He bounced his head up and down, grinning. I tried to read him, if he was genuinely happy or if he was struggling. I couldn't tell. With Derek, I just couldn't tell.

"So," he said. "What's the plan? You guys getting married, or what?"

"I don't know," I said. "We haven't thought that far ahead. I'd like to."

"I always figured you for a married guy."

"Oh, yeah?"

"Sure. As soon as you found the right girl."

"Sounds like you've spent some time thinking about this," I said.

"Man, you have marriage material plastered all over your face. Why do you think all the chicks like you."

"Because I'm rich."

"Well, that doesn't hurt," he said.

Derek, having dispatched his plate of food, wiped his hands on the front of my shirt, then patted it.

"Excellent food," he said. "Now. Can you tell me where Emma is?"

I pointed to the corner of the room. She'd been watching us since Derek arrived. He pressed his hands together and plowed forward through the crowd.

Julia came up, giving my side a squeeze. I gave her a kiss, then put my arm around her shoulders and kissed the top of her head. "You having a good time?"

"I'm having the best time," she said. "And so is everyone else. But are you? Eddy, are you?"

"I'm having a wonderful time," I said. "Best party since the peeing contest."

"Did you really?"

"Of course."

"Did you win?"

"I thought I did, but there seems to be some dispute over that. Maybe we can have a rematch later on, after the children have left."

"Keep it in your pants, cowboy," she said. "It's mine all mine."

"I see Nico's in rare form," I said.

"Nico the clown. I guess that's what makes him so loveable, but he never turns off the clown. Except when he's painting, of course."

"Did you see—Derek came."

"I saw him," she said. "How's he doing?"

"He's doing all right," I said. "Yeah, I think he's doing all right."

"He looks thin."

"He is thin, but he ate a plateful of food. I'm glad he came. It's good for him."

She led me by the hand to the balcony, where we were alone. I wrapped my arms around her.

"I'm happy," she said. "I'm the happiest I've ever been."

"I'm glad," I said.

"Do you know why?"

"No, tell me."

"I'm happy because I met you, because you're in this world. If I weren't with you, Eddy, I'd be happy knowing you existed. I'm happy because you love me and treat me with kindness. You bless me, my mother, my whole family with your generosity." She squeezed my arm. "I'm happiest because I have part of you growing inside me. I never used to believe in miracles—but it's a miracle if there ever was any. He's going to be just like you, Eddy, a gift to everyone around him."

"Or she," I said. "Could be a girl."

"Or she." Her eyes lighted up. "Maybe we'll have twins—a boy and a girl. Wouldn't that be something? It could happen. Things like that do happen."

I kissed her and held her.

"I think about months from now when our baby is born. I picture the three of us together. It's so beautiful in my mind, Eddy, it's like it's really happening, right now. But what if you're not here? What if. . ."

"But I *will* be here," I said.

"But what if you're not? What if something happens? Oh, Eddy, I don't know if you should race Harry—I have a bad feeling about it."

"You think I'd let something happen to me?"

"But still, what if?"

She started to tear up. I held her tight and rubbed her arms and rocked her, and tried to reassure her nothing bad was going to happen. She left, her tears wiped but not yet dry, to fix her makeup. A short while later Philippe came up. He stood beside me, leaning against the railing. The lines of the old medieval buildings seemed timeless against the gray-black sky.

"And so. . ." said Philippe.

"And so it goes," I sighed.

He turned toward me. "You don't look like a man who's near death."

"It's the shirt. I bought it just for the occasion."

"Yes, well, you could have done better. It's wrinkled already and I see you've spilled your plate of food on it."

I nodded slowly gazing at the birds in their compact flock, skimming the water. "Derek came," I said.

"I spoke to him briefly. He seems to be on the upswing, relatively speaking."

"He'll be all right," I said.

"If your easy confidence could be bottled, James. . . Ah. . ."

The birds were a good distraction. I watched them, as I often watched them, allowing their graceful flight to mellow my thoughts.

"Philippe?"

"I am listening, James."

"I've been a fool, haven't I?"

"How so?"

"I guess. . . thinking I could live as a wolf, alone, without true love for all these years."

"It is natural," said Philippe. "It's called life, James. Do not apologize for living life."

"Still, I've been a fool. All those wasted years."

"They led you to Julia."

"They did," I said.

"The world is stitched together with fools," said Philippe. "You are bound to your fellow man."

"I suspected early on she wasn't a student. It didn't add up. I should have asked her about it. I should have told her it didn't matter to me what she did. Instead, she went on working that job."

"What job?" Philippe, who I thought already knew, cocked his head in surprise.

"She works at the university cleaning classrooms," I said. "She'd open a book and pretend to be studying, but she'd be on the same pages day after day. It took me a while to notice. I was curious, so one morning I followed her. She went into one of the buildings, ducked into a bathroom, and came out wearing work clothes. A few minutes later she was pushing a trash can going around to all the classrooms before classes started. Every dime she made, from that job and working for Nico, she sent back home to her mother. And that, my dear friend, is why I have to race Harry."

Philippe took me by the arms and we embraced. He pulled back.

"Will you look after her?" I said.

"I won't need to," he answered. "You'll be here."

"In case I'm not; will you?"

"Of course."

We watched the birds. It was nearly dark. The sound of the party behind us was a form of music. I placed my hand on Philippe's and squeezed it.

A while later there came a loud noise from the corner of the room. Derek had taken a glass and smashed it on the floor. The room simmered and then became silent as he ranted on about his affliction. Those who knew him presumed he meant his alcoholism, but it soon became clear he meant his art. He picked up a bowl from a coffee table and threw it against the wall, then took a painting, one of his own, ridiculing it, and smashed it over his knee. Two young men moved to stop him. They seized him, pinning him against the couch, when I came forward.

"Let him go," I said.

I brushed them aside, angry at the force they'd used. I lifted Derek from the couch. He raised his head in desperation and shame.

The bottled-up anger I'd held for so long, sparked by Derek's outburst, uncorked. I took a second painting from the wall and, pausing to look at the waiting room of guests, struck the corner of the coffee table multiple times. I kept hitting it until I was exhausted and drained. I held a piece of the wooden frame, my hand bleeding, then let it drop to the floor. Nico, who stood nearby, told everyone to go back to drinking. He shooed them away, waving his arms like an angry bear. From the far side of the room Philippe made an announcement that there would be a pissing contest from the balcony in five minutes. He urged contestants to drink up—men and women alike—to increase their chances of being only the third person ever to hit the canal in one continuous stream.

Nico stood between Derek and me and the rest of the room. Derek wept on my shoulder and then, unable to contain myself, I wept with him.

"To hell with fate," I said to him. "To hell with it."

The Race

The day of the race I woke to the sound of birds. They were the birds of summer's wane. As a boy I'd lay in bed wondering about the big secrets of the world and imagined myself doing important things. The birds in the very early moments of daylight were personal hymns, and I associated the sound with the coming of a new discovery or a new threshold to be reached.

I lifted my arms from my sides, opening and closing my hands. I looked at my arms and flexed the muscles, keeping them straight. I dropped them silently to my legs, brushing off the light covers, and tensed my thighs and felt the sculpted separations of the muscles there. I felt the ribbed sequence of my stomach and the promenade of my pectorals. I lifted my head to peer down to the canal. Its mystic stillness satisfied me. I waited, but nothing emerged from below the surface of the water.

I got up from bed and stood behind the gauzy curtains of the window, looking out at the day. It was going to be a good day, I told myself. It was going to be something to remember.

I gazed back at Julia, who lay curled away from me, her body brightly lit by the emerging sun. I gently pulled away what little bit of sheets covered her so she was fully exposed. It occurred to me that if something should happen, this would be our last time together. I tried not to dwell on it but still, there it was. I thought of our child growing inside her. She had become more beautiful now that she was pregnant. I nudged her onto her back and began making love to her. She had been asleep and woke to the easy rhythm of my body moving against her. She opened her eyes, barely. She smiled, clutching the back of my neck. I lost myself in her cheek and spilled hair. I remained where I was afterward, then rolled onto my back. She lay her head on my chest, listening.

"It sounds good," she said. "I think it's a winner, Eddy."

"You think so?"

"I know it is. You'll ride like a god today."

I put the coffee on and we sipped it on the balcony, watching the sun lift above the bent old buildings, and then she made me a fry breakfast. She didn't know what a fry was and so I described it to her. She also made me hash browns for additional fuel. We sat down and I ate every bit that was on my plate, washing it down regularly with water from my water bottle. I glanced at the clock periodically, and we made idle conversation discussing baby names. I put on my cycling bibs and jersey, socks, shoes, and gloves, and then rolled my bike through the living room to the front door. I filled two water bottles and slipped two power bars into the back of my jersey.

"Are you sure you don't need a ride?" she asked.

"No," I said. "Philippe hired a guy he knows who works at a cycling shop. They're picking up Harry and me in the van."

"I'll be there," she said.

"You don't need to be at the start. Just meet us in La Roche-en-Ardenne in a few hours."

"How long will it take you?"

"I'm not sure. It's 110 miles, but because I've not ridden it before I don't know how long it will take. You have plenty of time. Go back to bed." I flicked the end of her nose playfully.

"I'll see you off if you want," she said, "but I know you probably want to be with the men."

I kissed her. "Really, you should go back to bed. I would." I brushed her cheek with the back of my gloved hand, and then my exposed fingers caressed her more delicately.

"Okay, cowboy," she said.

"So, I'll see you later?"

"I'll see you later."

"Remember—we're riding up to the top of the hill where the castle is—you can't miss it."

"In La Roche," she said. "Right."

"Take your time driving there. It's beautiful scenery."

I gave her another kiss, sat my helmet on top of my head, letting the chin straps dangle, and slipped on my cycling glasses. I wheeled the bike outside the door, then picked it up and carried it down to the courtyard where I waited for Philippe. I sat on the edge of a low retaining wall surrounding a large tree, legs crossed, trying to stay relaxed. The van arrived on time, five minutes later. I loaded my bike in the back and then got in.

"Hey," I said to the other three—Philippe and the guy from the cycling shop up front, and Harry, who was beside me in the back seat.

The start of the race was just outside Leuven. Philippe had driven Harry and me earlier in the week to show us the route—from Leuven to La Roche-en-Ardenne—through some of the most stunning countryside in Belgium. I could feel Harry eyeing me from behind his dark cycling glasses.

"Is Julia coming?" Philippe said, turning to look back at Harry and me.

I nodded. "After a few more hours of beauty sleep."

"She's going back to bed?"

"I hope so. I told her she should."

"I don't think Emma can make it," said Philippe.

"Yeah, I talked to her. She has to work. She said she could have taken it off but I told her not to—she needs the money."

"Isn't it funny," said Harry, "how Marta started it all and she's not here. I think that's funnier than hell, don't you?" Neither I nor Philippe answered him.

"Marta?" said the driver, looking at Harry in the rearview mirror. "Who is Marta?"

"Marta's my ex-girlfriend. She's the one who suggested James and I race. I think James had a crush on her—didn't you, James? Yeah, he had a crush on her. She had it for him, too, for a while. She said we ought to have a bike race—just the two of us. But that was months ago." Harry paused and looked out the window at the passing landscape. "It seems like a whole different time."

Philippe turned back around and we remained silent, listening to the radio playing low and muffled up front.

When the van stopped, we all got out. Harry removed his bike first. Philippe explained that the van would be riding just ahead of us and would have support if either of us needed it. If one broke away, the van would stay ahead of that rider mostly, but would fall back to check on the second rider occasionally. Any delays caused by traffic lights, trains, or anything else were to be expected, but a breakaway rider with mechanical problems should be waited on. We each had a map. The ride was nearly 110 miles, finishing at the top of the castle ruins in La Roche-en-Ardenne. The morning was nearly perfect, relatively cool, with low humidity and no rain in the forecast.

Harry had his chin strap secured and was already clipped in his left shoe. I stood with the other two talking about nothing, laughing, as they had coffee from Philippe's thermos. At five till 9 I secured my helmet and straddled my bike and clipped in. Philippe wished us both luck, he and the mechanic got in the van, and they started off. Harry and I followed about thirty meters behind.

The pace was steady and slow and we peddled in middle gears, warming our legs in preparation for the more rigorous challenges ahead. We rode with one hand on the handlebars or none at all, passing the map Harry had pulled from his jersey between us to confirm the route ahead. The countryside was flat, then unfurled into slightly rolling hills, but because of our pace it was easy and neither of us breathed hard. Dew still clung to low-lying fields, and we passed through cool spots beneath canopies of trees that hung over the road. There was little traffic and so we rode side-by-side where there was good visibility, then went single file over the small hills, each taking a turn pulling the other.

"You ever been to the Ardennes?" asked Harry. "I mean before Philippe showed us around?"

I shook my head. "No," I said.

"This was where Hitler's army had its last stand. Where they tried to make a final assault. I wonder why Philippe chose the route he did. He could have taken us anywhere. Why the Ardennes?"

I took a drink, then slipped my water bottle back in place. "It's hilly and beautiful. The hills are for separating the wheat from the chaff, and the beauty is for a distraction."

"Maybe," said Harry. "Who knows? I can never figure Philippe out." He'd taken out a protein bar and extended his hand, offering it to me.

"No, thanks."

"You hear about Rick?"

"You mean about him packing his things?"

Harry chewed and talked simultaneously. "It's about time. I'd have left a long time ago."

"I hope he finds happiness."

"I think he has, from the sound of it," Harry laughed. "Elle says he's gone off the deep end—acts like the two of them were never married, like she's a total stranger."

"Good for him," I said.

We peddled and Harry finished his protein bar. He stuffed the empty wrapper in the back of his jersey and wiped his mouth. "What do you have against Elle, anyway?"

"Not a thing. Is that what she says?"

"I get the feeling you have something big against her. Not that I care, really. It's just something I noticed."

"Well," I said, "I wouldn't worry about it."

"I'm not worried about it. It's just something I noticed."

We went along single file as traffic picked up. Each of us took three to five minutes in the lead, then peeled away, allowing the other to move up and take over. When Harry followed me he nudged the nose of his front wheel just behind my back, trying to show how good he was at dragging, but when I followed him I stayed a foot back. The pace was still easy. The road split and traffic eased up and we rode abreast again, separated by several feet.

We were outside Sint-Truiden, thirty miles from Leuven, when Harry said his right wheel felt strange. We pulled off. I waited, taking a drink from my water bottle, as Harry examined the wheel.

"Is it low?" I asked him.

"It's not low," he said with a mystified expression. "It's wobbling."

The van stopped and the mechanic, whose name was Marcel, removed the wheel and looked it over. He told Harry he had a bent spoke.

"It will probably be fine," he said, "but I can swap it out if you want."

Harry thought it over. "How much?"

Marcel furrowed his brow, then turned his head to Philippe and back again. "Nothing," he said, "of course."

"Sure, go ahead and change it."

Marcel pulled another wheel from the van. The wheel was sure to fit—Philippe gave him the make of our bikes several weeks ago so that he'd have the right replacement gear. He locked the wheel in place, checked that it was true, and leaned the bike to Harry.

"You're good now," he said.

Harry took the bike and got back on it. As the van eased away and he began riding again he said, "Pretty casual for such a big wager, don't you think?"

"What do you mean?"

"Just that who'd think we had a hundred thousand euros riding on this race if they saw us right now?"

"It'll pick up, don't worry."

"I hope you have it covered," said Harry.

"The bet?"

"That's a lot of money for whoever loses. I hope you have it."

I said nothing and looked away. I knew it was Harry's insecurities again, but still, it bothered me. I wanted to beat Harry for many reasons, whether there was a bet or not. The bet added insecurity to Harry, but considerably more pressure on me. I tried not to think about the money. Thinking of the money would only hurt my chances. I felt good—the riding was a piece of cake so far. I needed to save my mental energy for the difficult part ahead.

We rode into Sint-Truiden and each of us turned our heads up to look at the town hall and the church towering overhead. The church was chalk-colored, while the town hall was salmon below and darker stone on the bell tower. We passed between the two stone structures standing like goliath king and queen chess pieces, through the great plaza that had but a smattering of pedestrians, and agreed to stop to fill our water bottles. It would be the only major town we passed through until La Roche-en-Ardenne.

Outside of Sint-Truiden it flattened out. For the first time we increased our cadence, which pushed the van to speed up. The pace wasn't fierce, but quick enough so that conversation evaporated and we gripped our handlebars earnestly. The coolness of early morning gave way to more humid conditions and we began to sweat underneath our helmets, forcing us to wipe our brows. The van steered onto a less traveled road where the surface wasn't as smooth. Harry accelerated, pushing past the van briefly until Philippe waved his hand and Marcel sped up. I went along with him, unconcerned, positioning myself just off his back wheel. Harry snaked left and right across the barren road as I shadowed him, using him, until he eased off and returned to a consistent but easier pace.

I remained on Harry's back wheel, forcing him to do the pulling, making him worry about where I was. A while later he accelerated for real. He rose out of his saddle to gain immediate speed, then sat back down, shifted two gears higher, and powered forward. He went a quarter of a mile before glancing to his right to see where I was. I had little difficulty staying with him and hovered just over his right shoulder. Again, he eased up. He gave me a nod and grinned at me casually, but I knew it had shaken him the way I'd stayed with him.

For the next few miles we backed off the pace and enjoyed the hazy, green fields dotted with cows, tidy farmhouses, and columns of trees. A tractor going the same direction slowed us down briefly. It pulled a flat-bed wagon carrying two rolls of hay and had that fresh, earthy manure smell. The farmer waved as we passed and we waved back. I took a long drink from my water bottle.

We came off the loose road onto smooth asphalt again where a series of rolling hills lay before us. I swerved out wide, suddenly accelerating. I blew past Harry, who wasn't ready for it. When he did try to keep pace, already several lengths back, he didn't have it and I pulled farther ahead over the first hill and down it. I coasted until reaching the base of the next hill and then pumped faster, viscously, and Harry fell farther back. At the last hill I looked back to see Harry a quarter of a mile behind, his body lurching side-to-side in panic. Instead of backing off, I pushed the pace over the next ten miles and didn't look back again until a sharp curve over a stream. Harry was nowhere to be seen.

I passed near Liège, and then the route turned southwest as it followed the Meuse River on the way toward Huy. The Meuse is a sweeping, serene waterway along which hamlets arise from the rocky banks, glimmering like pewter pearls. The road dipped away from the Meuse occasionally to circumvent a sudden hill of rock, but it remained flat and I maintained my breakaway. The breakaway had been planned. When Philippe took us to review the route, I thought I'd try to make a move just after Sint-Truiden when the hills began. I didn't know Harry would try a modest breakaway of his own before this but it helped, draining him of confidence and lowering his guard for my attack. It was a perfect combination of strategy and fortune, and now Harry was some distance behind, in all likelihood losing even more ground. I unzipped my jersey to mid-chest to allow air to cool me. I motioned to the van to slow down and I pulled alongside it to exchange my empty water bottles for full ones.

"How do you feel?" Philippe asked me.

"Good," I said. "I feel really good."

"That was impressive. He wasn't expecting it."

"He shouldn't have tried it on the flats."

"Agreed. It set you up perfectly. No issues?"

"None," I said. "I really do feel great."

"You're doing very well," said Philippe, nodding. "Be strong."

I gave the van a tap and it dropped back to find Harry.

The Meuse was to my left and I looked at it occasionally, its smooth and glistening presence reassuring. It wiggled its way through carved-out slopes of fissured rock, then open pasturelands and small stands of woods. There were brief, moderate climbs where the road went around a rock outcrop, but these were nothing significant. I knew, however, that these were body blows to Harry, each one softening up his resolve. The first half of the ride had been easy. It would be in the Ardennes where we'd be tested and the outcome determined.

I wasn't very hungry, but I knew I'd better eat as I went along. I took a package of energy gel from the back of my jersey and had trouble opening it. I held it with both hands when I veered too far into the road. There was no traffic coming, but I instinctively overcompensated, swerving back to the right. I skidded off the road and onto a grassy bank, bouncing over the uneven terrain until I hit a rock, and then soared over the top of my bike.

As I lay on my back gathering myself, I felt my arms and legs for broken bones. I seemed to be all right. I stood up and checked on my bike lying several meters away, the front wheel still spinning. The front tire was flat. I unzipped the pouch beneath my seat and pulled out a spare tube. I rummaged through the pouch but couldn't find a lever to pry off the tire from the rim.

"Christ," I said to myself.

I removed the wheel from the frame and pressed the valve to deflate the tire completely, then attempted to uncrimp it from the rim with my fingers. I winced, bending back the tire as much as I could, but I couldn't get it started. Moments later the van went by, and then Harry after it. The van made a sudden deceleration, pulled to the side, and began backing up as Harry continued on. Philippe was first out of the van, then Marcel.

"A flat?" he said, his face contorted in panic.

I nodded. "I don't have any levers."

Marcel opened the back of the van and brought out a tool kit, but then realized he had a spare wheel. He grabbed it and ran to the bike. I stood wiping my brow, smirking at Philippe.

"The best laid plans," I said.

"Harry should have stopped," he said, angered.

"Maybe he didn't see me."

"What? Of course, he saw you. It's completely unacceptable that he didn't stop. Every rider knows that."

"We're not professionals."

"We discussed it. Trains, traffic lights, old men crossing the road—all things you must deal with. But when you come upon a leading rider with mechanical problems, you wait for him."

"Apparently, he doesn't."

"Well—I'm going to have a talk with him. It's completely unacceptable."

Marcel slipped the good wheel in place and adjusted the brakes so they were even on either side of the tire, and I quickly straddled the bike and began again. The van pulled alongside me, Philippe leaning out the window.

"How do you feel?"

"I feel great," I said.

"How is the bike?"

"It's good—I think it was just the tire."

"You had a good five or six-minute lead on him. I'll wager he's now a couple minutes ahead."

"It shouldn't be a problem. There's plenty of road ahead—more hills than he'll want to deal with."

"Don't try and get it all back at once."

"I'm good," I said.

Philippe pulled himself back inside the van and told Marcel to find Harry. I'd resumed my aggressive cadence easily and smoothly and knew I was gaining on him. I took water and relaxed, letting the road come to me. I ate a banana and then, twenty minutes later, spotted him—a quarter mile ahead.

The route headed due south into the Ardennes. Soon I was a mere hundred meters behind. Harry saw me as he navigated a turn and it prompted him to rise out of his saddle—a panic move—and I caught him as he sat back down. He bore down, gritting his teeth in frustration and anger.

217

"Bad luck back there," Harry wheezed.

"Could have been worse," I said.

Harry, who found it hard to talk and peddle at the same time, said, "Glad you're okay."

"I've had harder falls."

"You all right?"

"I'm fine."

"The bike?"

"The bike's fine."

"I wanted to stop. I saw the van pull back and figured there was nothing I could do. You understand."

"Sure," I said. "I understand."

"You—you would've done the same, I'm sure," he breathed hard.

I pulled out a power bar and nibbled from it casually. I sat up on my seat peddling without hands as Harry labored desperately.

"Harry," I said, falling forward onto the handlebars.

He wouldn't look all the way over, but turned his head to indicate he was listening.

"I'm going to head off now. See you around." I patted him on the back, which was drenched with sweat.

I shifted two gears higher and pulled away. The van accelerated to remain ahead of me, and Harry was left behind. Soon after, the first real hill presented itself. It was steeper and longer than any of the hills we'd hit so far. I took a drink and then lowered my head and pumped my legs steadily, not overdoing it, knowing that even a modest pace would leave Harry farther behind. I downshifted so that I peddled in quick, nearly effortless strokes. I reached the top breathing heavily, but my legs were unphased. Before descending I looked back to see Harry struggling, his bike jerking as he peddled, only halfway up. I flew down the hill, reaching forty miles an hour and allowing the momentum to glide me up the base of the next hill before I started peddling again. There were two more hills in this series, the last one having a sharp turn to the left at its summit.

For the first time during the ride, I wondered what Julia was doing.

She was probably nearing La Roche-en-Ardenne, or may already have arrived. When Harry and I went on the scouting ride with Philippe, we sat at a café down near the old Sherman tank. I told her I wanted to celebrate there after the race. The race itself finished at the castle ruins, not far from the café, up a brief but very steep spiraled entrance to the old citadel. That's where Julia would be waiting. I told her to wear the blue dress I'd bought for her. I didn't care what else she wore, but I wanted very much to see her in the blue dress. I was going to see her at the finish line at the castle ruins, and then we'd walk together—everyone, not just the two of us, but Philippe, Harry, and Marcel—down into the small town and sit at the café beneath the late afternoon sun and recount the race. I was going to get drunk and buy everyone drinks, and we wouldn't leave until the sun went down, and then I'd let her drive me home and I'd curl up on my side watching her at the wheel and I'd cup her breasts in the blue dress and fall asleep, my nose pressed to her arm. I kept thinking of her in the blue dress sitting alone at the castle ruins, waiting for me with her wry smile.

The next series of hills approached. These weren't as steep, but there were more of them, and there was one near the end that was steeper than the rest. Philippe dropped the van back to check on me.

"Do you need water?" he asked.

I handed him my water bottles one at a time and received full ones.

"Have you eaten enough?"

"I'm good," I said. "I had a power bar not too long ago."

"Don't neglect it."

I gave him the thumbs up. "I'm good."

He said he was going to drop back to check on Harry. There were about thirty miles to go.

The next hills weren't too difficult, though for the first time my neck began to ache. When I could, I arched my back and stretched my shoulders to try to relieve the discomfort. A short while later, as I was coasting down a long, gradual decline where you could see the bucolic fields and hamlets of the Ardennes, I felt the fluttering. It was a single flutter, a prolonged skip, and then my heart resumed its normal beating. I took in a deep breath to relax my breathing and backed off the pace. I had to be a good deal in front of Harry. If I kept it at a moderate pace, I'd arrive in La Roche-en-Ardenne well in front of him. I wished the van was back so I could follow it. All I had to do was follow the back of the van and let it take me the rest of the way.

The road became loose again and then deteriorated into crushed gravel, making it treacherous. I kept taking big, long breaths and sighing casually, as if it would somehow deter another occurrence of the fluttering. I wondered where Philippe and the van were. I figured they ought to be back by now unless Harry was having difficulty. My mind went over the possible things that could have happened to him. It could be anything—from bike trouble, to a physical problem, to issues with the van itself. The road wound around a small brook laden with ancient, arching trees, and then emerged into open fields, green and brown. I didn't remember seeing this part of the route on our drive with Philippe, and then it dawned on me: I must have taken a wrong turn. I stopped my bike, straddling it, and looked around. Nothing was familiar. I began peddling back the way I came with urgency. When I got to where the gravel met the paved road, I stopped and looked at the map. It took a while to find my location but once I did I saw my mistake; I should have stayed on the paved road. Quickly, I folded the map and got going again. The delay had been considerable, about twenty minutes. I had no way of knowing whether I was behind Harry or still ahead of him. I couldn't assume that I was ahead and pressed on, grinding the pedals in a steady, ferocious pace. I sped downhill around a curve, then another in the opposite direction, leaning over the bike keeping my body low. I passed through a small hamlet and blew on through a red light, then began a long climb up a winding portion of the road. I wasn't far into it when I spotted the van heading downhill toward me, and then Harry about a quarter of a mile ahead going up. The van passed me—I heard it screeching to a halt and turning around—but I had to keep going. I gritted my teeth and pushed on the pedals with maximum power, visibly gaining on Harry. The van pulled alongside me, Philippe nearly out the window.

"Where were you! Are you all right?"

"Took a wrong turn," I said. "How far to the end?"

"About twelve miles. James, are you all right?"

"Fine," I said, breathing hard.

"Harry's struggling. Don't reach too far—you've got time to reel him in."

"It's getting hot," I said.

"What?"

"It's hot. It's really hot."

Philippe looked at me and I knew he was concerned. I labored against the long hill, head dropped, back arched, hands on the lower part of the handlebars. Philippe glanced ahead to Harry, then back to me, sizing up the situation.

"That's it," he said. "Nice and steady and you'll reach him in a couple miles."

The van moved ahead. Harry was close enough now to remain in constant sight. I felt myself being pulled along even as I labored against the heat and my exhaustion, and Harry grew larger and larger until finally I was beside him. Harry, his face disheveled, mouth rimmed with salt, flinched with surprise.

"Brutal," he said, taking in breaths in loud, long gasps.

"It'll be over soon," I said.

"Wrong turn?"

I nodded, saving my breath.

"Figured," he wheezed. "You had a good lead."

We rode together keeping a steady pace. Harry knew I could take him at any moment and was waiting, saving himself for the final attack. He had nothing left to stay with me when it occurred.

"It's a lot of money," Harry said, moving his head over to look at me.

"Not for you," I said. "Not for me."

"It's a lot of money," he repeated.

I said nothing. I was gathering myself mentally. We were only a few miles from La Roche-en-Ardenne.

"You think you're going to win," said Harry. "Maybe. Maybe not."

"So?"

"So we could call it a draw. Nobody loses out. No hard feelings."

"No hard feelings here."

"We're friends," Harry forced a smile. "Why not keep it friendly?"

"It's only money," I said. "Our fathers' money."

"Somebody's bound to have bad feelings."

"Not me. But then I'm pretty sure I'm going to win."

"James," Harry said, waiting a few breaths before continuing. "I don't want to lose."

"Nobody wants to lose," I said, breathing hard. "Somebody has to."

"You don't understand. I really don't want to lose."

"What are you saying?"

Harry's voice fell eerily. "I have enough left to do something about it. It's not something I would be particularly proud of, but my shame would pass. Over time it would be a small detail lost to the years."

"Wha—what are you saying?"

Harry reached down and lifted the small tire pump that was secured along the frame of his bike, and extended it near the spokes of my front wheel. I swerved away from him.

"Are you crazy? Put that thing away."

"James," wheezed Harry, following me weakly. "Nobody has to be humiliated. I concede—you win. Let's talk about it."

"You've lost it," I said. I tried to shake him by making sudden changes in direction, but he was able to stay with me. He was putting everything he had left in keeping with me.

"James, let's discuss this like two grown men. It was a foolish bet to start with. We have no business betting that kind of money on a bike race. Money that's not even ours."

He swatted at my wheel several times, but each time I was able to make a quick move away from the pump. There was a wild fanaticism in his eyes.

"I don't. . . I don't *want* to have to do this," he gasped, taking another swing, barely missing my back wheel. "Be. . . reasonable. . ."

He swung again and the pump hit my tire, bouncing off. I bore down, deciding my best hope was to power straight ahead as if I were in a final sprint to the finish. I moved ahead of him, gradually pulling away.

"James. . . James!" he cried after me.

His pleas grew fainter, and then stopped altogether. I knew I'd expended a great deal of energy, but so had he.

The road, which had been following the Ourthe River for some time, hugged it more closely. A mile later it bent away from the Ourthe and climbed up a long steep grade to the top of a hill near Hotel Le Chalet, where I looked down on La Roche-en-Ardenne to see the bridge over the river as it swept back in a wide loop. I allowed my legs to rest as I turned to the left onto Avenue du Hadja and began coasting down. My head hung low; my chest expanded and contracted as I tried to catch my breath.

I made a sharp right and continued down as I approached the bridge. It was here that I had a second, more disturbing fluttering. My heart stopped, hanging for an eternity it seemed, before resuming its rapid beating. A sudden cold chill swept through my body. Sweat flowed into my eyes, making it difficult to see. I realized it wasn't just the sweat blurring my vision—everything went double. I closed my left eye, eliminating my depth perception but preventing the double vision. I crossed over the bridge and made an immediate right onto the Rue de Cielle. Once I passed the few taller buildings to my left, I could see the castle ruins sitting high up on the hill. I peddled steadily but cautiously without any depth perception. I wasn't afraid of Harry catching me, but of succumbing before I made it to the top.

I passed the Sherman tank and then made the first left that I could, heading directly toward the base of the castle. I nearly hit an old man grinding his way across the road, and came to a near standstill to avoid a collision. I started up again and was now at the base of the long ascent to the castle without any momentum. I shifted into low gear—it was the only way I'd make it up. My feet went around in a frantic blur.

I was happy. This would be my final climb. When I was done I'd embrace Julia, and we'd walk down the hill to the café and sit beneath an umbrella away from the sun, and I'd have a cold beer and something light to eat—I could never eat anything heavy just after a long ride, only fruit or small bits of cheese with crackers or a baguette—and I'd place my hand on her thigh feeling its firm smoothness against the calloused palm of my hand, and her mother would have her security, she'd live the rest of her life in relative comfort, and she'd get to know our child—and Philippe would be there with us, a surrogate uncle, always in our lives, and there would be no more pain for her or for me—there'd only be the joy of our family—the joy neither of us ever had. . . These thoughts burned in me like a glowing fire. The warmth spread through my chest and into my arms and legs. It flowed into my neck and eyes. My remaining open eye flickered. My legs moved without effort—I couldn't feel them at all—I couldn't feel anything—and my mind was at peace. I gazed up and saw in a blur the top of the hill. I thought I saw Julia in the blue dress running toward me, arms open, her hair flowing in slow undulations like simmering embers. Her mouth, parted, open, came toward me and I went to kiss—

Philippe, days later, recounted those final moments on the hill: I was near the top, a mere forty meters away, when I faltered and then fell over. I lay disoriented, moving only my head as I attempted to understand where I was. I staggered to my feet and attempted to climb back onto my bike when Harry approached, churning his way slowly up the steep ascent toward me. I dropped my bike and waved for him to stop. He had no intention of doing so and slid to the right, intending to pass me by. Just before he passed I lunged, throwing myself onto his path, forcing his bike to run me over, and sending him sprawling to the asphalt. We both tried to get going again—Harry mounted his bike first and pushed off. He began riding away from me when Philippe, out of the van and running down the hill toward us, thrust his cane into the spokes of his front wheel. Harry fell hard to the ground. As he lay there clutching his knee, Philippe leaned over and whispered in his ear, "Say one word and I'll tell Marta and Elle both what a coward you are." He hopped over to me. I was already up and riding unsteadily, wobbling, nearly blind. He led me the rest of the way to the top where I collapsed in Julia's arms.

They rushed me to the local hospital and then transferred me to Leuven, where they performed emergency surgery. The surgery lasted seven hours. It was touch-and-go and the doctor, when it was finally over, told Philippe I almost didn't make it. But my heart kept beating, as weakened as it was, refusing to give in.

The doctors said I had a good chance of living for many years. When Julia pressed them on what specifically that meant, I stopped them. I didn't want to know. A full life can be lived in weeks. A full life they had given me, and a full life I had every intention of living.

Julia and Philippe took turns staying with me during those first few days of recovery in the hospital, and were joined by the others whenever they could make it. Harry, in particular, was a frequent visitor. I suppose he felt bad for many reasons. I was the only true friend he had and my near demise seemed to affect him considerably. He joked less and listened more. Philippe told him about my condition leading up to the race, though he didn't tell him about my financial situation. I considered telling him, but in the end decided against it. He'd already paid the bet—the money was wired into my account before my surgery was over—and it just didn't seem to matter.

The pain was nearly unbearable. Each day I'd take more frequent and longer walks around the room, and then down the long, sunlit hallway. On the sixth day I abandoned the walker. Julia walked beside me, for reassurance, but I leaned on her arm only once, when I tripped over my slipper, which had slid partially off my foot. I slept a great deal, but otherwise we read or talked. We began organizing her mother's care. Surprisingly, Gia had decided to return to Italy to look after her. Gia came often to the hospital and we went over the medications, the tests her mother still needed, and her daily regimen. I was worried that it might be too much for her to handle, but Julia had no qualms and told me she was confident that Gia would do a fine job as caretaker. She said that Gia was young and impulsive, but otherwise was organized and smart. We called her mother a few times and I talked to her, though I couldn't understand what she was saying. She cried a lot and thanked me, and I felt embarrassed. The warmth I'd imagined she possessed was confirmed. She insisted we have the child in Italy, and I couldn't see any reason not to.

My father called the day before I went home. Julia answered, then handed the phone to me. He asked how I was doing and if I needed anything. I told him I was doing much better now and would soon be released. He told me how things were going at the brewery, and mentioned how my mother was planning a new rose garden. He told me how much I was missed at work and hoped that sometime soon I'd return. I listened vaguely as I picked at the turkey sandwich I'd only half-eaten. I could sense he wanted to say more, and I waited for it, but there wasn't anything. Julia sat near me on the bed; I stroked her hip and smiled at her. He said he needed to take a call and repeated again how glad he was that I was doing all right. I told him to give my mother my regards and I'd talk to him soon. I hung up and offered part of the turkey sandwich to Julia. We shared it, then took a slow stroll down the hall. I told her of our brief conversation, but then changed the subject. We still had not decided on a name for the baby.

I was released the following day during a light rain. It was a struggle to climb the stairs to my flat, but I did it and was proud of myself as I stood catching my breath. I opened the door to the balcony and looked down at the canal and the raindrops exploding on the surface. Julia had done some rearranging of furniture, which I should have done long before. The flat felt bigger and airier and she'd expanded the area for the photographs—adding another table and setting up a large corkboard to display them. The bathroom was still a darkroom. In the bedroom, above the bed, she'd hung one of the photographs I'd taken of old hands alongside one she'd taken of her own. We lay down on the bed listening to the rain.

Of Damsels and Dragonflies

Six weeks after the surgery, Harry and I cycled out to where we'd had the picnic. It was a pleasure ride, a ride for reflecting and reminiscing. We were to meet Philippe, Elle, and Julia, who were driving out. Beyond our picnic spot, through the woods, was a pond. Philippe said the pond was seldom used and was perfect for wading in and getting cooled off. The ride was slow and easy, but even so I had to stop several times to catch my breath. Harry waited patiently each time.

When we made it to the cemetery we parked our bikes along the road beside the tall field now turned gold in early autumn. We sat against a tree with eyes closed, waiting for the others as if we'd been there all day.

"Get up, you two," Philippe said as he walked past us. "Such clowns! Always in need of attention."

We stood, amused with ourselves, and helped carry the things to the pond. I fell back with Philippe, leaving Harry with the two women up ahead.

"How's the ankle?" I asked. I noticed he was limping more than usual.

"It hurts today," said Philippe without slowing down.

"I can carry that." I reached down and took the swinging plastic bag from his hand. "See? It helps balance out the load."

"Look what I'm reduced to."

"I see nothing but a giant," I told him.

"Who's leading the way?" said Harry, who strolled casually between Elle and Julia, almost loping forward, the canvas sack of food and utensils draped over his right shoulder.

"Philippe!" called back Elle. "You know which way to go?"

"Forward!" directed Philippe, lifting his cane. "Always forward!"

From the woods was a clearing and the pond. The pond was mature with weeds and wildflowers laced around its edge, all but for a section directly before us which appeared as a natural access point. Elle and Julia ran forward for a closer look. Two frogs soared into the water, frightening them, causing them to laugh giddily. Harry and I laid out the blankets as the two women held onto each other and peered into the water, and then they walked up to the blanket still arm-in-arm.

We sat on the blankets, reclining on elbows. There was a breeze and it pushed the weeds from left to right making a rustling sound like sand blowing on the beach. Elle laid her head on Harry's stomach. She reached back to touch Philippe's leg, stroking it affectionately. I had my head on Julia. She used the back of her hand to rub my temple. There came the sound of a large dragonfly above us. The dragonfly hung for a moment, watching us curiously, then raced off. It had been a spectacular specimen. Green and blue with flashes of gold along its abdomen. It was big and proud and haughty—the king of the meadow—the size of a small bird.

Julia and Elle entered the pond. We watched them, and then Harry and I strode down, stripped off our bibs, and waded in. I floated toward Julia, who straddled me underwater and laid her arms on my shoulders. Elle did similarly with Harry, leaning her cheek on his shoulder as he slowly took her around the pond, leading her as if in a dance.

I leaned back to wet my head, and with me came Julia, clinging to me like a nursing babe. We kissed, as Elle and Harry kissed, the hot sun on our heads and shoulders, lips like melted chocolate bars, cheeks burnt but cooling with each dip. I held her aloft effortlessly and felt slight nips along my knuckles, and I smiled knowing they were curious minnows. My hands traveled around her form and I walked in slow motion as if on the moon over the muddy bottom. We moved through some reeds and traveled across duckweed thick and fluorescent green. We came around and met Elle and Harry, and the women opened their arms in a welcome and the four of us drifted in place in the center of the pond, and then Elle and Julia slid off and we all lay on our backs in a four-pointed star, holding hands. The clouds rotated against the sky. There were no ripples as there are in a lake or the ocean—all was stillness and calm. Then, there came a disruption.

"This looks too fun," said Philippe, who made an opening between Elle and me. "I can't feel a thing," he said. He lay back onto the water like the rest of us. "My leg doesn't hurt at all."

Like Philippe with his ankle, I rarely had a waking moment when my chest didn't feel uncomfortable or hurt. The sensation was one of being burdened with a fifty-pound sack, always there, pushing on my ribs. Now, my chest felt big enough for the love of Julia with room to spare. It was big enough for Philippe and Derek and Harry, a different kind of love, a love without expectations or amorous desires. It was big enough for Elle, who taught me many things, who was desperate and searching, but pure in heart. It seemed as if my heart had doors and they were flung open, and all walked in and out freely. Each person brought sacks of goodness with them and exchanged them for sacks I'd stored over a lifetime. These were sacks I didn't know I possessed until recently. My heart was no longer a vault of pain and fear, but a cathedral of empathy and compassion.

We lay on the blankets drying in the sun, our hearts still trotting, skin tightening as water drops shrank and then disappeared into the warm breeze. It was Philippe who spoke, breaking the silence.

"There is nothing more," he said. "We go about our lives living, loving, playing out our little dramas, and that is as it should be. Remember these days when Leuven was the center of the world, when there was peace and prosperity, when we were young, before the change sure to come. We try and grasp these moments, but they are slippery, they have an agenda all their own. Let the breeze and hot sun caress your unblemished skin. Let the foibles of your desires pour like thick cream over your souls. Allow the beauty of your youth, especially you, my two damsels, to dance in celebration while it can. We each have our time; this is ours, it is *yours*, to do with as you may. The stars have aligned for us. We must honor such a gift by looking forward, always forward. This is not a farewell, but a toast to all of us. Santé, my friends. Santé."

We remained at the pond for much of the day and then all agreed it was time to go. We dressed, and packed, and gathered the blankets which before being taken from the ground held the impressions of our bodies where we had lain, and then we meandered through the woods and back to the cars.

"I'd like to see the horses," said Philippe, who drove separately. He began the short walk through the cemetery to the fence and the field where the horses were in spectacular play.

Harry lifted his bicycle into the trunk of Elle's car.

"You coming, James?" said Elle, sitting erect in the driver's seat with her shining sunglasses and big smile.

"You go ahead," I told them. "I'm going to ride back."

Harry, who was hanging out the passenger window nodded and said, "Enjoy it, James. Take your time and enjoy yourself."

I said nothing. I patted Harry's forearm, and then moved to the back window and leaned over and gave Julia a kiss.

"Oh, just stop it, you two." Elle rolled her eyes. "No kissing in my car, unless I'm involved."

We paid no attention and allowed our lips to linger, tasting the warmth of the day. I reached inside and placed my hand on her stomach and held it there and she smiled at me, squeezing my wrist. I tapped the side of the car and they drove off. I watched the car shrink until it turned a corner by some trees and was gone. I straddled my bicycle, clipped in my left foot, and secured the chin strap of my helmet. I gazed to the fence to see Philippe leaning slightly to one side, his hand on top of a rail. I thrust my hand into the air in triumph and Philippe, upon seeing it, pumped his fist three times. I turned, pushed off, and began the slow easy ride back to Leuven, my arms and legs in pleasant ache from the day's folly.